Praise for *Backward Glass:*

"Get ready to slide down into the past with David Lomax's *Backward Glass*. It's cold on the way down, hot on the way up into the future, and it is always, always riveting, no matter which direction in time he takes his courageous and intelligent teenagers. I'd read this again and again. Actually, the future me has already done so, I can assure you."

—Christopher Barzak, author of *One for Sorrow*

BACKWARD GLASS

To my wife, Christina,
without whom none of it is possible.

BACKWARD GLASS

DAVID LOMAX

Woodbury, Minnesota

First Edition
First Printing, 2013

Book design by Bob Gaul
Cover design by Lisa Novak
Cover image © Alex Stoddard

Flux, an imprint of Llewellyn Worldwide Ltd.

Library of Congress Cataloging-in-Publication Data (Pending)
978-0-7387-3751-5

Flux
Llewellyn Worldwide Ltd.
2143 Wooddale Drive
Woodbury, MN 55125-2989
www.fluxnow.com

Printed in the United States of America

INVICTUS

Out of the night that covers me,
Black as the Pit from pole to pole,
I thank whatever gods may be
For my unconquerable soul.

In the fell clutch of circumstance
I have not winced nor cried aloud.
Under the bludgeonings of chance
My head is bloody, but unbowed.

Beyond this place of wrath and tears
Looms but the Horror of the shade,
And yet the menace of the years
Finds, and shall find, me unafraid.

It matters not how strait the gate,
How charged with punishments the scroll.
I am the master of my fate:
I am the captain of my soul.

—William Ernest Henley

THE RULES

1. Going backward, it only opens from eleven until midnight, only in the years that end in seven.

2. From an even-numbered decade, you can go back on even-numbered days. Same for odds.

3. Once you've gone back, you have to wait until midnight. After that, you can go home again anytime.

4. When you go uptime to your home, you can bring the chosen kid from the past with you.

5. The mirror only picks one kid every decade. It never picks anyone older than sixteen.

6. You can't ever really change anything.

7. When you go downtime from your own mirror, you can take the kid from the future with you.

PROLOGUE

Here's what you need to know: You're my son and you're something like negative twenty-two, because that's how long it will be before you're born. I have a story to tell you. Most of it happened right here in Scarborough, forty, fifty, even sixty years ago, but it happened to me. Last year. 1977. The year I turned fifteen.

I wish I could begin on that cold day in January when I met her, but I should tell you about the dead baby and the list with my name on it. A year and a half ago, my parents moved us into this house, the one the long-termers in the neighborhood call "the old Hollerith place," far enough out of Toronto for me to call it the boonies.

That's what we do. My dad moves us into a place to fix it up, and then after puttering around with it for a few months, he wants to move again.

This was the worst change yet. Two months into the ninth grade and thirty days to pack up. I spent weeks grousing, sleeping, arguing, dragging my feet.

Still, when we drove up in the moving van on the first of December, and I got my first look at the old Hollerith place my dad had been raving about, I quit complaining. I didn't want to, but I could see what he saw in it—a grand old falling-apart house with a lot of history bearing down on it. It even had a second building on the property, screened off by high hedges.

As we piled out of the car, my dad saw the direction of

my gaze. "It's a coach house," he said. "Or a carriage house. It's part of the property. It's ours."

My mother laid a light hand on my shoulder. "The people who lived here were well off once," she said. "Kept their horse and carriage there. Who knows what happened? At one point, they turned it into a proper house and rented it out. The real estate agent admitted to your dad that it hasn't been much of anything for a while now. The neighborhood kids have been going in there and drinking and whatnot."

Inside the main house, up past the squeaky porch and through a well-worn door, I got that kind of combination disappointment-thrill that you only have when you're trying your hardest to hate things that turn out to be cool. My bedroom was the attic.

And with that, my two months of held-up resentment boiled away. First, a mysterious extra house at the back of the property, and now an attic bedroom. I could be Greg Brady up there, the lord at the top of the house. As I trudged up the old-fashioned too-steep stairs, then tugged to pull my staircase down, I could already imagine the calls from the first floor that I'd be able to deny having heard, the arguments I could escape.

The room was even better in person, though I guess not everyone would have thought that way. My dad had come the day before with some bus-driver friends from work and moved in most of our furniture. My bed, dresser, and bookcase now made a small island in an ocean of history. Scattered far into the dusty shadows were tables, credenzas, rolltop desks, sofas, and piles of dining room chairs.

"Oh, my God," said my mother behind me. "When he told me there were a few sticks of furniture here and there, I didn't expect a bonfire in the waiting. I'm sorry, Kenny. We won't keep you in this. There's an old nursery downstairs we could repaint."

"But it's—" I gave up. "It's fine, Mom. I like this room. I want this one."

And just like that, I was committed. Two turns of emotional judo, and she was the one doing me a favor. I was halfway down the stairs before I realized what had happened.

The hedge around the carriage house had grown tall and untended, and the effect was that you couldn't see the squat building at all until you had squeezed past onto its scrubby yard. The outline of the wide entrance that once admitted horse and carriage was still visible as a ghost of newer bricks inset with a low door that didn't even seem to have a latch. Clouds of dust billowed from a hayloft window.

From head to toe my dad was dark grey, out of which his eyes and teeth shone with a mad gleam. I shook my head. "Mom's never letting you back in the house like that."

He shook right back, shedding clouds from his curls and wild beard, but not getting noticeably lighter. "She can hose me down when I'm done."

My dad gave me what he called, "The nickel tour. A dime would be a rip-off." The main floor was all one space, half kitchen, half living room. The hayloft, accessible through a bare, rail-less stair was, like my room back at the house, both for sleeping and junk storage. It hadn't seen electrical service in years, and the gas was shut off for safety reasons. The roof was collapsing, the floor unsafe, and the place filled with mold. "Late 1800s this place must have been built. Same as the main house. The outside walls show a lot of care. But all this?" He pointed with a crowbar at the wall we were to demolish. "Maybe twenties or just before. In a hurry, too. We can do it much better."

He gave me a pair of gardening gloves and sent me upstairs with a hammer and a chisel, and instructions to get underneath the wall panels any way I could and just start ripping.

I got good at hammering the chisel in and working it around until I could pry an edge out. That's when I'd get to smash away with the hammer for a while, weakening the plaster's hold until I could pull the board out whole. Underneath, the bricks of the exterior wall were motley and old, but they felt solid. I finished as high as my shoulders on one of the short walls, and started on the more difficult long back wall.

Then the prickling started under my T-shirt.

I remember that shirt. It featured Speedy Gonzales, my favorite cartoon a few years before, and was now old enough to be on my mom's "tear-it-up-for-dusters" list.

Suddenly, it felt like I had bugs crawling on my chest, or like I had put my hands on those electricity balls at the science center. I gasped and started scratching and feeling around, then began coughing on the plaster dust I had sucked in.

"What's wrong?" my dad called up. I waved him away, and held my breath until the coughing fit stopped.

The prickling stopped as well. I sat up and inched back toward the wall.

Prickling again.

I turned to my dad, who was still frowning in puzzlement from below. "Lung full of dust? I'll get masks this afternoon. Your mother would kill me if she saw these conditions."

I shook my head. "Not that. There's something weird. When I get close to the wall here, I get this electricity shooting through me—like when you rub a balloon on your hair, but stronger."

His frown deepened. "Can't be. Place doesn't even have power. Everything's dead."

He came up the stairs cautiously and moved me back with a gentle hand. The farther I got from that point in the wall, the more the prickling subsided.

"I don't feel it," said my dad. He reached for the strip of lath I had been working on and tugged the board smoothly away, twisting at just the right points so it came off in one easy piece, which he tossed over the side. He did the same for two more pieces; then, "What's that? Did somebody—?" He reached into the space behind the lath, where something black and smaller than a loaf of bread nestled. "Did somebody throw their garbage in here? Their lunch or something?"

He pulled it out, a blackened bundle, crusty flakes drifting from it as it came out of the hole. A folded square of ancient paper fell away. I picked it up, eyes still on the parcel in my father's hands.

"Is that newspaper covering it?" I said. I could almost make out words, blacker ink set in folds and crevices. The piece in my hand was different, though, a page torn from a book.

He picked at it. "Yeah. Somebody's old fish dinner?" He held it to his nose. "Doesn't even smell. Imagine how long it's been there." He shook his head and grinned. "That's why I love doing this stuff, you know? You find bits of people's stories in the dust. History class, but way better. Who was the guy, Kenny? What was he doing here? Was he a worker? The owner?"

As he talked, he kept picking at the bundle, and finally found an edge that he could pull. More black flakes drifted away. "There. I've got it. Oh, Christ," he said. "Oh, Christ." Suddenly cradling the thing with more care, he sat down heavily. "Oh, Christ, Kenny, get your mother. Tell her to call—the police or something. Just tell her to come. Tell her to come and see." His voice had a heaviness I had never heard before, something deep and shuddering. "Oh, Jesus, Kenny, look at the little thing."

"What is it?" I said, though I had by this time looked and seen exactly what it was. The little blackened, mummified foot sticking out of the crystallized newspapers couldn't be anything else. I wanted my dad to tell me it was a doll.

He bounced it just slightly in his hands, judging. "Oh, Jesus, Kenny. It's so tiny. Couldn't have been a day old. Get your mother."

As I stumbled down the stairs and out into the tiny yard, I unfolded the piece of paper that had fallen into my hand. Blinded by daylight, and desperate to reach my mother, I couldn't read the words at first, but when I did, I felt a tingling less physical than the electricity under my T-shirt a few minutes before, but no less real. It was a list of names and dates printed in a neat old-fashioned style.

1917	Rose Hollerith	January 29, 1901
1927	Curtis Hollerith	September 2, 1917
1937	Lillian Huff	February 3, 1920
1947	Margaret	January 2, 1930
1957	Anthony Currah	March 27, 1940
1967	Jimmy Hayes	January 22, 1951
1977	Kenny Maxwell	June 19, 1962
1987	Lucy Branson	October 12, 1970
1997	Melissa Peat	January 15, 1982
2007	Keisha Blaine	March 2, 1992
2017	C.M.?	2000?

My name. My birthday. On a browned and crinkly piece of paper put in the wall—how many years before I was born?

I stuffed the paper into a pocket, and amid the excitement of my mother's moans, my dad's stricken face, and the three calls to the police that it took to bring a squad car, I didn't think about it again until late that night. On my bed at the center of the wide, low attic, I took it out and read the list again. Only then did I notice, scrawled at the bottom, the faint and urgent message that had waited for me all those years in that wall.

Help me make it not happen, Kenny. Help me stop him. Clive is dead all over again.

Part One

Time Travelers' Rules,
Winter 1977

ONE

The Rules

1. Going backward, it only opens from eleven until midnight, only in the years that end in seven.

I don't mean to sound morbid or callous, but there's nothing like the discovery of a dead baby to get you noticed at a new school. And after the number of times we've moved, I'm the guy who would know. By the time I went for my first day at Jane Ewart Collegiate, I was already well known. "You're in the old Hollerith place, aren't you?" said the secretary who took me to my guidance counselor. "I read in the Saturday *Star* about what you found. That must have been awful. My grandparents used to live around the corner from there, and there were stories even back then. Anyway, I'm sure it's a nice place now." I thought I caught her communicating something to my counselor with her eyes, but I might have been wrong.

It was just before lunch by the time they finally gave me a timetable and sent me to math class, but there was enough time for two kids to get in trouble for trying to talk to me about where I lived. As soon as class was over, they steered me to the cafeteria where I was soon surrounded by kids my age and older, half of them trying to get my story, and the other half trying to tell me theirs. It turned out pretty much everyone knew about the Hollerith house, though nobody could actually remember anyone by that name who lived there. A kid from the twelfth grade told me his uncle had once fought off someone who'd been prowling around their house and chased the guy all the way to the carriage house.

"Remember the skipping song?" said a girl from math class. "My mom always said it had something to do with that place."

"Skipping song?" said the senior.

Another girl chimed in. "Lover sweet, bloody feet, running down the silver street. Leave tomorrow if you're called— truth and wisdom in the walls. Crack your head, knock you dead, then Prince Harming's hunger's fed."

A hush spread out around the girl who had spoken, and I don't think I was the only one to shiver. "I never heard that song," said another kid from math class, turning back to me, "but I sure heard about Prince Harming. He's a complete legend around here. My dad says he was probably just some guy who was shell-shocked from the war or something. He killed some kids or something back in the twenties."

"It wasn't the twenties," said the skipping-song girl. "My dad lived around here when some girl disappeared after World War II. And he doesn't kill people. He's after girls; he's some kind of perv."

After that, everyone had to chime in. Their stories were different, but they all featured that same figure, Prince Harming. Either he wanted to crack your head open to scoop out your brains, or he wanted to catch your reflection in a magic mirror and steal your soul. Or kill you and take you down an invisible hallway. Most of them admitted they had heard the stories in the schoolyard when they were younger, but some of them got it from parents or even grandparents.

I was a curiosity like that for a few weeks, but while I was living it up on stories of that dark hole and the crystalized newsprint flaking away from the corpse of the baby, I held back that list of names and dates. Something about that piece of paper was mine and mine alone. Even when the other kids lost interest in me around Christmas, and I realized I hadn't actually made any real friends out of my notoriety, I wasn't tempted for a moment to bring out the note. I told myself I was just being practical. Who would believe I hadn't just written the list myself and stained it with tea to make it look old? But it was more than that. I hadn't shown it to my parents either. That was me on that note. It was my own private piece of impossible. It wasn't asking for anyone else's help, just mine. *Help me make it not happen, Kenny. Help me stop him. Clive is dead all over again.*

In any case, my dad certainly wouldn't have wanted to hear anything more about the carriage house. The only definite thing that had come out of the police investigation into the dead baby from the carriage house wall was that the little building itself was closed pending a further investigation into its building code violations.

The same cop who shut the carriage house down came by, trying to stay friendly with my dad, and let us know the case was going into the cold file. "Coroner—couldn't set a date of death. Without that, there's a million ways it could have gone. He says that baby could be anywhere from thirty to a hundred and thirty."

"Surely you could narrow down a list of potential parents," said my mom.

The detective shook his head. "Kidding me? You know how many owners this place has had? I did a search." He got out his notes. "Guy called Hollerith built it in 1889. One wife, one daughter, one son. Old money. German or something. War breaks out, the first; he joins up on our side, but gets killed in a training accident before he ships. Widow sells it in the late twenties. Guy called Huff—wife Joan, daughter Lillian —buys, but only lives here a couple of years before moving out and leaving it empty. Eventually it's bought by a family, name of Garroway. Garroway's daughter, Margaret, went missing in 1947, age seventeen. Looks promising, right? No go. She would have had to have had that kid real young, then figured out how to take apart the wall to put it in. We've got a bunch of people that can tell us that wall was around long before forty-seven. Which gets us to the creepiest part of the whole thing. You take a look at the newspaper covering that— you know, the baby? Dateline 1947. Couple of days *after* the Garroway girl went missing. Best suspect? Not so good."

I sat motionless through the mention of the names from my list. My mother hadn't wanted me around for any discussion of the baby, but I flat refused to stay away. This was all right in the middle of my dead-baby popularity at school.

The detective went on to explain that Margaret Garroway had only one surviving relative, her father, now in his eighties in a retirement home. "And that guy—numero uno when she disappeared, but no proof. Says she was rake-thin all the way up to when she went."

"So not the Garroway girl," said my mother. "Who came next?"

The detective shrugged. "Truth is, could have been anyone, anytime. That carriage house was too easy to get into, too hidden. Another funny thing, though. The newspaper was odd enough, from '47 like I said, even though the coroner figures the body's older than that. The baby was also wrapped in cloth, swaddled like. Coroner says we gotta start looking later. Says the polyesters in the cloth weren't even made until the mid-sixties. So I say, first you tell me forty-seven. Then you tell me the body's at least fifty years old. Now you're telling me fifteen?" He waved his hands. "Crazy as nothing."

Then it all went away. When my dad shut up the carriage house, it was like he was closing off the story itself. He started tearing up carpets in the main house and running the floorboards through a planer. Any mention of the other property would be met with his warning to stay away. My mom was happy to back him up on this.

But I couldn't give up on it. Despite the new lock and boarded-up windows, I often squeezed through the hedges that cut the carriage house off into its own little postage stamp of land, sat on a pile of lumber, and enjoyed the silence. After

Christmas, nobody at school talked much to me anymore. On the first day back, I went for lunch at the same table I had been guided to on my first day. The girl who had sung the skipping song raised her eyebrow at me and went back to her pizza slice. A couple of minutes later, her friend showed up, carrying a tray. "Is there any chance you could let me sit there?" she said. "We were going to study for a science test."

"I'm good at science," I said.

"You're in grade nine," she said. "This is grade ten science." She looked her tray and shifted as though it were heavy. "Most of the grade nines sit over by the back doors."

I looked over at the three kids from my math class who were seated just a few feet away, but all of them were studiously involved in a card game.

The note mentioning my name, which I always kept in my back pocket, carefully transferring it whenever I switched jeans, burned for attention. "I found something in that carriage house," I said, scooching over to make room for her to join me at the table. I bumped into a card player who pushed back, but there was still enough room for her. "It's a note with dates on it, and somebody asking for help."

"Just find another table, okay?" said the skipping-song girl. "Nobody wants to hear you make up more stories about your haunted house anymore."

One of the card players giggled. Nobody met my eyes except the girl with the tray. After another moment of silence, I got up and took my lunch over to the garbage. Only one bite taken from my peanut butter sandwich, but I threw it and my whole apple away.

I then realized something that would come to me again and again that year, the year I found the backward glass and went inside: if the note was meant for me, then it was mine alone. Nobody else, not my parents, not the police, and not the kids at school, could be expected to care about it. The urgency of that note, the *Help me make it not happen, Kenny*—that was meant for me. Nobody else was supposed to be obsessed about it but me.

Which is how I ended up there, on a Sunday near the end of January, after three weeks of eating my lunches alone, looking at footprints in the snow leading out of the tiny door. I was all alone in the forbidden yard. My dad was rehanging doors and my mother reading a mystery novel.

I examined the tracks. They went up to the front door, which was hanging slightly ajar.

Heart pounding, I closed it again, and looked back at the footprints.

One set.

Leading away.

I stepped back. Had the guy gone in a window? There were only two on the ground floor, boarded up tight. The hayloft window was clear, but it was fifteen feet up and there were no ladder marks in the snow, nor any easy handholds for climbing.

I called out a couple of hellos.

Nothing.

The creepiness that had made my hair stand on end began to give way to annoyance. This was my place.

I looked back toward the main house, but it couldn't be seen through the high, unruly hedges.

I pushed the door to the carriage house open and stepped in, holding it open behind me to admit the weak January light.

"You're crossing a police line," I said, trying to sound bold and official.

Nothing.

I waited, letting my eyes adjust. No one.

The lower floor was bare now, the musty old couch long since left by the curb, but upstairs the jumble of disused tables and desks remained. I walked up in the dusty light and looked around. My eyes kept wanting to come back to the dark hole left by the last panels my dad had torn away. *Help me make it not happen, Kenny. Help me stop him. Clive is dead all over again.*

Nobody there. An odd, low dresser with a full-length mirror stood near the back. Was there dust scuffed away from its surface? Maybe with a flashlight I could have been sure.

This was stupid, I told myself. My dad forgot to lock the door. Somebody came up and went inside, then it snowed while he was there, and then he walked away again.

But the snow had fallen yesterday, and I had seen it untrammeled last night.

I walked back downstairs and dragged my feet to the door.

Snap. Rustle.

The sound came from the hedgerow. "I hope you know you're trespassing," I said.

No reply. I looked into the thick hedges, snow-blind after the dim mysteries of the carriage house. But I could still tell height, and this was a kid, no taller than me.

I strode forward, shielding my eyes. "You're not allowed to come here," I said, maybe a little louder and harsher than I had intended, but I was trying to build up steam. "Cops closed it off."

The figure withdrew to the other side of the hedge and took off toward the creek.

"Stop!" I hesitated for a moment, then ran to the box-wood shrubs my dad had planted, the easiest part of the hedge to slip through.

The guy was a good runner. He sprinted ahead of me, dodging trees and jumping bushes. When he reached the creek, I got a better look. A dirty white jacket, too thin for January. A foolish-looking orange woolen hat with one of those knit balls bobbing on top.

It's funny how you can switch from feeling one way to something totally different. I had wanted to catch this kid and give him a shake, tell him he better get off our property or else.

Then, in the middle of running—I was lonely. Just like that.

"Hey, wait," I shouted, gasping. "I just want to talk."

The kid veered away from the creek again. We were coming up on the fences that separated us from the subdivision, and it was either climb a fence, go back to our house, or descend to the muddier ground near the trickle of water that was Manse Creek. He headed to the house.

I tried to cut him off, but he was too fast, and I was breathing hard.

Then I got it. He was doubling back to the carriage house. I'd been tricked. I put on a burst of speed, but then slowed. Why hurry? There was only one way out.

I switched to an out-of-breath jog, keeping him in sight through the winter-bare saplings that dotted the ground. He twisted sideways and slipped through the hedge, losing his hat on the way. I saw a hand flash back through and grab for it, so I put on another burst of speed.

The hand disappeared, leaving the orange hat caught in the hedge. I snatched it when I got there.

Before I had even begun to worm my way through, I heard the door slam. I rounded the front of the little house, pushed open the door, and stepped through.

The dark was almost total, cut only by the dimness making its way through the hayloft window. I was worried that the guy might be right beside me, but then I heard a scrape from the second floor.

"Who are you?" I said.

"Are you the one?" came a gruff voice from the shadows. Was he trying to disguise his voice from me, trying to sound older than he was?

"Am I what one?"

"The one the mirror chose? This time, I mean. It's me in ten years."

"Who are you?" I said again. "Look, it isn't safe up there. I'm sorry I scared you before."

The shadowed figure above made a dismissive sound.

"You didn't scare me. This is 1977, right? Are you the one who scratched that message in my drawer?"

"What message? What drawer?" I was beginning to wonder if this was my first encounter with a junkie. "I don't know what you mean," I added. "Look, my name's Kenny Maxwell. I live here. Well, not here, but in the big house."

There was a long silence. "You're Kenny." It was something halfway between a question and a statement. The kid rattled a piece of paper. "So you did write out those rules."

"What rules? What are you talking about?"

"The note Melissa brought back. That she got in the mail." He sounded impatient now, and the gruff was slipping out of his voice. "Do you know what's going on? Have you gone back?"

I held out my hands to calm him down, but I didn't step any closer. "Back where? I don't know any Melissa."

"Don't know much, do you?" I didn't answer. After a long pause he spoke again. "I'm going. It's your note, so you can have it back, I guess. Jeez, I thought you'd have more answers. Help Kenny. What am I supposed to help you do? I guess we'll figure it out, but I've stayed too long as it is. Bye."

Bye? "Wait," I said. I held out my hands, ready for him to rush me, but there was a quick rustle above me behind the furniture.

And then nothing.

"Do you need help or something?" I said after a moment. There was no reply. "What's your name?"

But I knew I was alone. That way your voice is when it's

only you in a room. It was impossible, but I knew it was true. I walked up the stairs.

My dad hadn't finished stripping the lath, so the dark space where the baby had been still dominated the back wall. To the right as you came up the stairs was the cluster of old furniture, much more carelessly placed than in my room. A bed had been ruined with a pile of chairs and two well-worn school desks. I picked a path between dressers, chests, and a pile of splintered remnants.

I wasn't at all scared of the kid jumping out at me. He was gone, I was sure of that, however impossible it was.

It was the note that guided me. He said he was leaving it, and there it was, a new piece of paper sitting on the top of that same low dresser I had noticed before. I picked it up, but couldn't read it in the dim light.

I looked at the mirror, then down at where I had been standing. Yes, this was the thing the kid would have ducked around. I squatted to open its four stubby drawers. Nothing. I ran my hands over a surface that looked to have been finished and refinished several times. The wood framing the mirror at the top was scroll-cut in fancy loops, but everything else was square and functional. I guessed the idea was that the lady of the house would sit in front of it to put on her makeup and jewelry. But if that was so, why did the mirror need to be so tall? It rose a little more than four feet above the dresser. Had it been tacked on later? Maybe. As near as I could tell, it didn't have single scratch on it, and it threw back the dim light perfectly.

No kid hiding. No ghost jumping out.

"I just wanted to talk," I said again, but my voice sounded stupid to me in the empty place, so I went back down and into the light, feeling the paper between my fingers as I went.

As soon as I got outside, I closed the door, sat down on the step, and looked at it.

The first thing that struck me was the lettering. Clean, like letters printed in a book, not punched into the paper the way a typewriter does.

The Rules

*The mirror works January to December, on years
ending in seven. It takes you backward from eleven
until midnight. If you're in an even-numbered decade
(like the eighties or the sixties), it opens for you on an
even-numbered day. Odd decade (seventies or nineties),
odd days. Once you've gone backward, you have to wait
until after midnight to return. The mirror picks one
person every decade, and never picks older than sixteen.
But you can turn seventeen and still use it.*

*There are other rules, but I didn't say them
before, so I shouldn't this time.*

*Good luck,
Your friend for all time,
Kenny Maxwell*

TWO

The Rules

2. From an even-numbered decade, you can go
   back on even-numbered days. Same for odds.

What do you do when you're confronted with something
that's obviously crazy?

You don't talk about it, that's for sure.

I put the note and the orange hat with the list under my
mattress, and spent the day thinking about how nuts I was for
not throwing it all away and telling my dad I had seen some kid
trespassing.

It was the twenty-third of January, so don't think it wasn't
lost on me that at ten-thirty that night I was supposed to be
half an hour away from ... something. Odd day. Odd decade.
Takes you backward.

My parents are strict early-to-bedders, so the house was
quiet. I sat by my window and looked out, though not at

the hedges and the carriage house, since my window faced the street. A new snow was falling.

I continued the argument I had been having with myself for hours, one voice insisting that there was a rational explanation for all of this, the other pointing out all the irrational and unexplainable elements. Whenever that hopeful voice, the one that wanted something magical in the carriage house, finished with its best arguments, rational me would simply shrug his shoulders and say, *Then why aren't you out there? It's because you don't want to be disappointed, isn't it?*

And that was it. All these weeks I had been keeping the list secret, telling myself stories about what it was, how I fit into it all. I didn't believe in ghosts that needed to be saved or set free, but I wanted to. If I went out there, and nothing happened, my ticket into the story I had been living in my head would turn out to be a forgery I had made myself. But if I stayed here, I would always have the ticket to look at.

I stayed.

Eventually I fell asleep.

————

School the next day was hell. Every moment irritated me. Normally, I just did as I was told, and tried to finish my work quickly.

But not today. I failed a math quiz, fumbled at marking another kid's when we were supposed to take it up, stumbled when I was called on, and actually grumbled slightly when Mrs. Bains told us to take out our grammar exercise books.

Why hadn't I gone out there? An odd-numbered night. *It takes you backward. It opens for you.*

Once home, I had time to myself. My mother got off work at five, and my dad after that.

I dropped off my backpack and squeezed through the hedges. There were no new footprints. The door was still unlocked. I spent my hour and a half of freedom rummaging through the old furniture, but there was nothing there. When I figured I was in danger of Mom getting home, I took some balled-up newspapers from the wall and headed up to my room.

Nothing interesting. It was amazing how few pictures they had in those old newspapers, and how long they took to say anything. One of them had a variation on the local Prince Harming skipping rhymes scratched in faded pencil in a margin: "Lover sweet, bloody feet, running down the silver street. Leave tomorrow when you're called, hear the wisdom in the walls. Crack your head, knock you dead, then Prince Harming's hunger's fed." I tore that part of the paper off and stuck it under my mattress. Why did it matter to me? Why did I shiver every time I heard that name? The kids at school had thought it all had something to do with my house, but for them it was just a game. They didn't have a note signed, *Your friend for all time, Kenny Maxwell.*

A call for supper. Interrogation about my day. Merciful escape back to my room. Homework. My dad calling lights out. Tossing. Turning. Sleep.

Tink. Clatter.

I looked to the ceiling and rubbed my eyes.

Something hitting one of my skylight windows and falling down the roof.

I went to the window and opened it. "Hello? Who's throwing that?"

A figure came into sight. "Who do you think, retard? Where's my hat?"

My mouth hung open. "You're a girl." The hat had hidden a huge mane of curly hair, and she wasn't trying to disguise her voice now.

She folded her arms. "And you're an airhead. Are you going to give me my hat, or what?"

"Who are you?" I said.

"I'm Luka."

I frowned. "Luka?" It didn't even sound like a real name.

Luka threw up her hands in annoyance. "My real name's Lucy, but my mom took me to *Star Wars* on my seventh birthday, and I kind of made her change it. It's not my fault. I was a spazzy kid. Go figure. Are you coming down or what?"

I had no idea what she was talking about, no idea what half of her words even meant. Airhead. Go figure. Spazzy. *Star Wars*. But one thing she said stood out. "Lucy?" I said. "Lucy Branson?" She nodded. "I'll give you your hat if you tell me where you disappeared to," I said.

That stopped her. "But—didn't you say you're Kenny? Didn't you—oh, I get it. You didn't do it yet."

"Do what?"

"Write the note, genius. Okay, fine. Come down. I'll explain. But you'll never believe it."

THREE

The Rules

3. Once you've gone back, you have to wait until midnight. After that, you can go home again anytime.

Getting downstairs was easy. If I was careful and stuck to the floorboards my dad had fixed, I could blend in with the creaks and pops of the old house settling down for the night.

I surrendered the hat as soon as I got outside and Luka put it on.

It couldn't have been more than a couple degrees below freezing, and there wasn't much wind. We stood for a long moment.

"Who are you?" I said, but before she spoke, I added, "Not just your name. What's going on?" When I asked that, something stiffened in my spine. I was still scared, not of this kid, but of something out there in the night. But that didn't matter. That was my name on the note I had found. Someone was asking me for help.

She dropped her hands to her sides and looked at me directly. "My name is Luka Branson. I was born October 12, 1970. I live at 428 Larkfield Drive. I'm sixteen years old."

My heart thudded painfully. "How is that possible?"

"I don't know. We're just starting to figure it out. It goes every ten years. A few days ago I met the girl from 1997, ten years up from my time. She got those rules from you." I opened my mouth, but she held up her hand. "Come on. There's something I want to show you."

She grabbed the shoulder of my coat and pulled. I let myself be dragged through the hedge.

"See that?" she said, pointing to the winter-brittle tangle of tall weeds that choked the carriage house's tiny front yard. "That's a swimming pool. And right there?" She pointed to the far corner of the hedge. "That's where Larkfield curves out to Manse Creek Road."

"There's no Larkfield going onto Manse Creek," I said.

She looked at me like I was an idiot. "Don't you get it? Time travel. I'm from 1987."

I shook my head.

She looked into my eyes. "Come on," she said. "I really thought you'd know more stuff than this."

As she dragged me farther from my house, I looked back, worried.

She must have read my mind. "Look, if you got out okay, you're not going to get caught now. Even if you do, just say you went out for a walk."

I couldn't imagine just how badly that would go, but I figured she was right about the first part, so I let her take me down to the creek.

"This used to be a bridge," she said, pointing to a bend where both banks were about eight feet high. "I mean, it will be. It's confusing, right? I keep thinking I'm in one of those Mad Max movies, you know? After the world's been destroyed. I go to these places, and some of the trees look the same. Like that one. Tom Berditti's dad put a tire swing on it a couple of years ago. But now it's not there. Yet, I mean."

She walked me down the creek, pointing to things I couldn't see, things that wouldn't be here for years—a whole subdivision, paths to and from the creek, bus stops for routes I had never heard of, and things she called "super mailboxes."

She was entranced with the world of the past. I was more interested in her.

"How did you get here?" I asked as we walked out onto Lawrence.

"You know that," she said. "The mirror."

"But how?"

"That bus stop looks so new! In my time, it's all beat up. When did they put it in?"

"I don't know. I don't care. It was here when we moved in. Look, how did you know about the mirror? Does it just take you back? Does it go forward as well? How does this work? I don't care about this stuff about the neighborhood. I want to go to the mirror."

She threw up her hands, then tapped her watch. "Fine. I

was just killing time anyway. I can't show you anything until midnight."

When we got inside the carriage house, there were two minutes to go. Luka took out a flashlight and guided me upstairs through the maze of junk to the low dresser where I found the note. She looked at me and pursed her lips. "Look, I can sit around talking at you all night, or I can show you. What do you want?"

Blood pounded in my ears. "Show me."

With that she grinned, shone her flashlight at the mirror, and touched it with her other hand. For just a moment, her palm lay on the surface, fingers splayed. "It's hot," she said. "You have to be ready. Cold when you go down, hot when you go up." She beckoned. "Take the flashlight in your other hand. You have to hold my hand all the way through. There's a space in between going in and coming out. Are you coming?"

"I'll be able to get back, won't I?"

She rolled her eyes. "Real adventurer, aren't you? Yes, you'll be able to get back. When you're in the wrong time, you can always go back. After midnight, I mean. I haven't figured everything out yet, but I know that. Melissa took me through with her last night."

I knew I had to go through. My name on a list. My name on a note. "How is all this connected?" I said, fixing her with my gaze. "Do you know about the dead baby? The one in the wall? Do you know about Prince Harming?"

She shrugged. "Kind of. There's some story in the neighborhood about a guy who kills kids or smashes their heads in or something. But that's all the past. All I can do right now is take you to my time." She saw that I was about to ask more questions and held up her hand. "Look, I'm from the future, all right? You're the one from the past. I came back to get answers from you, not sit around explaining things. Are you coming or not?"

I had already made my decision when I left my room. I took the flashlight, grasped her hand, and let myself be dragged along as she stepped up onto the low surface of the dresser and, with some effort, pushed through the mirror. I could see her, like a fun-house effect, going from two girls, to one-and-a-half, to one, to just a double arm, shortening as it pulled me in.

If she hadn't warned me about the heat, I might have let go. As it was, I flinched. On the skin of my wrist I could feel first the freezing surface of the mirror, then the pore-opening fire of whatever lay beyond. It was like sticking your hand into burning Play-Doh.

Up to my elbow disappeared. The tugging from the other side grew stronger. I felt Luka's other hand encircle my wrist, and almost stumbled as I got both my feet onto the surface of the dresser and ducked my head.

As my eyes moved toward the mirror, I turned my head and closed them. The cold mirror flattened my ear at first, then my head went through a heat that felt like it would burn my eyebrows off. I had taken a breath and closed my mouth, and now I imagined I was in some kind of burning, molten silver. We moved through that hot blindness for just a step—

Then I was falling—out of the other side of the mirror

and into something soft that went "Ow!" and punched me hard in the shoulder.

I opened my eyes to darkness, then brought the flashlight around to Luka's face.

She put a finger to her lips. "Don't talk loud or you'll wake my mom up. Welcome to 1987."

FOUR

The Rules

4. When you go uptime to your home, you can
   bring the chosen kid from the past with you.

My first impression of the future came from a small room that
must have been decorated by someone with a great interest
in horses and someone called Bon Jovi. I shone my flashlight
beam all around. I guess I had been spoiled by the distant
walls of my converted attic, because it seemed claustrophobic.

"This is the future?" I whispered.

"What did you expect, space ships and flying cars? Come
here, I'll show you." Luka dragged me to the window. "Does
that tree look familiar?"

"Kind of." To me, one tree pretty much looked like the
next, but there was something in the way its lowest main
branch jutted almost straight out, then changed direction and
thrust upward. The street itself was just a quiet suburban subdivision. Did the cars look different? In the dark, I couldn't

tell. Maybe that one's bumper was a little more rounded, and the same with the roof on that other one two doors down.

It was the weather that convinced me. "You've had more snow," I said.

"You're right. It's been cold since New Year's."

I lingered a moment at the window. I could see now the fascination she had felt just a few minutes ago on my side of the mirror. That whole world out there was the same, but not the same. I was out there somewhere, ten years older. My parents, too. Every problem I knew about in the world had moved and changed into something else. All because I had stepped through with Luka. I pointed my flashlight back at the dresser. "How did you get it?" I said.

"My dad bought it at a garage sale just before you moved. I was, like, nine. The mirror won't break, you know. I once threw an ashtray, full force. Not a scratch."

"Do you know me?" I said. "I mean—me now?"

"Like I said, you moved. Just after we moved in. I don't really remember you."

We were by this time sitting in front of her bed, the flashlight between us. "So what's cool about the future?" I said at last.

She shook her head. "It's not the future, dummy, it's just 1987. What do you expect, jetpacks and flying cars?"

"No, just—do you have anything cool?"

Luka gnawed her lower lip, then came to a decision. "Fine. Come with me. But once we get outside this room— no noise. I don't want to know what would happen if my mom found a boy here at night."

She insisted on turning the flashlight off for our journey downstairs, so I had to rely on her to lead me.

In the basement, Luka turned on a light, then picked up a black plastic rectangle with numbered buttons and pointed it in the direction of a large TV. Without her approaching it, and with a kind of muted *thoom,* the thing turned on. Then she went to it and touched a grey box on a shelf on the TV stand. She took away two smaller rectangular grey boxes away from it. Each one had a cross and two red buttons on its face.

She handed one to me. "You're gonna like this."

"What is it?"

"Nintendo. It's what's cool in the future."

Two hours later, she practically had to rip the controller from my hand and force me up the stairs. "It's almost three in the morning back in your time as well. Didn't you say it was a school night?"

It was. Sunday here was Tuesday back home.

I didn't care. I had been Mario. I had jumped onto turtles and mushrooms, leaped hammers and jets of fire, fallen down pits, and climbed into elevators. The future was cool.

I told Luka as much. She shrugged. "It's better than Atari because they have more games. Melissa, in ten years? Has way better stuff. And Keisha has even better than that. Anyway, come on. I still have to show you that drawer."

We started up the basement stairs. "How do you know about them? Keisha and Melissa?"

"Even, odd? Forward, backward? My theory? It was really only for backward. I think it's kind of cheating when

I bring you forward like this. That's why it'll let you go back anytime. Kind of putting things right again. Anyway, hush."

Luka made me hot chocolate in a microwave and told me to drink up. "You have no idea how cold you're going to be. Trust me."

"So who made it?" I whispered, looking at the mirror when we were back in her room with the door closed.

She shrugged. "We don't know. In 1997? They have this thing—it's like all of the computers in the world connected together. They call it the Internet."

"Can you talk to it?"

Another eye roll. "No. But you can type in things and search for them. Melissa and Keisha think maybe it has something to do with your house."

"So you really met them?" I said.

Her shrug was minimal, cool. "Sure. I guess I almost had a heart attack when Melissa first came through. Eleven o'clock at night, this girl just steps out of my mirror. Keisha came to her a few days later."

"What about the one further up from her? Initials C.M.?"

That stopped her. "How do you know anything about way up in 2017?"

"So you haven't met C.M.?" Oh, this was good. I knew something she didn't.

"Of course not. Think about how hard that would be. Melissa can only come back to see me on odd-numbered days. I'd have to get her to take me with her to her time, then wait a day until Keisha could pull us up to 2007, and another one for that other kid, whatever his name is, to come back to

Keisha's time. I'd be gone for three days. My mom would kill me."

I pursed my lips. "So we can't ever go far from our own times?"

"We're working on it. Sleepovers. Lies to the parents. We'll think of something. We have a whole year, right? That's what the note said."

I rubbed my neck. "Yeah. But a year for what?"

Luka looked right at me, and an electric moment of communication passed between us. I had never had that with anyone before, but I knew that I knew what she was thinking, and I knew she knew I was thinking it, too. A year for what? Just for having fun, for doing something no one else on earth could do? A year for seeing the world stuttered ten years back and forth? A year for seeing that there never were any jetpacks or flying cars? Or a year for something more?

"What are you getting at?" she said.

"The dead baby," I said. "The girl that went missing." From my pocket, I took out the list I had found on my first day in the new house, the paper that had fallen away from the tiny, blackened corpse. I spread it in front of her and aimed my flashlight at it.

She stared at it long enough to read the words three or four times. Then she ran her forefinger over the writing at the bottom, the message to me. "So it really is about you and me," she said.

"What do you mean, you and me?"

Luka pursed her lips. "I should have shown you before,"

she said. "I just—I got so used to keeping it a secret. I never showed anyone. Since we moved in."

Without another word, she stood up, walked to the dresser, and pulled out its top drawer. She brought it back and lay it upside down, the beam of my flashlight revealing the rough, scratched letters.

Luka, help Kenny. Trust John Wald. Kenny says he is the auby one. Save the baby.

"Okay," I said after a long, long silence.

"I found it years ago," Luka said. "What's that mean, an *auby* one? Did they misspell Aubrey? How is that even pronounced? Is it aw-bee or oh-bee? Or oh-bye?"

"No idea. But that's our names."

"I know." She grinned and so did I. "This is the coolest thing that's ever happened in the world. I mean—it's really you. There's really a Kenny."

"Hey!" came a voice from the hallway. I heard a door open. "You on the phone with your stupid father again? Hell's the matter with you?"

Luka's eyes grew wide, and she snapped off the light. "Go," she whispered, pushing me to the dresser. "Remember, it'll be cold." I was already pressing my hand on the glass. Just as I felt it give, she leaned forward and kissed me on the cheek. "For luck," she said, and was gone like a shot to her bedroom door, opening it and charging out to meet her mother. "I'm not talking to anyone," she said. "You were having some drunk dream."

The last thing I heard in 1987, before I shoved my face into iced molasses, sounded like a slap.

Luka wasn't kidding about the cold. It touched every part of your skin, no matter how much clothing you wore. And it held on. I closed my eyes as I pushed through. The journey didn't seem so long this time, maybe because I had done it before, maybe just because I was coming home. No matter what reassurances Luka had given me, a part of me had been terrified of being trapped.

I took a large step through the bone-chilling cold of the mirror and felt the air of the carriage house. My forward hand found a grip on the frame and I pulled myself out, feeling like I was climbing out of a mountain of slush.

I collapsed, curled and shivering with the transit. I had never felt such cold. It went beyond skin, beyond lungs, bone, teeth. My memories, my thoughts, my whole life was freezing, clenched into a shuddering ball. The excitement of time travel drained out of me. It would be good to sleep here. Maybe if I could do that, I'd wake up and it would all be over. My mother would have more hot chocolate. My dad would tell me to take a day off school.

In the end, I only got up because of that rational inner voice, the one that had told me I didn't want to come out here and be disappointed.

There was also the kiss still freezing on my cheek. That was worth getting moving for.

By the time I got into bed, my clock showed almost four. I had never been up this late in my life. Before I gave in to sleep, I thought ahead enough to take a final look around my room and make sure any signs of my nighttime journey were gone, my clothes scattered in their usual way, the note and the list back under my mattress.

Next thing I knew my mother was shaking me and telling me I was going to be late.

For a second day, though for different reasons, I went through the motions of school, mechanical and uninspired. Whenever I could, I replayed parts of last night. Nintendo. Welcome to the future. Nintendo. The feeling of pressing my hand onto an unyielding surface only to have it melt away. Luka. Nintendo. If I closed my eyes, I could still see Mario running and jumping through castles and fields.

And feel that kiss.

At eleven that night, I sat by my window, wishing it faced the carriage house. It was an odd-numbered day now, so if the note from future me was for real, nobody should be coming through. But didn't that mean this "Jimmy Hayes, 1967" might be waiting for me ten years back? Did he even know about the mirror? Had he already gone to 1957?

Luka had done it. She had just stepped through the mirror and into my time. Melissa and Keisha as well. And there was a note, two now, asking for our help. I had to go, didn't I?

But ten years. No one in the world would know me. I would be a four-year-old out there. What if I got caught? What if Luka was wrong and the mirror broke? Why didn't any of these other stupid kids on the list have these fears? What kind of idiots were they?

I couldn't do this.

I couldn't.

At eleven thirty, I crept down to the first floor and spent fifteen minutes assembling the most complete survival-in-the-past backpack I could think of. Two flashlights, a handful of chocolate bar, a half bottle of juice, and all the quarters I could find so at least I'd have some money. Some of them had post-1967 dates, but I figured they'd still be more convincing than paper money, which I'd checked and found all marked 1972.

Two minutes before midnight.

Help me make it not happen, Kenny.

Help me make it not happen.

Kenny.

I put my hand on the mirror and pushed.

Either I was getting used to the resistance, or it was getting easier. The cold was still there, worse than any January wind on bare skin, but I pushed through faster this time, got my hand on the other side, braced it on the mirror in the past, then pulled my head and shoulders after it.

For all my caution, I misjudged my balance. I got a look at a flickering light, and maybe two figures near it, then I tumbled out, the mirror loosening its grip on me, and fell onto the floor of the carriage house.

"There he is," said a voice from below. "Get him!"

FIVE

The Rules

5. The mirror only picks one kid every decade.
   It never picks anyone older than sixteen.

Boots thumped up the stairs, and before I could get on my feet, someone grabbed me. Two someones. They grasped my arms, pulled me up, and marched me down the stairs. I slipped once and cracked my knee, but they didn't let go.

The flickering came from a Coleman stove. The bigger of the two kids holding me turned me toward him. "Well," he said. "If it isn't the kid from the future. What've you got for us, H. G. Wells?"

He was bigger than me, seventeen or eighteen maybe. "Here," he said, "let's have a look at the backpack." He took it from me. I held my hands at my sides and shivered. The hand warmers helped, as did the flickering flame of the Coleman stove, but I was still almost incapacitated by the chill of time travel. "I'm Rick," he said, opening my backpack and looking at my thermos, wrapped coins, spare batteries, pen, paper, and Hershey bars. "No smokes? What's your name, kid?"

"Kenny Maxwell."

"Well, Kenneth Maxwell," he said, "welcome to the past. Have a seat."

He put a hand on my shoulder and I let myself be guided down. He sat too, and waved to the other kid to do the same. "Listen, Rick," the other kid said. "Maybe I should go. We don't want my folks to wake up."

Now that I could see him, this other kid was only an inch taller than me. He had a mess of sandy hair and looked nervous.

"Sit down, Jimmy," said Rick. "You got no curiosity? Kid's from 1977. Isn't that right, H. G. Wells?" I nodded. They had seen me come out of the mirror and seemed to know what was going on. Why deny it? "So, what's happened in the future, Kenneth? We've been waiting a while for you. We were beginning to think you'd had a nuclear war up there and you weren't coming. You look kind of good for a mutant monster, though. Did the Ruskies attack?"

"No," I said. "Not even in 1987 or 1997 or 2007." Instantly, I knew I had said too much.

Rick leaned forward. "Really? Time traveler knows a lot. Who you been talking to, H. G?"

"A girl. She came back from 1987. She told me about the other ones." I tried to think about what Luka had said. You were only allowed to go forward if you were going with someone from the future. Maybe Rick didn't know that.

Rick took my things out of the backpack, giving Jimmy

a running commentary. "Nice flashlight. Bet I can get a buck or two for that. Chocolate's always good. What's this? Trying to make a black jack?" He took my quarters out of the socks and as soon as he saw what they were, vanished the money into his pockets. The Hershey bars he shared around, even handing one to me and insisting that I eat it. "Come on. We're all in this together, right?" He looked at Jimmy, who nodded reluctantly.

As Rick did all this, I studied him. His head was covered in a cloud of black curls and his face still troubled with acne. His hands were huge, but his shoulders weren't as wide as I had thought at first. Once he had finished with the backpack, he made me turn out my empty pockets. He took my hat and gloves and gave them to Jimmy.

"What's your story, Kenneth Maxwell?" Rick said. "How'd you find out about my little mirror here?"

His mirror?

Thinking as fast as I could, I told him an edited version of the facts. My encounters with Luka, my journey into the future. He was interested to hear that the mirror was still in the carriage house in my time, and even more interested that the place itself was gone ten years later. He wanted to know if I knew who my dad had bought the house from. I told him nobody had lived in it for a few years, and I didn't know who was there before. "Hear anything about the Beech family? No?"

He didn't ask about the other kid's family. Jimmy sat looking miserable.

"You ever think about what you could do with this?" Rick

said. "Friend of my dad's deals in old stuff. This one time, I helped some old lady clean out her attic after her husband died. I found these boxes of old magazines and comic books. The old lady paid me a dollar to take it to the dump, then my dad's buddy paid me twenty bucks for the stuff. Twenty bucks. That's nothing compared to what we could do. Go back ten years, buy up a bunch of cheap stuff, then go up to your time or that girl's and sell it all for a mint."

"I don't think that's what it's supposed to be about," I said, reaching out to warm my hands in the small flame of his Coleman stove.

Rick looked up sharply. "You don't think what? What's what supposed to be about, Kenneth?"

I flinched from his anger, but pushed on, pretending it was like the impersonal cold or heat of the mirror. "The mirror," I said, not even wanting to look up to the second floor, not wanting to let him know how much I just wanted to run back into it. "I don't think it's about us getting rich. I got a— there was a note. Left for me. It said my name. Somebody was asking me for help from the past. Something about a baby that got killed."

Rick greeted these revelations with a long, stony silence. "Well," he said at last, "nobody here's asking for your help."

Fine, I wanted to say, I'll just be on my way, then. But I didn't want to let him know just how much I wanted out of here.

"Yeah, that's right," said Jimmy. "Things are just fine here. How do we know you're telling the truth, anyway? Maybe you broke into my folks' house to go into the mirror.

See, Rick, I think we gotta get rid of that thing. There's no telling who could—"

Rick raised his hand to shut Jimmy up. "So what are you here for? That's the question, isn't it? You came here to help somebody, is that it?"

I studied his face for a moment before answering. It wasn't a bully question, the kind where there's no right answer and you're just going to get interrupted or pushed or hit whatever you say. He actually wanted an answer. "How could I not go?" I said. "It's time travel. And there's something about a baby. I think I'm supposed to save it. It was—it was hidden in the walls. Like someone killed it and hid it there. With a note asking me for help."

Jimmy shook his head. "Man, that's crazy. I mean, you're lucky it was us here. This old place—technically, my folks rent it from Rick's dad, but he doesn't come out here much. All kinds of stuff goes on here. I'm not even allowed to be here. Kids with wild parties. Pete Masterson's crew gets drunk here sometimes. Like if it was a Friday or a Saturday night, and you came out of there—no way."

"That's why he's got us," said Rick. His gaze still hadn't left my face.

Jimmy swallowed. "Sure, Rick, sure. But he should just stay home is all I'm saying. You know? I could even—we could give him back his stuff, too. We could give it back and just push him back through and—that's it. Too dangerous, you know?"

"Jimmy, shut up a minute, will you?" Rick said it without any inflection. He scratched his chin and kept looking at me. "What about it? Is that what you're going to do? Never come back?" He waved his hand impatiently when I hesitated. "Not what you think I want you to say. The truth. Are you coming back?"

A long moment stretched between us. Jimmy cleared his throat. "Uh, Rick? My dad? He could wake up any time. He don't find me in the house, he'll come looking, you know?"

"Fine." Rick didn't even look at him, just kept his gaze fixed on me. I realized I had gotten it wrong. There was still baby fat in his face, still a kid in there. "Get out of here, then. Leave the kid's stuff here."

Jimmy hesitated briefly at the door to give me a look that might have been an apology. Then he was gone.

Rick let another long moment of silence follow the click of the carriage house door. "How old are you, kid?" he said at last.

"Fifteen." He looked at me dubiously, and I amended, "In a couple of months." Still a lie. My birthday wasn't for half a year.

"You can take your backpack," he said.

"Thanks," I said. Wondering if he might change his mind, I got up and went to pick it up.

"Can you believe it?" he said. "Eight years ago, I found a diary. Most of it makes no sense. But it talked about the mirror. About when the guy was a kid and he went through it and met his own mother before she was his mother. Crazy stuff. He said how the mirror was unbreakable, how it chose one kid every ten years to get to go back in time."

"And you waited," I said.

"Not at first. Didn't believe it. But the idea was cool."
I nodded. I had felt the same way about my list. "Last year
Jimmy tells me about this mirror. He's up here one day fool-
ing around, and he throws a baseball right at it. For kicks.
Doesn't break. He brings me in to see it. Man, I couldn't lay
a scratch on that thing." Rick scratched his chin and looked
at me.

"You're too old, aren't you?"

His eyes narrowed. "Is that it? The diary didn't say anything about age. There's a rule?"

"I got a note," I said. "I mean—I sent it, I think. To
the girl twenty years later. It says the mirror never takes
anyone older than sixteen."

Rick closed his eyes and shook his head. "Found that
goddamn diary when I was nine years old underneath an
old floorboard. Too old."

"But not Jimmy."

His eyes were still screwed shut. "Jimmy goddamn
Hayes," he said. "Kid's got the guts of a bed-wetting chip-
munk. January second." He shook his head. "I let him stick
around while I was going to go in, right? I didn't even tell
him about the diary. I just wanted to amaze him. Stole
some smokes from my dad, brought Jimmy in here, and
just casually leaned against the mirror. Nothing. I got so
mad, I pushed him into it." He opened his eyes for the first
time in a couple of minutes and looked right at me. "Took
him three hours to come back. He ended up in some basement. Thought it was me playing a joke, and started yelling
for me. Someone came, and he ran out of there. Spent all

that time wandering around, then snuck back in a window. Course, at the time, he didn't even know what was going on. I had to explain when he got back." Rick dropped his cigarette and ground it into the floor. "So you think it's all about this dead baby? Some kind of mission in the past?"

"I don't know," I said. "I mean—I think so. The girl from 1987, Luka. She found a message as well. It told her to help me."

"But how can you save the kid if you've already found its body?"

I held up my hands. "I don't know. I don't get it. But somebody asked for my help."

Rick closed his eyes and drew in a deep breath, then let it out through his teeth in a long sigh. "You're a weird kid, you know that? Okay, H. G. Wells." He stuck his hand in the inside pocket of his jean jacket and brought out a squat leather-bound book with pages sticking out of it.

"What is it?" I said, looking at his outstretched hand.

"The diary. I can't make much sense of it. There's the mirror stuff, and some stuff about jobs he had, but the rest? Guy thinks he's two different people or something. Take a look anyway."

"Why are you giving this to me?"

He looked away. The light of the Coleman stove caught a bitter twist in his face. "Comic books. That was my big idea, you know that? I mean, I thought about stock market and crap like that as well, but I figured who wants to figure out how to invest in stocks. I figured I'd get all the other kids who could go into the mirror—we'd pass stuff up and down the line and make some money." He shook his head. "Christ. Time travel—and I wanted to sell comic books. Go on, H. G. Wells. Take it. Save the baby. Maybe there's a reason the damn mirror didn't open up for me."

SIX

The Rules

6. You can't ever really change anything.

Luka, when she next made it to my time more than a week later, was astonished by my story, which I told her over some microwaved lasagnas she had swiped from her mother's fridge and "nuked" just before coming through. The cold of backward time travel didn't affect inanimate objects. Your clothes and your possessions didn't freeze, just your skin and everything underneath.

She felt sympathetic at Rick's disappointment. "Can you imagine? He knows all about it, and then he has to watch some wimp go instead?" As a card-carrying member of the wimp party myself, I didn't like this judgment, but then I didn't like what I had seen of Jimmy Hayes either. "So what's with this diary he gave you?"

I brought it out from hiding. "It's not just one diary. This crazy guy must have somehow got a hold of old diaries from two other people—I think it's Rose and Curtis from the list. So he cut them all up and pasted them in here, but the paper's old. Anyway, listen."

I read her the first two entries, which I had puzzled out in the last week.

January 18, 1917

Dear Diary,
Am I a fool to love Clive Beckett?

Should I run through my mirror into the past and warn my six-year-old self never to smile at him or think him fine? I have given him everything, and now all he can give me is the role of the faithful girl keeping the home fires burning.

But, Diary, oh what news I have! I have already told you not to suspect me of madness when I wrote to you about my magic mirror. Now I have found it is not mine alone. Two days ago, as I was combing my hair for bed, a little boy stumbled through.

This boy's name is Curtis, and he is a glum little thing, just nine years old. The mirror is so much more than I thought. This Curtis is from ten years onward. I asked him what he is doing in my house, in 1927, and what do you think he said? He is my brother, not even born in this year. Further, he said that another child, someone called Lillian, comes and visits him from ten years further. Am I, I asked him, Mrs. Clive Beckett in your time?

I think I am a shrewd enough judge of character
to sense that there was something this little boy
wasn't telling me. He told me that, yes, I am married
to Clive Beckett and we have three children and
live nearby. But each answer was preceded by such
stammering and looking off that I wonder if he is my
brother at all.

He said that he would come again in two days
and bring more news from ten years on.

How vast the world is, and strange.

That entry, along with all those pasted onto the left-hand pages of the book, was in the same hand that had written the list I had found weeks ago. The right-hand pages were in a more childish style and quite often from ten years to the day after the ones they faced.

January 18, 1927

Rose is the girl in the past. That's my sister who died
when I was two. She said I should keep a diary of
what happens, but I won't let her see it. Seems nice
so I don't want to tell her the truth. Lillian came
through again. She is nicer than Rose and doesn't ask
lots of questions. I wonder if I will meet her when I
am older in her time.

The last third of the book was mostly unreadable. When you could make out the writing, it was lists of words, sometimes rhyming or connected. Now and then there was a sentence, but you couldn't string much of it together: "Shatterday shatterdate cursed on the track effect cause effect cause change it stop it switch the track and shatterdate the nightmare save the girl and catch him just in time to shattertrack shuttle-track."

And so on. An entire page was devoted to variations on the Prince Harming skipping song, which Luka said was around even past her time. One of them was just a few words different from the rhyme I had found written on the page of an old newspaper: "Lover sweet, bloody feet, running down the lonely street. Leave tomorrow when you're called, truth and wisdom deeply walled. Crack your head, knock you dead, then Prince Harming's hunger's fed."

"You think it means something?" said Luka when I showed it to her.

"It's about walls," I said. "Both versions. Deep and walled, in the walls. And there was that baby. And the note."

"And you still want to go back?" I could tell she didn't totally believe me, but I nodded, resolute. "Okay, but not yet. I'm going with you, but it's going to take some time to set up."

"What is?"

"You'll see. I'm going to make it safe. Just—until then, don't do anything stupid, okay?"

As it turned out, I didn't get much chance for stupid for another month. A big storm dumped a ton of snow on us in early February, and I would have had to take a shovel to dig out the giant drift against the door of the carriage house. Luka still came back, and on even-numbered nights, I'd sneak out and sit in the little area bounded by the hedges and talk to her through the dormer window. She wanted me to clear the snow away, but I was too scared of being found out.

Crazy, right? A mirror ready to take me back or forward in time, an impossible note asking for my help, and I was scared of getting in trouble from my parents. In my heart, I knew I wasn't that different from Jimmy Hayes.

But all snow melts if you wait long enough, and the day it did was an Easter weekend for Luka. Her mother had taken off and left her alone. We made big plans. My parents were both at work when I got home, so I didn't even drop off at home before going to find her. Having pushed the door open past the dregs of the snow, she was out and about in 1977 for the first time in weeks, and she had a present for me.

"A rabbit's foot?"

"Not just any rabbit's foot, dummy. This is from the junk house over on Homestead."

"Granny Miller's place? Did you break in there?" I might have only been in the neighborhood a few months, but I knew that the old lady who ran the convenience store down the street was crazy. The story was that all the stuff she couldn't sell in her store went into that place, that it had been years since people could even fit in there to live. "It's even supposed to be haunted and stuff."

Luka shook her head. "Nah, nothing like that. I got it right from the old lady herself a couple of years ago when she finally cleared that place out and let them demolish it." She took my door key and clipped the dyed purple charm onto it. "I found it a few days ago and it got me thinking. Do you know what her real name is?"

"It's not Miller?"

"Uh-uh. Miller was her first husband. But if you go down the side of the house, that's not the name on the mailbox. And that phone booth outside her house? I ripped this out of its phonebook, just to bring you proof."

She thrust a page at me and underscored a name with her fingernail: L. Beech, 38 Moores Road.

I took a moment under her gaze to make sense of what she was saying. "As in Rick Beech?"

"Right. As in, his grandmother owns the store and the junk house. Back then in the sixties, his dad even owned your house." She paused, waiting for me to say something. "You're having some kind of thought," she said. "Out with it."

"Rick's twenty-eight now or something," I said. "Right now, I mean. I wonder if he's around the neighborhood? What if he could tell us about some mistake he's going to make in life, and we could tell him to avoid it."

Luka raised an eyebrow. "You're only thinking about this now? Sometimes Kenny, I swear, for a smart kid you're such a dunce."

She went on to explain how she and Melissa and Keisha had tried testing the limits of our time-travel powers and advantages. Melissa thought of it first. She wanted to know who her first boyfriend was going to be, and she wanted Keisha's help doing it. Keisha found a listing in the phonebook for Melissa's family, but every time she called to ask future-Melissa about her life something went wrong. Melissa wasn't home, or the phone was busy, or Keisha's phone wasn't working. Nothing seemed to work.

Melissa asked her to just visit. Again, everything got in the way. The bus broke down. A car accident delayed her for more than an hour. Once, when she actually made it to just across the street from Melissa's house, and thought she saw older Melissa coming out, a car drove by, hit a puddle, and drenched Keisha with icy slush. By the time she recovered, grown-up Melissa was gone.

"It's like you can't mess up time," Luka said. "Keisha says it's God, but I asked her where exactly the time-travel mirrors come into the Bible. Melissa says it's fate, but I don't even think it's that."

"Then what?"

She shrugged. "It just didn't happen that way. Think about the Melissa's-first-boyfriend thing. Let's say his name is Chris. Let's say she didn't like him in the end because he cheated on her. So Keisha finds that out and tells her. Is she going to go out with him?"

"Probably not." I figured that was the answer she was looking for. Going out with people and cheating were things I had no idea about. I was about a million light years away from a girlfriend. Did Luka have a boy up there in the future? She never talked about anyone. She was two years older. I figured that meant she'd never be interested in me.

"Exactly," said Luka. "No way. So she never goes out with that guy. She goes with Joe instead. But doesn't that mean she would have told Keisha about Joe, not Chris? And if she told us about Joe and how he was no good, doesn't that put her back to Chris? The point is, it just didn't happen. If we try to make something happen when it didn't happen—it doesn't happen."

When I couldn't wrap my mind around this, Luka insisted on a demonstration. We went back to my place and got out the phonebook. There were four listings for R. Beech, so we called them one by one. The first was a woman, second was an old man. Holding up the phone so we could both hear it, we hit paydirt on the third. "Hello, is this Rick Beech, formerly of Manse Creek?" said Luka in her most formal voice.

He replied immediately, almost before she had finished speaking. "Luka? Is it you? This is the call, isn't it, the one you told me about?" She tried to say something, but he rushed on. "Look, there isn't much time and there's so much I want to tell you. Is Kenny there? Kenny, listen. The baby. It isn't him. You have to go to 1917. Rose is the key. You already know Wald's okay, but so is—"

The phone and the lights went dead at the same time.

SEVEN

The Rules

7. When you go downtime from your own mirror,
   you can take the kid from the future with you.

A transformer had exploded somewhere in the city, dropping over us a fifteen-mile cloak of darkness beginning at Manse Creek and extending exactly to Wellesley Street, the address at which we had called Rick Beech. Eight car accidents and the transformer explosion itself sent eleven people to the hospital. One died.

"Did we do that?" I asked Luka that night. She had gone off to the carriage house half an hour after the lights went out so as to avoid my parents when they came home. The power outage had dominated both dinnertime conversation and the evening news. By the time I snuck out to the carriage house, I had all the statistics memorized.

"No way," said Luka. "You can't change anything. That power-out was going to happen anyway. Look, here's your pepper spray. You won't need it, but I'm giving it to you any-way. You flip this and press here. *Don't* spray me in the face. Two flashlights each and a surveyor's map from sixty-five."

"So why are we going, then?" I didn't take the pepper spray or the surveyor's map.

She read my expression right away. "Look, I don't know," she said. "I know what you're thinking. We have to go back. We have to save someone. Someone wants our help."

"But you say we can't change anything. So why are we going?" I didn't want to be stubborn. The truth was that I was desperate to go. But why?

Luka rolled her eyes. "You're thinking too much. If we can change things, we caused the power-out and killed people. If we can't change things, we can't save anyone, so why bother? Look, Kenny, if you think too much, you never do anything. I can't get into the mirror to go back without you going first. Are you coming or not?"

It was hard to argue against her. I steeled myself against the cold, grabbed Luka's hand, and pushed my way in.

Something was different right away. Normally you took a step in that molasses space in between the two sides of the mirror, your eyes shut tight against the heat or cold, and then you were through on the other side. A second step this time, and I wasn't out.

Luka squeezed my hand. "It's okay. Stop for a second. Don't move."

If I held myself as still as I could, the cold of downtime travel matched with the uptime heat behind me and settled into a kind of buzzing, the kind you get when you lick a nine-volt battery.

"When you get used to it, you can open your eyes," said Luka.

In front of me was a cloud of floating image-fragments, as though the mirror had been shattered in the act of reflecting a scene and kept holding the same view. An image of the floor of the carriage house floated past me. There was a piece of paper there. A note?

"It's getting bigger," said Luka. "The space in between the mirrors. Look behind you, but move really slow so it doesn't hurt. If you wait long enough, you get used to it."

Another cloud of images showed the carriage house as we had just left it.

"It makes it safer," said Luka. "This way you can look and figure out if anyone's there before you go through. Come on, let's go."

As soon as we were through, I shone the flashlight about the carriage house. No trap. No ambush. Just the same silent, junk-filled space, barn-like in the crisp winter air.

I pulled Luka through. "Weird," she whispered. "I've never gone from a place to exactly the same place before. It's like we haven't gone through at all."

"Look at the wall," I said, and turned my beam on it. The wreckage and gaping holes she had been looking at all day in my time were gone, replaced by a seamless but battered back wall. There was a dead baby inside there.

Remembering the image-fragment I had seen in the mirror, I shone my flashlight at the floor, and there was the note I had seen. Luka and I read it together, though it was addressed to me.

"I guess you're not coming back. I understand. Bet it all wigged you out pretty bad. I got Jimmy to go back two more times, but it's getting harder to convince him. Sorry about everything. Rick Beech."

"This is good," said Luka, stuffing the note in my backpack. "Come on."

I hadn't thought much beyond coming back through the mirror, but Luka clearly had a plan. She took me outside and around to the front of the main house. There were no lights. Some stubborn muddy patches of snow still hung on in the shelter of the house, but there was a spring scent in the air and a wet bounce in the ground.

Luka picked up a pebble and cocked her arm to throw. I caught her hand. "He won't have the attic," I said. "Second floor. That one."

It took three pebbles before Jimmy came to the window. Even in the dark I could tell his eyes were wide with fear. "Come on down," I said.

"Two against one? No way."

Luka sighed. "We're not here to get you. We want to talk. We've got a plan."

Jimmy squinted. "Hey, you're a girl."

"I hear that a lot."

It took some convincing, but he came down. He stayed by his door for a long time, studying us. "So you're the girl from way in the future?" he said at last to Luka.

"No," she said. "You're the boy from way in the past."

Jimmy frowned and I saw his lips moving as he worked that one out.

"Never mind that," Luka said. "We've got a plan. You say it's not safe in the carriage house because Pete Masterson and all them go there. There's a fix for that. You just have to listen."

As soon as she laid it out, I loved the plan. Jimmy was equal parts terrified and confused. He had trouble getting his mind around the way we knew about people and places from his time. Between the two of us, Luka and I finally managed to convince him to go to the carriage house and help us pry the mirror from its frame with some screwdrivers Luka had brought along. Once it was out, I tested it; my hand still went in, still felt the uptime heat.

"Rick and me—we were just gonna make some money," Jimmy said as we took the mirror out toward the street. "He said we'd just use it for money."

"That's not what Rick said in the future," I said. "I called him. He knew things about people from way in the past. Rose, and someone called Wald. He knew things. That means we must have found them out."

Jimmy shook his head, but Luka interrupted him. "Look, all you have to do now is go get Rick. We'll meet you there."

I saw Jimmy look longingly at his bedroom window, but in the end, he did what Luka said.

How can I explain what that walk was like? Midnight, ten years in the past. Somewhere in the world, I was four years old right now. It was a comfort that at least we had the mirror with us, though carrying the thing took a lot of getting used to. If your bare flesh touched its surface, you'd sink in, so we wore gloves and let it mostly lean its solid back against our arms. It was about four feet high and two wide, and no heavier or lighter than it ought to be now that it was out of its frame and off its dresser. To the two cars that slowed down as they passed us, we must just have looked like two lunatic kids carrying a perfectly ordinary mirror down Manse Creek Avenue at about one in the morning.

We walked in the general direction of the lake, mostly on the side of the road. Luka pointed out houses that had later been knocked down and ones that had yet to be built.

When we turned onto Homestead and could see the place Luka called the storage shack, Rick was waiting on the doorstep with Jimmy.

He stood as we approached and ran a hand through his hair. "Holy crap," he said. "When Jimmy—I almost didn't think he was serious. Hey, can we just forget about what happened the last time? I was an idiot."

Luka interrupted. "Kenny wouldn't have come back if he wasn't ready to forgive and forget."

I didn't say anything for a moment. All of their eyes were on me, even Jimmy's. I felt like whatever I said, it should be the right thing. Forgive and forget was good, but it wasn't enough. "We called you in the future—in my time. It didn't work out, but you tried to tell us things about what happened in the past, something about the baby that died. You were with us. You were one of us."

Rick raised an eyebrow at all this, but didn't say a thing.

He just nodded, opened the door to his grandmother's junk house, and motioned us in.

The place was a dump. It had clearly once been intended for people to live in, a tiny bungalow with two bedrooms, a kitchen, and a living room. No indoor bathroom. The bedrooms felt like they were designed for midgets.

Every space was filled with junk. Faded boxes advertised toys, gadgets, household utensils, things I couldn't even guess about. The kitchen counter was covered with rubber overshoes and something that called itself a waterproof scarf. Other rooms held cigar cutters, pipe maintenance kits, junior golf kits, ladies' massagers, mustache trimmers, and a million old magazines.

"It's a family joke," said Rick. "My dad begs her to get rid of it. She always says next summer she's gonna clear it all out and sell it. For the last ten years at least."

As we carried the mirror in through the crowded kitchen, I yelped in pain and danced back. The mirror would have dropped if Rick hadn't leaned in and grabbed it. "What's going on?" he said.

I dug frantically in my pocket and brought out the rabbit's foot Luka had given me. In the darkness of the junk house, a web of fine blue sparks danced in the fur. "Felt like I had a live wire in my pants," I said, staring at the others.

Jimmy had shrunk back to the entrance of the house. Rick and Luka put down the mirror and leaned in. She touched it. "Tingly."

"It was burning before," I said.

I reached out to hand it to Rick, but then clutched it

tighter. "Wait," I said. Holding the keychain out, I turned in a circle. Weaker, weaker, weaker, and then when I turned back toward Rick, stronger. I took a step. Stronger still. There was no movement, but I kept thinking the rabbit's foot was struggling in my grip. Another step and I was surprised it didn't jump out of my hand.

Rick reached out, touched it, and recoiled.

"It's getting stronger," I said. "Move the mirror away."

"It can't be that," Luka said. "I've been in and out of the mirror a bunch of times with that thing." But she moved it anyway, giving me room to step forward again, closer to the kitchen counter.

I don't know why I wanted to get closer. I had a half memory in my head of something like this, but couldn't bring it to the surface. I took another step, finding I had to switch hands because my right was almost numb from the strange electricity.

"Kenny?" said Luka.

"Yeah."

"Why is that box moving?"

I had been concentrating so much on the sizzling object in my hand, I hadn't even noticed, but now I did. A cardboard box on the counter. Smaller than a loaf of bread and so covered in dust that you couldn't see what the once-colorful pictures and writing were advertising. Its movement was slight, like there was a mouse inside making halfhearted escape attempts.

Rick picked the box up and blew the dust away, though

when he did, I had to step back because the tingling in my hand grew to a genuine pain.

Luka directed her flashlight beam at the box. "Holy crap."

"You got that right," Rick said. He read from the box: "Lucky-for-you rabbit's foot. Genuine talisman of good fortune from ancient times. Only left hind feet. Just thirty-five cents."

Luka took the box from Rick, broke the seal, and opened it up. You could pick it out easily. One foot, packed in with the rest and dancing with blue sparks. Luka steeled herself and put her hand around it, then held it up to me.

I yelped and dropped mine, the shock so intense. Luka did the same.

They landed close together. An electric blue tentacle darted out of the keychain I had been holding and struck the one from the box. It wasn't a spark. It wasn't quick or thin or jagged enough. It was more like an arm made up of silvery blue ripples, and it lingered for a good two or three seconds. Along its length, flickering back and forth like eels, were ghost images of the rabbit's foot, for all the world like one thing remembering its life, another imagining what was yet to come.

Then, with a final crack, the glowing connection moved the two keychains apart and collapsed.

"Holy crap," said Luka into the ringing silence of the room.

"What the hell was that?" said Rick, looking at the two good-luck charms. "Is this one … are they … ?"

"The same rabbit's foot," said Luka. "Your grandmother

gave it to me. They're the same thing." She kicked the one she had given me a safe distance away, then asked me to put the other one back in its box.

"So … it does this because it can't be in two places at once?" I said.

Luka shrugged. "What am I, a scientist? Come on, it's getting late."

We found a place for the mirror in the larger bedroom, then Rick wanted to sit in the hallway between piles of horrible oil paintings and boxes of mason jars and talk for a while, mostly about setting up some rules. "For the house, I mean. If you're seen coming and going in daytime, it's gonna be trouble. I'll make copies of the key and leave them in front of the mirror."

We agreed to all of this. Rick would have talked more, but Jimmy started getting increasingly nervous, and even Luka began to yawn.

The goodbye was awkward. "You guys—you guys'll come back, right?" said Rick.

We promised we would.

I had intended this time just to power through the three steps it now took to cross the slow, buzzing space between the mirrors, but the moment we were inside, I heard a gasp from my right, and I turned my head and opened my eyes before I knew what I was doing. Luka must have done the same, because we both winced and cried out in pain at the same time.

Or maybe it was surprise.

Just more than an arm's length away stood a girl, brown-skinned and wrapped in a colorful cloth. Around her swirled another cloud of images, like ours but dimmer.

After a moment of silence on both sides, the girl broke out into a wide grin. "Greetings," she said in a musical accent. "I have not yet met any of the blessed from your mirror."

"Our mirror," said Luka. "You mean ... are there other mirrors?"

The girl's eyes widened. "Have you not looked down the hallway?"

As soon as she said it, I couldn't help but steel myself against the buzzing pain and look beyond her. They got dimmer as they stretched away, but there they were, more clouds of images, two at a time, stretching far beyond the limits of vision.

"It is the same in both directions," said the girl. "Do not ever use them, though. You are blessed only for your own mirror. If you go through another, you may never return. Even a key will not open them."

"A key?" I said. "The mirrors have keys?"

The girl raised an eyebrow. "How little you know. Are there no elders to teach you of the mirrors?" Before we could answer, she continued. "You do not find it. You make it, and you must have patience, too. Take a—" She stopped and her eyes darted to the image-cloud she had been heading toward. "You must not stay here," she said. "My uncle is after me. I hid the mirror, but he will find it soon. Have you seen him? A fat man with a scar above his eye?"

"Is he Prince Harming?" I said.

Now her gaze was fixed on her image-fragments, and she talked quickly. "What? No, he is no Prince. No doubt you are talking about some part of your own story. If no one has told you, hear me now. We each have our own stories in the mirrors. My uncle has kidnapped my mother as a child. I must help her before he forces her to take him into the glass."

"How?" said Luka. "I thought only the kids can go through."

"Once blessed, always blessed," said the girl. "But an adult needs a child to open the mirror first." She hazarded a glance at us. "I wish I could tell you more. Look for an elder, one you can trust. I must go. You, too. Do not let him catch you here."

With that, she moved uptime in the direction of 1977. The cloud of image-fragments flared for a moment as she went through, then dimmed again so as to be barely visible.

"Come on," said Luka. "We should go, too. Besides, if you squeeze my hand anymore, my fingers'll fall off."

She said she couldn't stay long, but we ended up talking for another hour in the carriage house, mostly just trading back and forth the new ideas and new words we had just been introduced to. Other mirrors? Keys that you could make? Adults going through?

"This is even better than we thought," Luka said before she finally went back through the mirror to her own time. "Now everything's going to happen."

Part Two

_____

The Curse of Prince Harming, Spring 1977

ONE

And then—nothing happened. Seriously. You have to realize how hard it was to use that mirror for more than your own personal ten-years-to-the past. I sneaked out of the house two or three times a week and went back to see Jimmy and Rick. Luka came sometimes as well. Now and then we saw other kids going through on their own missions, but sound carried strangely in the place between the mirrors, a place Luka started calling the Silverlands, and none of us wanted to leave our own mirrors for fear of getting lost or stumbling through one that wasn't our own. We were usually confined to a few mangled sentences. What year are you from? What country? Once, far in the distance, I saw a kid being pushed roughly through by a grown woman, but neither turned my way. I kept in mind what the girl in the sari had said. Their stories were not mine.

Our own mirror kids still met as often as we could. Three-way meet-ups were rare, as those required some way to fool parents for a whole day. Melissa made it back to my time in late April, but I didn't get to her time or backward to Anthony's. I heard stories, though. In early May, Jimmy went back with Anthony to 1947 and spent a whole day with him and Margaret Garroway. He caught the two of them kissing in a barn where they sheltered from the rain, and Anthony had to admit that, yes, there was something going on. When we asked Jimmy if Margaret knew she was supposed to go missing in a few months, he blushed and said he didn't know how to talk about "stuff like that."

About the bigger mysteries—the baby, the disappearances, and the riddle of Prince Harming—we learned nothing. In every decade we could, there seemed to be nothing more than rumors and legends. Jimmy confirmed that the scratched message to Luka on the underside of the dresser drawer existed in his time and ten years before: *Luka, help Kenny. Trust John Wald. Kenny says he is the* auby *one. Save the baby.* And the note for me: *Help me make it not happen, Kenny. Help me stop him. Clive is dead all over again.* I had read that note so often that it had aged more in six months with me than it had in all those years inside the wall—however many they were. But what could I do? Short of going missing for a few days, I couldn't make it further back than 1967. None of us knew what *auby* meant. Luka brought word that Keisha had found a reference to a John Wald in some eighteenth-century book on magic as a kind of mystery man in the north of England who saved children from fires and drowning, but what good was that? Why would I ever describe this or any John Wald as an *auby* one?

Jimmy grew on us. The kid had never met a shadow he wasn't scared of, but his wide-eyed wonder and open-mouthed gullibility made it fun to tell him all kinds of things, both true and otherwise, that the future would bring. I once had him convinced that Luka was actually a clone, and that the real Lucy Branson controlled this body from the safety of her own time.

In June we finally had a four-way meeting. Melissa lied to her parents about going to a friend's for a sleepover, then came back to Luka's time, while Luka, having told the same kind of lie the previous day, waited in mine. Then I went back to 1967 to get Jimmy, and Luka went up to 1987 to pull Melissa through. As long as she didn't leave the mirror in her own time, Luka could keep it open to 1977. They all slept in the carriage house that night, and I met up with them the next morning, a Sunday for me.

It was my first time meeting Melissa, but still I felt like I had my three best friends with me.

We sat on my sun-warmed driveway and Luka and I did our act of reading out the newest pages of the journal that I had puzzled out, she over-acting as Rose and me as Curtis. Some of the early pages were dull, so I chose something that began on our exact date, sixty years before.

June 7, 1917

Mother says I'm getting fat and that's just fine by her. "Nothing like a plump, healthy girl." She says it in a sing-song voice while she cleans or does dishes. I tell her my stomach has been hurting. I want her to take me to the doctor. He would tell her. Then we would know and we would not have to continue in this lie.

But she won't. She is hateful in her cheerfulness.

June 9, 1927

Lillian told me a ghost story. It's about a bad man called Prince Harming. Well, not a ghost story but a scary one. This Prince Harming lost his own soul a long time ago when he killed his brother. He did it when he was a baby, strangled the other baby in the crib or something. Now he tries to kill children because if he kills the right little boy, he can eat his soul.

Mother got angry again at nothing, so I went to the creek to the cave that used to be Rose and Clive's and just stayed there for a long time and was sad. I scratched my initials into the wood next to theirs so at least it will make a difference to something that I was alive.

July 10, 1917

Now I see her plan. For weeks playing up my ill health. She insists I dress in heavy layers. Is she hiding it from herself or me?

In any event, yesterday she announced that I

*must move to the carriage house for my health. It
is too dusty in the main house. We are much fallen,
she says, from earlier times. There will be no more
carriages or horses for Holleriths, so we might as well
make use of it as a real property, and I will be her
little pioneer, she says, though I simply must come
over for breakfast. She has it all planned out.*

*Curtis came back again. Always angry. Mother
hit him, he says. Caught him stealing biscuits from
the pantry. He says she is forever shouting about one
thing or another. I ask if it's me she's shouting at, but
he doesn't like to talk about me. He says I don't visit.*

I complained about all the work it was to puzzle out
the old handwriting, but Luka said I should go on. "At least
you're finding some stuff out. It's driving me crazy that we
can't get back to those times. I can't wait for summer."

I stood up and flapped my arms against the chill. "Yeah,
but everything I find out just brings up more questions. What
are these health problems? What's she so worried about?"
Luka didn't reply at first. I looked around at her. "What?"

"Are you that dense? Seriously?"

"I'm with Kenny," said Jimmy. "What?"

Luka shared an eye roll with Melissa. "You dummies,
don't you get it? Look, January she talks about how she's missing Clive. End of February she's got this 'terrible suspicion.'
March she's really sick. By June her mother says she's getting
fat and is ignoring something, and in July she wants to hide
Rose away in the carriage house. She's pregnant, dummy."

I turned to face the hedgerow and thought about the dark space in the wall where I had ripped away the lath six months ago, before being driven away by the prickling in my skin.

"That is some sad stuff," said Jimmy. "Can't she just, you know, take care of it?"

Melissa gave him a scornful look. "In 1917? An abortion?" Jimmy winced when she said the word.

"That's just not possible back then," said Luka.

We went down to the creek and searched out the place Curtis called the cave. You could see there had once been something there, a space underneath three large rocks nestled into an overhang. Mud and erosion had covered the hiding place years ago. Jimmy and I got a couple of sticks and dug. We found some large pieces of broken furniture buried in the dirt that looked like they might have once been used as makeshift tunnel supports. Luka and Melissa took the top of a small table to the creek to wash the decades of muck away until we found where CB+RH were scratched deeply into the wood.

The bigger surprise came when Luka dashed another bucket of water on the tabletop and revealed further initials below CH. LH as well as AC+MG. Further below that, KM and LB.

"Great," said Melissa after our shared moment of stunned silence. "Lillian Huff from the thirties, Margaret Garroway from the forties and Anthony Currah from the fifties. Then Kenny and Luka? Nothing for Jimmy and me?"

"That's fine by me," said Jimmy. "I don't want to get stuck in no long-ago past."

I ran my fingers over the initials. Not as deep as Clive had carved, but deeper than Curtis. I looked at Luka. "I never did this."

"Don't look at me. I'm five right now. In my time there's a bridge here. These rocks are gone."

We dug for a while more, but didn't find anything. It was getting close to the time I should be expecting my mother home from work, so Luka took us back to her time for some Nintendo, but before we could even get the TV turned on, Melissa surprised us into seriousness.

"Is it a curse?" she said, as Luka served us all sodas in her basement.

"Is what a curse?" said Jimmy.

"You know, how everybody says this neighborhood is haunted. I know that girl you met called us the blessed, but seriously? Margaret Garroway going missing in September? And a really long time ago some little boy went crazy and cracked a girl's head open. Maybe it's the mirror. Maybe Prince Harming lives in the mirror. Keisha left me a note a couple of nights ago saying she found something out about him, but she hasn't been back."

"Aw, that's just a story anyway," said Jimmy. "Like the boogie man. Or Santa's evil brother."

We all turned to look at him.

"What, your mom never told you about Opposite Christmas, when Nefidious Claus comes to take the presents away if you were bad?" We continued to stare. Jimmy's head sank. "Man, I had the worst childhood."

"Why cursed?" said Luka. "Look at the fun we get to

have. Anything can be bad or good. And like Jimmy says—Prince Harming is just a story to frighten kids."

"Here," I said. They all turned to me and frowned. "It's a story here. I've lived in a bunch of neighborhoods, and I never heard about this Prince Harming before. And what that girl said? She said we all have our own stories in the mirror. She was running away from her own uncle, and he didn't sound too nice. Just because they're stories doesn't mean they're not real, and you know it. The mirrors are around here, and so is Prince Harming. Everybody talks about him, all the way back to Rose. There's even that skipping rhyme."

"Lover sweet, bloody feet," Melissa chanted.

Jimmy continued it from where he lay on a couch by himself. "Loudly yelling down the street."

Then it was Luka's turn. "Holler loud, curtsey proud, you shall wear a coffin shroud."

Jimmy finished it. "Go to mass, go to class, you'll go down the backward glass."

Melissa turned to him, mouth open. "What did you say?"

"What, go to mass? Are you Catholic? I didn't mean nothing by it."

"Not that," said Melissa. "The whole last bit together."

Jimmy frowned. "Go to class, go to mass, you'll go down the backward glass. Oh, wow. Backward glass. Like the mirror?"

We all stayed silent for a long moment to let this sink in. Our mirror? Our private story? Our secret tunnel? Connected to something in the real world, something other kids knew about? It was like reading the name of your imaginary friend in the newspaper.

I broke the long silence. "Mine's different." I opened the double diary Rick had given me. Inside, at the page with the skipping rhyme, I had tucked the piece of an old newspaper with the first variation I had found a few weeks after moving in. "'Lover sweet, bloody feet, running down the silver street. Leave tomorrow when you're called, truth and wisdom in the walls. Crack your head, knock you dead, then Prince Harming's hunger's fed.' Then there's this one from the book: 'Lover sweet, bloody feet, running down the lonely street. Leave tomorrow when you're called, truth and wisdom deeply walled. Crack your head, knock you dead, then Prince Harming's hunger's fed. Head will hurt, death's a cert. A dead man's sentence should be curt.' There's a bunch of these in here."

"Silver street?" said Luka. "As in the Silverlands?" Her name for that growing space between the mirrors had caught on. Jimmy reported that even Margaret and Anthony were using it. "We should be figuring this stuff out," said Luka. "We just have to—" Her head snapped up. "Oh crap."

"What?" said Jimmy. "Is someone breaking in?"

"Worse," said Luka. "That was my mom's car door. All of you—upstairs, now!"

She snatched chip bags and glasses out of our hands and began pushing us in the direction of the stairs.

"Go," she shouted several times.

Jimmy and Melissa crashed through Luka's bedroom door together, but it was Melissa's hand that touched the mirror first.

Melissa had just a moment to shrug apologetically at us before she pushed out of sight.

"Lucy Branson, what is all that noise?"

Jimmy hesitated before the mirror. I knew what he was thinking. If he pushed it in now, the mirror would be hot. Until Melissa pushed through the ever-expanding Silverlands and cleared the mirror, it was open uptime to 1997.

"Go," Luka mouthed.

"Do you have people in here?" Her mother's voice was quieter now, but full of menace.

Jimmy looked like a thousand volts of pure terror was sizzling through his fearful body. "Oh, man," he whispered, barely audible. "Oh, man, Kenny, we gotta go."

Further into the future? With my mother coming home soon? And Cindy Branson possibly guarding her daughter's mirror. "Just wait," I mouthed. "She'll clear the mirror in a second." It couldn't take much longer.

Jimmy gave me a look that might have had some kind of apology hidden under the fear, then pushed into the mirror and was gone. Out of the corner of my eye, I could see Luka squaring her shoulders and straightening her back the way she did before doing something scary. I realized it probably hadn't even registered with her why Jimmy and I had been hesitating. She didn't look at me anymore, just faced outward as we heard her mother's feet on the stairs.

"What's going on up there? You know my rule. You better not have a boy in your room. Is that it? Being a little tramp? Going to make the whole neighborhood hate me even more?"

"Mother, you're imagining things," said Luka. "I'm doing homework."

How many seconds since Jimmy had gone in? I pushed into the mirror. Still hot. I couldn't even think about what Jimmy would do once it crashed through to him what he had done. Thirty years uptime. What was taking him so long?

"Don't you 'mother' me. I'll send you to your father's whether he likes it or not," said Luka's mother. "And whoever that is up there, you better—"

It was too much for me. Hoping desperately that Jimmy was through and the mirror would open in the right direction, I stepped up and pushed my way in. I didn't care about the cold, didn't even let it slow me down.

The cold.

Downtime cold.

I was going home.

My T-shirt caught in a splintered bit of the frame for a moment, but I kept pushing. Inside, I paused to check that the rippling image-bits showed my carriage house, then charged out, shivering into the warm spring air.

I was so relieved to be back that I just sat on the dresser and rubbed my arms for warmth, then leaned back against the mirror to breathe a sigh of relief.

And sank back into it.

My back burned with uptime heat. I sprang away and whirled around. This wasn't supposed to be possible. The mirror shouldn't open for me again until eleven tonight. Even then, it should take me back, not forward.

I reached out and touched. My fingers sank in, burning as they went, freezing as I withdrew.

It was then that I saw the thread. It led from the sleeve of my T-shirt all the way into the mirror. I gave it a gentle tug and it grew taut. I remembered the tear as I caught it going in.

For want of a better object, I took out my house key and touched it to the mirror, exactly where the thread was. It clinked against the glass. I could move it right next to the thread, even let the thread in a little and pull it back out, then touch the key against the mirror again. Tap, tap. As soon as my finger touched, though, the mirror let it through.

Aside from the thread, this was the way the mirror normally worked. It wouldn't let through any inanimate object unless part of us went through with it first. If I put the key in my fist, it would go through.

I didn't move for a few long moments, thinking about what this must mean. Could you hold them open indefinitely like this? Could we have been going backward and forward at will all this time?

I heard my name called outside. My mother. Home for half an hour by this time.

I ripped the thread from my T-shirt. What could I tie it to? I couldn't pull it too far or it would tear away at the other side, and what if this was the only time this would work? What if I tried to show it to the others and couldn't make it happen again?

"Kenny!"

The key. I quickly tied the thread around it. Tension pulled it toward the mirror, but though the thread wanted to go through, the key just clinked against the glass and stayed there.

I heard my name again and fled down the stairs.

––––––––––

I was excited enough at my new discovery that, after my yelling-at for not being home and not leaving a note, I still risked staying up past lights out and went back to the carriage house.

Luka was waiting. "Okay," she said, pointing to the thread, "this is amazing. Why couldn't we have figured this out before? Do you realize how amazing? When we pass it on to the others, anyone can go as far back or forward as we like."

I felt the same breathless excitement, but I also had a lot of questions, having had time to think. It was an odd-numbered day, just after eleven at night. Normally, I should be able to go back to 1967, but the mirror heated our hands when we pushed in, telling us it was still connected to Luka's time.

I wanted to ask how this could work, how it could fit with all the other rules we had discovered, but another question surprised its way out of me first.

"Where's Jimmy?"

Luka frowned at me. "What? Didn't he go home?"

I explained what had happened, Jimmy panicking and going uptime. "I figured he'd come back and you'd see him as he passed through. But look." I pushed my hand in again. "If that takes me forward to your time, and it did the same for Jimmy, then he wouldn't be able to get back home. He'd be stuck either here or at your place. What?"

Luka's jaw was hanging open. "If he could even get back to my place."

"What? You can always go back to your own time."

She shook her head and pointed to the thread tied to my key at the surface of the mirror. "I don't think so, Kenny. Not if there's one of these things in it. Think about it. If this thread keeps the mirror open between your time and mine, how could he even get in on Melissa's end? We always thought the odd-even day was some kind of safety thing, right? So that someone couldn't be coming out of a mirror from the past at the same time someone was coming from the future? This must be the same."

"We have to take it out then," I said. "Jimmy'll be going crazy."

Reluctantly, Luka agreed. She went through to her time, reached out of the mirror and unsnagged the thread, then brought it back with her.

We didn't have to wait long for Jimmy. Within a couple of minutes, he came shivering out of the mirror. "You guys! I thought I was stuck in the future forever. What happened?"

I held up the thread with my house key still attached. "We made a doorstop, Jimmy. We just changed everything."

TWO

It took us the last two weeks of school to work out the rules covering doorstops. The anchors had to be objects that had spent some time with one of us, stretched between string that hadn't. We loved the new ways the decades opened up for us. Luka and I could rush home after school and go back and forth between our times depending on whose parents were home, what the weather was like, and what was on TV. She and Melissa were enjoying the same benefits, but Keisha hadn't been back to visit Melissa in 1997 since leaving the note saying she had something to tell about Prince Harming, so she didn't know if anybody further in the future knew how to jam a mirror open.

The mirror rules still frustrated us, though. The more I fumbled with the shatterdate book, the more Luka became obsessed with going further into the past, but the logistics of this still escaped us. Unless she wanted to go missing for a week, there was no way to get Luka further back than the fifties, and even that was difficult considering how fearful Jimmy was of the mirror.

On a day late in June, I took Luka back to 1967 so she could share her frustrations with Jimmy and Rick. They had come along with some hockey cards and wanted to convince us of yet another get-rich-quick scheme, selling these much more portable items through the decades. Luka refused even to take off the newspaper Jimmy had wrapped them in until we talked about what she wanted. "I want to go back," she said. "I have a plan about how to do it, but you need to get Anthony in on it. It's time for him to start helping us."

Jimmy and Rick exchanged a look. We were all seated around a "campfire" of flashlights in the junk house eating snacks from the future. "Uh, yeah," said Jimmy. "We been meaning to talk to you about Anthony."

Luka and I looked between the two of them questioningly. Rick sighed, pulled up a chair, and motioned for us to do the same.

"I still say it's nothing," said Rick. "But—fine. Go ahead, tell them."

Jimmy rubbed his forehead. "Last night? I tried going back to see him. It's been almost a week and nothing. The mirror's in the basement, so if he's not there, usually I just bug out. But then I hear something. A lady—crying. She's talking about, 'My Anthony, my little boy.' It was real heavy. Then there's another voice and he says he wishes they had reported it sooner. And the lady, she gets out how they didn't think much of it because Anthony's been spending a lot of time at friends' places lately, but now it's a week and none of his friends have seen him. Then the man starts talking about how he should take a picture away with him, and that's when I got out of there, 'cause all the albums are in the basement. I took a look out the window before I went, though, and sure enough there was a cop car."

Luka shook her head in disbelief. "This isn't right. It's Margaret that goes missing—have you even talked to her about that yet, Jimmy? And that isn't until September. Anthony didn't go missing."

"I kind of talked to Anthony about it a couple weeks ago," Jimmy said, "and he knows all about it. It's only ten years ago for him, right? He said he tried to bring it up, but Margaret wasn't interested. She said everything was going to work out."

"Anyway," Rick said. "The Anthony thing. Jimmy and me went to the library today. We looked up newspapers from ten years ago. We even asked my grandmother. She says Anthony was just fine when they sold the place to my dad and moved to Alberta a few years back. She knows other kids have gone missing over the years, but not Anthony. So it has to turn out, right?"

"But what about the guy?" said Jimmy. "I think we gotta tell them about the guy."

Rick rolled his eyes. "This again. Jimmy, there's no guy."

"What guy?" said Luka.

"It's nothing," said Rick. "Jimmy says there's been somebody hanging around here. He just got spooked is all."

"I had a good reason," said Jimmy. "This is some weird stuff. Rick didn't want me to say. He says it's just some kids or whatever. But I seen someone hanging around the neighborhood."

"Come on," said Rick, "you've been saying that for weeks. There's no evidence anybody's been around here but us."

"Don't be too sure about that," I said. It was the first time I'd spoken for several minutes. As the rest of them argued, my eyes had turned to the package of hockey cards Jimmy had given me. They all turned their flashlights my way.

"What do you mean?" said Rick.

I didn't answer right away. "Jimmy, where'd you get the newspaper to wrap these up?" I held the bundle he had given me up to the flashlight.

Jimmy frowned. "It was just lying around. We were sitting around waiting for you guys."

Luka had caught on and took the bundle away from me. "Oh, man," she said, reading the same date I had read just a minute before. "Will you look at that?"

June 3, 2007.

I held it up for them all to see, and as they read the article at the top of the page, the one that had been circled in black marker, I got a perfect view of the chill that ran through them.

Second Girl Attacked
in Cursed Suburban Home

A teenage girl is in hospital after an attack in her Manse Valley home left her with severe head injuries almost exactly ten years after a similar attack on another girl in the same house.

Keisha Blaine, who was home alone, managed to get to a phone after her attacker fled the scene, and was rushed to hospital with severe head injuries.

Police are now looking for a dark-haired caucasian man in his forties with a medium build, around 5'10".

Bizarrely, an almost identical attack happened to Melissa Peat on June 5 ten years ago. Peat, fifteen at the time, had injuries severe enough to put her in a coma.

Peat's attacker, also described as a dark-haired man in his forties, was never found.

"I am never leaving my house again," said Jimmy and looked around at us for support. "Come on, you guys. This is Prince Harming. He's cracking their heads open. That's what we've been hearing from way back. He's probably the one who made the mirror so he can get kids out of their time when nobody's going to miss them."

"And that explains why he attacked Melissa and Keisha right in their homes, does it?" Luka snapped. For all her bravado, though, she looked around furtively. Our ring of flashlights suddenly seemed small in the abandoned house.

"Point is he's been here," said Jimmy. "Someone has. Any of you guys bring that paper back? I didn't think so. How do we know he's not here right now? June 3. That was around when Keisha was supposed to come through, right? She was supposed to be bringing something about Prince Harming. Then what? Crack-bang is what. Then he goes for Melissa.

And Anthony's missing in 1957. And we know Margaret Garroway goes in September 1947. And a baby gets killed. It's time to quit this, you guys. Pretty soon we'll be the only ones left. And this paper, it was right here." He looked accusingly at Rick. "You said there wasn't a guy. Well, who left the paper, then?"

That shut us all up, and for a few long moments we sat in our circle of flashlights and listened to the small noises of the June night outside. Wind in the trees. A car passing by. Four or five streets away, a dog barked.

"Question is," said Luka, "who is it who was here? Look at this paper. It's not like it's new."

I took the paper from her and felt it in my hands. She was right. I could see how Jimmy could have just absently picked it up and used it for wrapping. It looked like it had been sitting around for years. "And what about this? Look what's written here."

We had only looked at the article at first, not noticing the words written on the old paper in what might have been fresh pen: "Better watch out. He's lurking around. C. M."

"C. M.?" I said. "I know those initials. They're from my list, the list of mirror kids. C. M. is from 2017. Jimmy, this isn't from Prince Harming, it's from someone like us."

"Yeah, sure it is," Jimmy said. "Someone just like us, only he doesn't ever talk to us and he leaves notes laying around. How do we know C. M. isn't Prince Harming? How do we know it isn't a trap?"

"What trap?" said Luka. "What kind of trap are you

being lured into when somebody warns you to watch out? Isn't that the opposite of a trap?"

"Look, none of this is getting us anywhere," Rick said. He took the paper from Luka's hands. "We have to be careful is all. We know Anthony ends up okay. We don't know about Melissa or Keisha or Margaret, though. So nobody travels alone if we can avoid it. Look out the mirror before you walk out. Start being smart." He glanced over at me. "Anyway, we can't quit yet, Jimmy. What about our big plan? What about... you know?"

Jimmy grinned. "Aw, yeah. You mean about Kenny's—"

"Shut up, Jimmy," said both Rick and Luka at the same time.

He shut up.

"What is this?" I said. "What's going on?"

Luka shook her head. "Rick's right. We're just not making any decisions right yet. We made a plan for one more meet-up at least. Wednesday for you. June 19."

"Hey, that's my birthday," I said.

Everybody looked away at the same time. Even with the flashlights all still trained on the newspaper, I was pretty sure I saw a couple of grins. They wouldn't say anything more, though, and it was late so we broke for the night.

Just as I was about to head through the mirror after Luka, Rick put a hand on my shoulder and with a jerk of his head indicated I should stay for a moment. Then he asked Jimmy to go wait for him at the front door. He nodded toward the mirror as Luka's trailing hand disappeared inside it.

"I see you looking, H. G. Wells," he said with a wry smile. "I see you worrying, too."

I shrugged. "I don't—what am I worrying about?"

He raised his eyebrows. "Eight years older one way, two years younger the other way." He held up his hand to hold off whatever dumb thing I would have said. "All I'm saying, Kenny, is there's always a way if you want a way."

I let out a heavy sigh, blowing away with it whatever useless denial I had been about to make. "How?" I said.

Rick grinned. "No idea. We'll figure it out, though. It's what we call a summer project. Now go on. She'll be waiting for you. Nobody goes alone anymore, remember?"

When Luka and I got back to the carriage house, she never asked what had delayed me. She insisted on walking to within sight of my front door and watching me go in. She wouldn't say why, but we were both creeped out by the Prince Harming rhymes. You'll go down the backward glass. A dead man's sentence should be curt. Bloody feet. Silver street. Crack your head. Knock you dead. I shuddered as I climbed into bed. Here it was the end of June, and yet September seemed far too close.

THREE

I spent part of my fifteenth birthday in the same year and on the same day that, about twelve miles away, I was celebrating my fifth.

Luka had put in a doorstop the night before so she could be waiting for me the next day, a bulky present filling up her backpack. She wouldn't show it to me until we had crossed to the far side of the creek.

"These trees are still here in my time," she said, leaning her back against the outside cedar in a small thicket, and patting the ground for me to sit as well. "That's why they're perfect for this. Happy birthday." She took out a large box, carefully wrapped, and motioned for me to open it.

Inside were seven small decorative wooden boxes. I had seen her looking at them on one of our downtown comic-selling trips. The curbside vendor claimed they were handmade in the Tatra Mountains in Poland. Their lids were inlaid with metal designs and colored glass. To the front of each one, she had affixed a small plaque with the engraved name of a month, June to December. Inside each was a small golf pencil and a few pieces of paper she had cut to fit in.

My mother raised me well; I said thank you right away.

"I know," she said, "you have no idea what they're for. But, look, I made them for me, too." She took out another set of the same boxes, engraved in just the same way. "I wanted to do a set for Keisha and Melissa, but maybe it's too late now."

"I still don't—"

"Here," she said. She picked up one of my boxes, August, and handed it to me. "Take it and walk around these trees. Keep it low to the ground."

I felt stupid, but she insisted. I walked around the outside of the thicket, looking like I was feeding chickens. "Now, inside," Luka said, guiding me into the cooler confines of the thicket. "Keep it low."

Near the knuckled roots of an old maple, my hand tingled and I instinctively withdrew it. "Hey!" Then I turned to Luka. "What—"

"So that's the August tree," she said. "Come on. I'll explain." She took me out and sat me in the sunlight again. "Look, we're kind of on our own in this, right? No Melissa, no Keisha. Jimmy's not much good, and Rick can't go along. That leaves you and me. So I started thinking. What if one of us gets lost or something? What if we need help? I mean if that kid Anthony had something like this, maybe we'd know what was going on."

Her idea was that whenever we went into the past, we'd take the boxes with us. If we were separated, one of us in the past and one in the present, we'd use them to communicate. Write a note, bury it around here, and the other person would come looking for it years later.

"Did you make these for Jimmy as well?" I asked. Jealousy is a crazy thing. In my head I knew Luka's only interest in Jimmy Hayes came from his access to 1957, and I had a strong suspicion that any talking they had done recently probably involved my birthday that night, but even the smallest sentence that might pass between Luka and Jimmy or more wincingly between Luka and Rick made me squirm like a stepped-on earthworm.

Luka rolled her eyes. "Please. Can you imagine trying to explain these things to Jimmy?"

The logic of it made even my head want to explode, so I just went along with her, and we established some rules. Each box was to be buried, at the latest, on the last day of every month, even if there was nothing to tell. If we were in our own year, then fine, we would bury it in our own year. We took each of our boxes around and mapped out where its future-past counterpart was.

Most of them weren't there. All we could find was a July and an August from each of us, and a December from me.

"What does that mean?" I asked, but Luka had no good answer.

"We better get going," she said. "Your mom will be home soon. I'll catch up with you later."

For my birthday dinner, I got taken to the Old Spaghetti Factory downtown. All three of my grandparents came. My dad sat himself next to my grandfather so they could argue about baseball, while his own mother made sure she pulled her seat up right next to me. Grown-up conversation was boring, she said.

Mostly she wanted to tell stories. My dad, the only son born to her before her husband went off and died in the war, was her favorite thing in the world, and she never tired of telling us about him. She told me the one about him breaking John Timson's nose, the one about him throwing Mrs. Bonder's vicious chihuahua at Victor Pike who was beating up Aunt Judy, and even the one about him deliberately losing a race to his best friend Lester Charles, because he thought that might get him in good with Chuck's sister. My mother didn't like that one.

The more we laughed, the more she told. How he got accidentally hypnotized at a show when he was eleven, how he hid a full-to-bursting water balloon on Mr. Verturer's chair in grade six so that when the teacher sat, it burst and made it seem as though he had peed his pants.

Just as dessert was being served, she came back to her favorite, the little hobo boy story. "This city in the fifties," she told me. "Nothing like it is now. It wasn't the Great Depression, but it wasn't a picnic either. Children had been orphaned in the war, you know, some of them brought over here when their parents were murdered. There weren't a lot of them, poor children, but they were here. Running from the orphanages. Asking for jobs or food when none of us had much to spare."

This was all a kind of rationalization, I realized, to explain why no one was doing anything to help the homeless boy that they had all seen hiding around the neighborhood. As the story went, my father finally took pity on the kid and hid him in the coal cellar for a few weeks.

What I always wondered was what had happened to the kid. After the crazy dad came and knocked my dad out, did he get the kid? Did my grandmother fight him off? That would be hard to imagine.

She smiled and shook her head when I asked this, then glanced over at my father, still deep in conversation. "Well, Kenneth. Maybe your father doesn't quite know everything about that story. There might be secrets an old lady takes to her grave. Or at least keeps for a while longer. Do you know what the last words I read from your grandfather were before he died? His last letter? 'Keep Brian safe,' he said. 'You and he are the only things in my world.' I never told anyone that, you know. Not fair to Aunt Judy, is it? Daughters are important, too."

It was late enough when we got home that, after waiting for my parents to settle into bed, I only just made the mirror before midnight.

Luka put a blindfold around my eyes and had me step in and pull her along. In 1967, Jimmy and Rick were waiting with the coolest present anyone ever had. They had cleared a space and set up a mattress and some pillows, all facing an old TV hooked up to a VCR from 1987.

"Okay," said Luka, "just to be clear, the birthday present is you get to see it before anyone else around. Well, not anyone. Keisha looked it up. It actually got released in May or something, but not everywhere. It goes out in wide release in about three weeks, your time." She turned to Rick and

Jimmy. "For you guys it's another ten years. If you talk about it, people are gonna think you're crazy."

"Talk about what?" I said. "What is this anyway?"

She held up a cardboard case and slipped a bulky cassette out of it. "I told you when we first met; I saw it on my sixth birthday, and it was the most amazing thing ever."

Rick groaned. "So this is a kiddie movie? *Cinderella* or something?"

"Bite your tongue," said Luka. "This is the best movie ever made. My mother didn't do Disney." She looked at us in exasperation. "It's—oh, I might as well just play it."

She had already fast-forwarded a little so that as soon as she pressed play, words started scrolling up the screen: "A long time ago in a galaxy far, far away."

They say you never forget your first time with *Star Wars*, and that sure is right for me. What I recall most about that night was my worry that I might forget some of it. That scene when Artoo and Threepio are on the surface of Tatooine and you can see the giant bones of some terrible desert creature in the background, I was only half there in the moment. The rest of me was trying to catalogue it, make sure it would never slip away.

I guess I succeeded, as did Jimmy and Rick, who were silent throughout the whole thing. About half an hour in, when Luka's running stream of commentary had extended to such trivia as pointing out when a storm trooper's helmet bumped against an opening door, the three of us begged her to shut up and let us watch the movie. She pretended to sulk for a few minutes, but I could tell she was enjoying our excitement.

When the end credits rolled, we sat like three patients recovering from electroshock therapy. Luka finally brought us out of it simply by getting up and pressing the eject button. "No," said Rick. "Show it again."

Jimmy stirred from his torpor and agreed, but Luka said no way. "It's past two in the morning. Kenny has to get home." She started disconnecting the VCR. "So do I. I have to sneak this thing downstairs before my mother wakes up. Anyway, you have to rest." She stood up, holding the tape like it was orders from rebel command. "Remember, we're on summer vacation now. It's time to get going. There's some kind of mission waiting for us in the past, and we're going for it. Tomorrow's mine and Jimmy's day to go back. Here's how we do it: Right now, I go all the way uptime, then Kenny goes up to his own time and leaves a doorstop between here and 1977. Tomorrow, at eleven, Kenny comes downtime here to 1967 and takes it out. Then I can go back to Kenny's time, and Jimmy in the meantime goes back to 1957. Jimmy, you have to be alone there for a few minutes. It can't be helped. Kenny then goes up to 1977 where I'll be waiting, keeps the mirror open, and pulls me back to now. Then all Jimmy has to do is stick a hand out and pull us back to 1957. Jimmy, you can take off then if you want."

The three of us just sat and blinked at her. We were still recovering from the explosion of the Death Star. Jimmy was the first to speak. "You know what's wrong with this? I just figured it out." He pointed at us each in turn as he spoke.

"Kenny's Luke, Luka's that princess girl, Rick's Han Solo—and I get it—fine, I'm the gold robot guy. But you know what's wrong with this? We don't got no little trash-can robot guy or no Obi-Wan Kenobi. We don't got nobody who actually knows what's going on. You think they could have done all that without the little robot guy or the Obi-Wan guy? We need an Obi-Wan."

Luka just shook her head. "We don't need an Obi-Wan. We're going back, we're finding out what's going on, and we're saving Margaret Garroway and Anthony Currah. If we can get up to the future, we're finding out what's happened with Melissa and Keisha, and maybe we're saving them, too. If we have to, we're stopping Prince Harming. This is our mirror. It's our year. And we're not letting anyone take it away from us."

I actually saluted.

FOUR

Luka's plan worked perfectly. I later found out she had pages and pages of diagrams in a notebook, but well before that I just learned to trust her about when we could travel in which direction. That night was a Thursday for me, a Friday for Jimmy, and a Tuesday for Luka. By a minute after midnight, we were in 1957, five years before I was born.

Jimmy took off as soon as he had pulled us through, promising to wait with Rick in 1967.

The Currah basement was the same as mine from twenty years up, but unfinished and dark. A metal shelving unit held all sorts of tools, paint cans, and cardboard boxes. Crates lined another wall. It was damp and dark. A tap dripped into a large sink.

Luka had come with her hand over her flashlight so we'd have the tiniest bit of light, and we stayed that way for a couple of minutes, listening.

Nothing.

The windows were set high on the walls, but you could see out of them. Once our eyes adjusted, we risked stepping away from the mirror and looked out into the darkness of 1957. No cars in the driveway. No streetlights.

After another couple of minutes, during which she examined the view outside every window, Luka pronounced it flashlight-safe. She found an open photograph album, and we flipped through some pictures of Anthony.

Was he still missing?

After a few minutes of snooping around, Luka began to shine her flashlight around the area in front of the dresser. "The thing is," she whispered, "of anybody here, we're the ones who probably know where he's gone. Into the mirror."

But what were we going to find, footprints in the concrete dust of the basement? Our own shoes would have scuffed any evidence there.

Luka took the top drawer out and turned it over. The words were still scratched into it, a little newer in 1957: *Luka, help Kenny. Trust John Wald. Kenny says he is the* auby *one. Save the baby.*

"I've still got no idea what I'm supposed to help you with," Luka said. "Doesn't sound like anyone's home. I think we should go upstairs."

I was getting less fearful as time went on. It was true that if we were discovered, all we had to do was escape to the mirror. Blood rushing with the thrill of the forbidden, I walked behind her.

I had never traveled through time to my own house before. The few times I had been to 1967 were late at night, and Jimmy didn't want to risk taking us inside, so as nervous as I was about where we were, I was equally fascinated by the opportunity to see the new wallpaper that my mother had pronounced hideous two decades from now, and the light fixtures that she had demanded my father replace before allowing family visitors.

Our flashlight beams didn't show much color, and I had seen many of these same views in the pictures I had found in my attic bedroom when we moved in, so the effect was of walking through a black-and-white photograph album emptied of people.

We padded quietly past the kitchen and the living room. In the hall, sitting directly in front of a much nicer front door than we had in my time, we found a large-lettered note: "Anthony, we have gone to Auntie Ellen's. Nobody is angry, just worried. Call us." They listed phone numbers to call, including the police.

We looked glumly at each other. "Maybe he's given up on everything here," said Luka. "Just wants to be with Margaret before she goes missing."

Anthony's bedroom was torn apart, every drawer turned out, the whole closet emptied. "This wasn't planned," said Luka. "Him going missing, I mean. Look at all the *Weird Science* and *Tales from the Crypt* comics. They don't even look read. He was bringing these to Jimmy."

From the angle of his mattress, I could tell it had been disturbed, but I looked under it anyway, finding nothing but two well-thumbed *Playboys*.

After a few more minutes of searching, we agreed we

weren't going to find anything. I asked Luka what she had expected. "I don't know. Something about Margaret's disappearance? I thought we might find some newspaper from ten years ago about it. Can you imagine what this has been like for him, knowing it's coming? Maybe he went back to stop it."

"Yeah, but would he think—"

A ferocious banging from the front door interrupted me. Halfway down the stairs, we both jumped. "Is that him?" I said when I had my breath back.

"I don't think so. I don't think he's that—"

The banging continued, heavy and desperate. We chanced a look down, and could see a large figure through the glass of the door, throwing himself against it time and time again. Then a voice, shouting, strangely accented, "Come out! Come out, ye twisted fool. I'll no be snared in years again."

"Time for us to go," said Luka. She grabbed my hand and pulled me the rest of the way down. My last sight of the door before she pulled me around the corner to the basement stairs was of it buckling and splintering under the onslaught, and of a wild and desperate face.

"Turn!" shouted that voice again, but we didn't. Luka kept a tight grip on me as we clattered down the basement stairs. "Turn. Who is it there? 'Tis old John. List to me. I am the obie one."

I was too scared to react, too scared to listen. By the time we had reached the basement, I could already hear heavy footsteps on the first floor.

"Wait," said Luka as I was about to go into the mirror.

She pulled out the string Jimmy had left in. "We don't want that to let anyone in behind us."

"Come, fool!" shouted that voice from upstairs. "I've waited ten long years while ye blinked in silver. Come and clash with me again."

"In," said Luka. She pushed me forward.

I steeled myself for it, and— "No, wait, something's wrong. It's cold. The mirror's cold."

Feet thudded down the basement stairs. Behind me, from within the mirror, a hand reached out blindly and impacted my shoulder, pushing me aside and off the dresser. Luka fell with me, her knee sinking into my stomach and her forearm almost breaking my nose. Both our flashlights dropped to the concrete floor. One of them shut off.

The room was a mix of cries. "Jimmy Hayes!" a new voice cried, much easier to understand than the hoarse gibberish of the one who had broken in upstairs. "Which one here is Jimmy Hayes?"

The door-pounder shouted something about having "found the twistit fool."

Luka crawled over me and managed to snare the flashlight, playing it around the room. Two tall, thin men faced each other in the almost-dark, one backing up, both screaming and impossible to make out.

Luka got up and moved toward me. In the swinging of her flashlight, I lost track of which man was which.

The gunshot shut everyone up.

One sharp crack, then a hundred echoes, and our eyes

blinded by the muzzle-flash. The large basement filled with the itchy smell of gunpowder.

"That's better," said a ragged voice. "Someone turn on the lights."

I didn't move, the shot still ringing in my ears, but Luka stepped over and pulled a string that hung from a bare bulb. I flinched from the sudden glare.

A man in a soaked and torn black raincoat stood, backed up to the storage shelves, holding in one hand a gun and in the other the shirt-front of another man. Both looked like they had spent weeks in the woods. The gun-holder was maybe a little older than my parents, receding hair leaving a sharp widow's peak on his forehead. Days of stubble covered his face. His hooded, haunted eyes stared the other man down with a wild fire.

I couldn't tell the other man's age. A thick beard covered his face, and long, unruly hair hung past his shoulders. His shirt and jeans were torn and ragged.

The two men both spoke at once, but the gun-holder spoke louder and shook the gun. "No! Listen to me! You know what this is, don't you? Bang bang!" He narrowed his eyes and pulled back as though trying to see something under the man's dirty beard. "Went the long way, did you? Couldn't catch me? Good. Too bad you waited all that time for this. Now, what's here?" His gaze flicked over to Luka and me, then his eyes focused more tightly on me, and his jaw hung for a moment in surprise. "It's you. It's you again. You're Kenny Maxwell."

And who was he? Was one of these men Prince Harming?

Neither looked anything remotely like royalty, though the bearded man certainly talked like he was from a foreign country.

The man in the raincoat began to shake all over, and the other took advantage of the moment. He surged forward, grasped the man's gun-hand in his own, and forced it upward. Though I was still rooted to the spot with indecision, Luka darted forward, having apparently made her own decision. The nature of that decision, however, was unclear. She reached for the gun, now pointed toward the ceiling, and covered both of the men's hands in her own, but from one of them—I couldn't tell which—came a sharp kick to her midsection that sent her flying to crack her head on the cement floor of the basement.

I scurried toward her, trying at the same time to make out the voices of the struggling and cursing men in front of the mirror. One called the other a fool, while the other kept shouting, "This can end it. Leave me be."

Luka was blinking when I got to her, and had raised her head. She tried to sit up all the way, but fell back. I caught her. "Don't try to get up," I said.

"We have to do something, Kenny," she said. "We have to stop this before someone gets shot."

I looked at the two men. They were evenly matched, like opponents who had fought each other more than once before, each well aware of the other's strengths. When the better-spoken man who had first fired the gun tried to shove his knee at the other, or hook his foot around the wild man's leg, the other man would shift or turn just enough to avoid the trick. For his part, the long-haired man kept straining at the gun, trying and failing twice to smash his forehead into the other man's face.

It was the gunman who turned to me first. "Help me, Kenny," he said. "This man wants to kill us all. Pull him off me and I can get us away. It's me. I'm your friend."

"Nay, hark not," said the wilder man, shaking his greasy grey hair out of his face. "Hear me, Kennit. Here is where thy troubles begin. Help me."

I looked back to Luka, but for all that she had seemed certain a moment before, she now shook her head. Two struggling madmen blocked us from the mirror that led home. What were we to do?

As my indecision stretched out, the gun-holder with the widow's peak seemed to be winning. "This is all it takes," he said between clenched teeth. "I can change everything back."

"Fool," gasped the long-haired man. "Nothing can change." Then his eyes darted back to me. "Kennit, help me. He'll shoot you. Help me. I'm the obie one. That's what she said. Rose. Said you'd know what it meant. I'm your obie one. Me, old John Wald."

It must have made sense to Luka at the same time as it did to me. She grasped my arm and I turned to her. The scratched note on the underside of the dresser drawer. *Trust John Wald. Kenny says he is the* auby *one.* And the rhyme, "truth and wisdom deeply walled." Or deeply Wald? And Jimmy's words just last night, which Luka mouthed now. "We need an Obi-Wan." I finished the sentence with her.

Not obie one. Not *auby* one. Obi-Wan.

That was enough. I wrenched away from her, her own feeble strength shoving me on my way, though I had made my decision too late. I got to the struggling pair just as, with a ferocious rush of strength, the gun-wielder spun John Wald around and threw him at me. We collapsed back in a clutter of limbs and landed on Luka. By the time we had all struggled out from the tangle of our own bodies, the man with the widow's peak was standing directly above us, his gun leveled.

"Stay where you are," he said to John Wald, who eyed the gun warily. "This is him. Don't you see? This is him. If I kill him, none of it ever happens. I live, she lives, everyone lives! It's all his fault."

"What's his fault?" said Luka, struggling to put some part of herself between me and that gun.

The gun-wielder's eyes narrowed on her. "You're his accomplice. But you don't matter. It's him who did it."

"Wait it," pleaded Wald, sitting up as much as he dared. "Will ye hear no reason?"

"Shut up," said the other. He turned to me. "This is it," he said. "If I kill you, it's all over. Do you see that? You started it all." He took his left hand from the gun and roughly wiped tears from his dirt-streaked face. "You were there. Every time. Always you. Pretending to be my friend."

"Kenny wouldn't do that," said Luka. "He's never even met you before, right Kenny?"

"Never met me?" said the man with a snort. "Wouldn't do that? When I was little, Kenny was, for just a while, my only friend." His hand grew firmer on the gun and he stood straighter. "Weren't you, Kenny? He said he'd help me. But you know all he did? Or had you done it already? Did you know, even then, that you had done it?"

"What?" said Luka. "Done what?"

He looked at her disdainfully. "Kenny Maxwell killed my wife," he said, and fired his gun.

FIVE

The thing about getting shot is that you don't exactly follow what happens next. It didn't even register at first that he had shot me.

The gun went off, and I felt a giant's fist punch me in the side. Luka later told me that she had seen in his eyes that he was about to do it, and tried to push me out of the way. At first I thought the pain in my side was somehow her fault, like she had punched me.

There was shouting above me and another gunshot, all the sounds retreating as though I had slipped into a deep grave. I found myself looking at the concrete floor as a film of milky white curtained my eyes. "But..." I was trying to say. "But..." I don't even know what the rest of that sentence would have been. I started breathing in tiny gasps to minimize the agony building in my side.

I think time must have sped up for me then. I didn't lose consciousness, but events started happening at a faster pace.

There were more bangs and scuffles and shouts. Twice some-one tripped over me. Groaning made the pain worse.

Rolling onto my back, I saw the raincoated man with the gun straining to turn it toward me, wresting against John Wald. "Leave off, ye mad fool," shouted the bearded man. "Tha canst not hold off what's done."

"Let me kill him," said the man with the gun. "Then it all gets better."

He kneed Wald in the crotch and pushed him as he dou-bled over. The barrel of the gun strained closer to me. Part of me wanted to close my eyes so I wouldn't see it coming, but before I could decide, another figure launched itself at the man, more like a jaguar than a person.

Luka.

She grabbed his gun hand and heaved herself up at the shooter. She didn't speak. She must have been too angry or desperate or scared for that. She just smashed her face toward his.

With his other arm, the man with the gun smashed her against the wall, but when he did, a splatter of blood came with her, and I could see that she'd bitten his cheek in her rage.

The bearded man rose up again, overcoming his pain. My shooter still had his gun, but he looked scared now. Before Wald could grab him, he snarled in frustration and backed into the mirror.

In the midst of my pain and the odd coldness flooding my body, I had a moment to be shocked at this. An adult going into the mirror.

What about the rules?

Strong hands rolled me over. I heard a man's voice, talking softer now, but I couldn't understand a word.

I tried to pay attention, but fingers started examining my wound, and I felt like throwing up. I began to tense and buck. The hands withdrew and instead turned me on my side so I could heave the contents of my stomach onto the concrete floor.

I heard Luka's voice again. "I have to go. That was—he went forward. I have to see if Jimmy and Rick are okay."

"Wait it," said the bearded man. "Boil some water and search me out a needle. I'll go along to aid thy friends, but we must first stitch this wound."

He probed my side again, and all I could get through the agony were confused impressions. More gibberish talk from the bearded man, impatience from Luka. More pain in my side. Some lost time. Minutes? An hour?

"I have to go," said Luka's voice. "Tell him I'm sorry, but I have to go. You have Anthony now. He can help."

A different voice. Anthony? "I think you should wait for John. What are you going to do against that guy by yourself?"

"Something."

More talk. Maybe more time passing.

I was picked up with what might have been gentleness, though I only felt pain. The veil of white that had descended across my vision had begun to thin, so I could see as we turned to the mirror.

"No," I said feebly. "No, it's going to—"

Burn was what I thought, but it didn't. I didn't see in

the mirror who was carrying me, but I saw the glass come toward me. I flinched and felt the chill of downtime travel.

We were going further into the past.

There followed an endless series of bounces and jostles. I could feel the wetness of my blood around the agony of my wound. I could make out the foreign man's voice, and the boy's.

If that journey was five minutes, an hour, or a year and a day, I couldn't have told you. Sometimes we were in light, but mostly not. Where were my parents? Were they going to find out that I was gone? Had those gunshots been loud enough for them to hear in 1977? Would my dad hold my shoulders when they took the bullet out like in the movies?

The giant who was holding me stopped and began to put me down. I tried to speak, but a voice said, "Hush now. Old John Wald'll stash us sound in the fool's mucky hiding hole. Hush."

My dreams were about pain. Spears and knives stuck in my side, usually from behind so I couldn't get them out. Luka was there, telling me about the bad man from the mirror, and how he wanted to crack my head open, but I kept trying to tell her that we had it wrong, what he really wanted to do was shoot me to stop his wife from dying.

I woke in a muddy hole with dim, grey light leaking in from beneath my feet. I could smell smoke.

I tried to sit and groaned in pain.

"Sounds like our patient is awake," said a voice from the direction of the grey daylight. A girl's voice. "Should I get him?"

"Let me," said a man's voice. "I must ensearch the stitches for corruption. Hast thy flashlight?"

A moment later, the wild, bearded man from last night folded himself into the entrance of the tiny cave. He shone his flashlight first at me and then into his own face. "'Tis only auld John Wald, a'here to spy thy wound."

His manner and his warm eyes assured me more than his words. His voice was different from the desperate croak it had been last night.

Unbidden, my hands had moved to protect the wound, but he gently pushed them aside, murmuring strange words and pulling off the woolen blanket I was wrapped in to expose a gauze dressing, only slightly bloody, and smaller than I had imagined.

Under that—I winced as he tugged the gauze away— was a wound smaller than a dime and puckered with ugly black stitches.

A brief examination and he pronounced it clean. Next he looked at my face. I can't say I wasn't afraid; my teeth were chattering and my heart pounding, but something about him didn't look scary. "Thou must have carps?"

"You mean ... questions?" I asked.

He nodded. "We hid thee here a night and day again, but now I can bring thee from the deeps."

He began to help me halfway upright so I could crawl with him from the cave.

The "hiding hole" from which we were crawling was too small to be called a cave. Long and narrow, it seemed to have been excavated by hand, though some care had gone into it as well. I could see bits of broken furniture that had been used to shore up the sides. The ragged man helped me negotiate the tight spaces. Even bowed down in this tight space, he had a kind of rough nobility about him. *Trust John Wald. Kenny says he is the* auby *one.*

All of a sudden, I knew this place. "Wait," I said to the bearded man. I took his flashlight and aimed it at a much-abused tabletop buried in the wall. Some decades in the future, I didn't know how many, Jimmy Hayes and I had dug this same tabletop out and we all stared at the carved initials in its surface. Some of them were fresh, some old. CB + RH. CH. Clive, Rose, and Curtis. They looked faded and worn, though perhaps not so much as before. And below, where before I had read the initials of Lillian Huff, Anthony Currah, and Margaret Garroway—nothing. Uncarved wood. The bigger surprise, however, came at the bottom of the list. KM and LB. Kenny Maxwell and Luka Branson. Even back in this time, whenever this was, they were not fresh.

We had carved them even further in the past.

But how far in the past was I?

"Fleet now," said the bearded man. "There's much to speak ere dark enshrouds us all."

I returned his flashlight and emerged from the cave mouth into a grey day on the shores of a much stronger Manse Creek. In my time, the hole had been halfway up the creek bank. Here, now, it was five feet of sloping sand from a deeper and wider stream.

Two girls about my age sat by a campfire. They looked up as I came out.

The taller one had bright blond hair in long curls. She wore a heavy wool coat, patched and worn. The other was her opposite in every way. Her dark hair was short, framing a round face that was both soft with plumpness and hard with some inner resolve. She stood and spoke.

"Kenny Maxwell," she said. "Welcome to 1947. I'm Margaret Garroway. Everyone calls me Peggy. This is Lilly Huff. And I guess you've already met John Wald. I know he looks like a rough sort, but he's okay. He's from the seventeenth century."

I straightened painfully, wincing and worrying about my wound. "How do you know who I am?"

Peggy shrugged. "You've heard of us, haven't you? Anthony's been talking about you for weeks. Isn't that what we do, talk about the kids further up and down the line?"

She put a cigarette to her lips and took a long draw on it. I tried to remember, had we figured out her age? Sixteen? Seventeen? Was she trying to act older, or was that how kids were in 1947?

Lilly looked about the same age, but she wasn't wearing makeup, and didn't have the same hard-bitten look. She remained seated, and now indicated a rock by the fire. "You've been through a lot. Care for a seat? John has cooked some fish for us. He's something of an outdoorsman."

I stood and blinked for a moment. How did they know this John Wald? And here she was talking about Anthony as though everything was fine. Wasn't he missing? And shouldn't I talk to Margaret Garroway right now about how she was supposed to go missing?

Lilly smiled, and I shrugged inwardly. They seemed to know what was going on. Best just to listen. Shivering despite the blankets, I sat, and when Lilly handed me some charred fish on a chipped, dirty plate, I wolfed it down.

The others ate as well, and I stayed quiet for a while, listening to them talk. If you didn't trouble about every word, John Wald became comprehensible. He gestured expressively as he spoke, perhaps used to not being understood.

Lilly complimented John Wald on the fish. Peggy wondered if it was going to rain. At this, John raised an eyebrow and examined the sky before nodding.

"I'll have to get home before that in any case," said Lilly.

Peggy tossed her cigarette in the fire. "Not me. Mother's gone to Auntie Nina's again and the ogre will be brooding. I could stay out another night if I choose."

You're supposed to go missing, I wanted to say. But there was something forbidding and sharp in Peggy's manner. "Where's Anthony?" I said at last. I would have much preferred to ask about Luka, but it didn't seem the time yet.

Peggy shrugged. "Back at home with mumsy and daddykins in the fierce familial embrace. Got away from the bad man, don't you know, thanks to John Wald here."

I was silent for a long moment, trying to sort it out. I was shot; the pain still throbbed, burning if I shifted or tensed. I was in 1947. This was the thing Luka had been dreaming of for months. I could ask what they knew about the dead baby. I could do what Jimmy had been avoiding for weeks; I could ask about Peggy's disappearance.

But before any of those questions—and I felt like a

traitor to Luka for acknowledging it, but it was true—before anything like that, came a much greater concern.

"I have to get home," I blurted. "My parents will be going nuts."

Lilly opened her mouth to say something, then hesitated.

"Come on, Lil," said Peggy. "Out with it. Rip the Band-Aid off already. Tell the kid he isn't going home."

SIX

It took a while to get the full story. Peggy and Lilly kept interrupting each other, and then John Wald had to tell part of it in his half-English gibberish. But between the three of them, they managed over the next half hour or so to tell me everything.

The trouble had started for them just about the way it had for us further into the future, with the disappearance of Anthony Currah.

"It was the man who shot you," said Peggy, "not that we knew that at the time. He came out of the future as far as we can tell. Seems able to get into the mirror. Caught Anthony alone. Screaming something about you, and being back from Wales of all places. Forced Anthony into the basement and through the mirror. Brought him back to now—1947—and hid him in the little cave. I came home to muddy footprints leading from my mirror and—nothing." She abruptly stood up, took out a cigarette, and turned her back, walking a few paces away.

"It was a terrible shock for poor Peg," said Lilly in a lower voice. "To me as well. John had just come through my mirror the night before. I brought John to meet Peg when she came back to my 1937 to tell me about her mysterious footprints. Her parents—well, they're not as … supervisory, I suppose, as most. John could hide out in the coach house for days, I reasoned. He helped us look. We scoured the countryside for days. Then it got worse. Peg came home to find her house broken into. I'll bet you can guess the one thing that was stolen."

"The mirror."

"Exactly. Ripped from its frame. I think Peg must have been going wild. I was in my time, so apart from John, she was all on her own. No going back to get me."

"What happened next?"

Peggy turned back toward us and fixed me with a hard but unreadable expression. "Anthony almost died is what happened next. The man made him put a doorstop in the mirror, then tied him up and left, taking the mirror with him."

"Five days he was gone," said Lilly. "And Anthony tied up all that time in that little hole. If the rain hadn't been making it through there, I'm sure he would have died."

"Five days," I said. "Looking for me? Wait." I held up my hands and tried to line the times up in my head. "This started, what, two weeks ago? That's when Melissa and Keisha got attacked."

They made me tell them what I knew about those attacks. "But wait," I said, looking at Lilly. "What about you? What happened when you tried to come through?" I looked back at the hole in the creek bank I had come out of. It wasn't large, and was mostly hidden by grass and weeds. "If he took the mirror away, where did he put it?"

Lilly opened her mouth to speak, then paused, thought for a moment, and tried it again. "That's ... part of what we need to talk to you about, Kenny. There's a lot this man doesn't understand about the mirror, we think, but some things he must understand better than we do." She looked at my face and shook her head. "Oh, I mustn't be making any sense at all. It was in water, Kenny. It was sunk in water. I found a doorstop in my mirror. Thinking it must have been left by Peg, I tried to come through, and I almost died. John says he's seen exactly that happen. You know, of course, that terrible heat or cold you go through when you pass through the place in between. Somehow it's worse when you pass from the mirror into water. It makes your muscles cramp and tighten. My lungs filled with water and I could barely drag myself back in time to save my life. I kept trying, but I could never go through. Wherever he had taken the mirror, he had sunk it in water."

"Why do you think he's looking for you?" said Peggy abruptly, directing a steady gaze at me.

"What?"

"Why is he looking for you?"

Kenny Maxwell killed my wife. I could still hear the words in my mind. I flicked a glance at John Wald, but he wasn't entering into this part of the conversation. Could it be he hadn't heard or hadn't made out that accusation?

"I don't know," I said. I just couldn't bring myself to say it. What if it was true? Killed his wife. What if I deserved what he wanted to do to me? "What happened next?"

Peggy turned away, finding something to look at up a bend in the creek. Lilly took over. "The man came back two days ago. Screaming. He thought Anthony was hiding things, mirror-secrets. He hauled Anthony out of the hole and into the creek where he had the mirror. I think he might have killed him, but Peggy heard." Lilly gave a little smile. "Our Peg is brave, I think, however much she wants to hide it."

"Doesn't take courage to scream and act the fool," said Peggy, her back still turned to us.

"As soon as he saw her," said Lilly, "he dropped Anthony and ran for her, started screaming. This man she had never seen before in her life, babbling about how he'd found her at last, he'd save her, never let her go. Is it any wonder, she isn't thrilled to be talking about it?"

"I'm fine," said Peggy. She walked back to us but didn't sit. She ran a hand through her hair. "He kept screaming about how he'd tell me everything and make it right this time."

At last, as she told it, the man must have realized he was terrifying her. He tried to reassure her that he was only trying to "stop the bad things." To prove his goodwill, he fished Anthony out of the creek, and the mirror as well. Tying Peggy as well—for her own good, he said—he brought them all back to the carriage house.

"Then came the gun," said Peggy. "He said it was all to make us happy again. If he could kill Kenny, everything would be peachy keen."

"He would have done it all, too, if it weren't for John," said Lilly, "though it cost him terribly."

Wald, also out looking for Anthony, returned to the carriage house in time to see the crazy man tying Peggy and Anthony to chairs. Wald attacked and they struggled. In the confusion, Anthony broke free and began to scream. People ran to help, but before they arrived, the crazy man escaped into the mirror.

"How could he do that?" I said. "I thought it was only the mirror kids? I thought it doesn't let in any one older than sixteen?"

Wald shook his head. "Does not choose." I frowned, and he rubbed his chin as though choosing his words carefully. "When it chooses the first time, we must be young. And when our year of seven is done, we think the glass is done with us. But ten years on comes another year of the glass. And ten and ten and every ten. If we're still alive, we're still the children of the glass."

"So it depends on what's his home time," I said. "Right? You can always go back to the time you're supposed to be in." I shook my head to clear away the questions this new rule brought up. "Anyway, that must have been when he came to Anthony's basement and got me." I turned to Wald. "But you were there. Breaking into the house. How did you get there? You didn't come through the mirror."

Wald gave a huge sigh and a sad, weary grin crossed his face. "The long path, lad. Pray thou never need foot it."

"He was arrested," said Peggy. She threw her cigarette butt into the dying fire and stared at the embers. "They were all idiots. Wouldn't listen to a thing I said. My father and Ben Wilkes from down the street came in to find me tied up and John bleeding from a nasty pistol whipping. I tried explaining, but—well, you know the neighborhood's reputation. Missing children and the like."

John nodded, staring into the fire. "I canna blame them," he said. "A good drubbing I took of it, too. That father of thine, hath a good kick in his foot."

John told of how he was arrested and charged with assault, breaking and entering, vagrancy, and half a dozen other crimes. Unable to prove his innocence, and carrying only serviceman's papers from thirty years ago, he didn't see the light of day until 1948.

"So, wait," I said. "That's happening right now? I mean—it just happened, right? How are you here?"

Peggy groaned. "Weren't you listening? 'The long path'? John waited. Yes, he's in jail now, one of him. Awaiting trial. He'll get out. Wait all the way until 1957 and come to help us. He broke into Anthony's house last night—in ten years—to catch Prince Harming when he came through the mirror. If you had let him in instead of running, he could have helped you sooner. Gave us a shock when we saw him, I'll tell you that for nothing, ten years older in a day."

He smiled ruefully and nodded.

"So Prince Harming," I said, "comes out of the mirror to kill me, and that's when—"

Wald nodded. "Would have been worse if thy Luka had not been there."

"Did . . . did she bite his cheek?"

Wald chuckled at that. "A high harpy that one, and fond like gold a' thee."

I told them I remembered some of the rest of it. "He escaped. And Luka followed while you stitched me up."

"Aye," said Wald. "She could not wait it. She guessed the mad fool had footed up the years to menace thy friends. I called her to stay whilst I stitched thy side, but she'd have none a' that. Rushed into the glass. Left one a thy doorstop strings that I might after-foot."

"And?" I looked at the girls.

Peggy looked over at Lilly. "You're the sweet one, Lil. You tell him."

"Tell me what?" I said.

Lilly took a deep breath. "It's the mirror, Kenny. Jimmy's— in 1967. Prince Harming must have done it when he escaped after shooting you. It's in water again. He's thrown it in the lake."

Part Three

*The Mirror in the Lake,
Summer 1947*

ONE

And so began my summer of exile.

I slept on the sofa beside the mirror, fifteen years before I was born.

I was trapped. The mirror was in the lake. Lilly, Peggy, and John Wald took me to the carriage house to the mirror. They took me to 1957 where Anthony met us in his basement. Jimmy had described him as a husky overconfident kid, but he was sunken now, his eyes darting all around. He was desperate that we be quiet in case his mother heard us, and seemed happy when I took Lilly and John into the Silverlands in the direction of 1967.

We couldn't go through. The mirror and its cloud of image-fragments were dark. If I hadn't been warned of what lay beyond, I might easily have died. John and Lilly held my shoulders as I tested it. The hand I stuck inside cramped agonizingly as the uptime heat gave way to chill water.

Then they brought me back. To 1957 where Anthony

apologized and said we couldn't stay. To 1947 where Peggy said she'd bring blankets out to the carriage house and sneak me food when she could. John Wald retired for the evening to a shelter he'd built in the woods. Lilly and Peggy went back to their homes. I asked Lilly to leave a doorstop open to her time, just in case Prince Harming, whoever he was, tried to come back from the future. He seemed to be the only one of us who had the secret of getting into a mirror that lay in water.

Most evenings, Peggy would head back to Lilly's time, pulling out the doorstop, so John Wald and I could go forward into Anthony's basement. From there, we would try the passage to 1967, but every time we went, the mirror was underwater. In daylight we could make out what we thought might be glimmers of sun through the water, but neither of us wanted to trust what it might be.

Over the days, I learned John Wald's strange story. He took me for walks in the woods, and in between teaching me how to build a simple shelter and make a meal from leaves and berries, he talked about his life and his long-ago year in the backward glass. By the middle of July, I could make pepperweed tea, dandelion salad, and a bland snack mix of nuts, seeds, and chewy stalks. I guessed he made a pretty decent wise old man, though I had been hoping for a little more wisdom about the way the Force worked and how to handle a lightsaber.

I grew used to his talk. Lilly, who came often and tried to make my exile bearable, brought dictionaries, Shakespearean English, Scots-English, and we used them to puzzle out his words.

He didn't know exactly when he was born, sometime in the 1600s in a small village in the south of Scotland. He was the son of a blacksmith. His mirror, the same one that all of us used to travel back and forth between our decades, hung in the manor house of the local baron. It wasn't until May of his year that John saw a child come through the mirror, then found that he too could enter it. His opportunities were few, but he took them where he could. In the end, he was tripped up by the mirror's rules. Fed too much beer at a year-end celebration by a strange, scarred servant he didn't know, he came back to the mirror too late and found himself trapped ten years in his own past.

Fifteen years old, and all alone in the world, he still managed to make his way. He tried to change his future, as many of the mirror kids do, by approaching his younger self, but a horse kicked him in the head, and so he learned his lesson and didn't try again. In the next few years, he fell in love with a girl in a neighboring village and ended up married with two children. Ten years onward, he saw his own self at the year-end feast, and realized that he, John Wald at twenty-five, was the strange servant who had kept his younger self out of the mirror. What else could he do? He had built a life. He didn't want to lose it.

Knowing he was trapping himself in the past, he became a willing participant in his own fate.

"But didn't it turn out?" I said. "You got to have your family, right?"

He shook his head and told me more. Eight years after his year of the glass, the plague came to his small corner of the world. His children died, then his wife, pregnant with a third. "Her last words to me were, 'John, will ye jig my belly? I haven't felt it move in an age.'"

He was quiet for a couple of days after that, but then one morning he took me out to pick what he called partridge berries and told me the rest. He had gone mad after the plague year. "We all did, those of us as lived. The world was dying 'round us."

He stopped and knelt by a clutch of low plants bearing red berries. "Here now. Pick these. We'll make a tea of it for pain."

"How did you end up here?" I said. It was the main question on my mind. "This is—hundreds of years from your time."

He tugged at a berry. "I found work digging graves and hauling dead. I stayed there, fitting my soul-broke body into the place it had grown up. And in that mad world, I came into a madder plan. I would wait until that cursed glass opened once more, but this time I'd go down and down the years, each time getting a child to take me through, ten years, ten years, ten years again."

Mostly Wald's old face—how old? Fifty? Sixty?—seemed crinkled more with kindness and sorrow, but now a wild fire jumped in him.

"I wanted the maker, see? There must, I thought, be some old wizard ahind the making of that glass. I'd place my hands athwart his reeky neck and twist the breath within him."

"So—what happened?"

Satisfied that we had enough berries, he straightened

and stretched his back. "Time zones, you call 'em," he said. I gave him a blank look so he went on. "You've seen that space between the mirrors, and you know it's long and full? In there I met a girl from the long-to-be, traveling back as I intended. We sat one night and talked, and she told me an answer to the thing I had always wondered. Did you ever not wonder, Kennit? What clock the mirror keeps? It's always an hour before midnight it opens, you know, wherever in the world. This girl from another mirror told me about time zones. Think on it—back in my day, there was no agreed-upon time the world about. Noon was when the sun was overhead."

"I don't get it."

"See'st it not?" he said. "All along, I had been scheming to follow that mirror back to its making. Now I saw I had it back-and-front. That glass isn't made in the long-ago, Kennit. It's from the long-to-be."

I stopped, stunned. "It's from the future?"

"How can it be otherwise? It keeps its days to a tune not yet sung in my day."

"So you—decided not to go into the past to find its maker? You're going into the future?"

He put a gentle hand on my shoulder and started me walking again. "Nowt for me there, a plague-burned world. I've used my days in climbing up the years. Three times I've had to take the slow road. I almost missed the glass in Rose's year, for they made me go to that long war in Europe, the one they said would end all wars. Then that mad fool got me coppered by the guard for grasping Peg as then they thought. Madness." He rubbed his thick-bearded chin. "To think that even now I'm clapped in irons ten miles off, yet talking to ye here and ten years older."

When we got back to the carriage house, he pressed the leather pouch of berries into my hand. "Tingle tree it's also called," he said. "For pain."

"But I don't—I thought this was for you. My wound's almost healed."

"Not for thee, Kennit. You'll find use for it in time." He rubbed his brow with one dirt-covered hand. "We cannot change what's been, Kennit. We know that, aye?" I nodded. "But there is a way to—to make what is. Yesterdays or tomorrows. There is a way to float above the—the stony world of minutes and hours. I cannot say it other ways. Keep the tingle tree. Find use for it in time."

And with no more explanation than that, he was gone, off to his forest shelter.

In my first few weeks there, I pressed my hosts—Lilly, Peg, and Anthony—about details regarding Prince Harming, but they didn't know much more than I had already learned from them. None of them had believed the local legends meant anything at all, though they had all heard variations on the rhyme. Peg wouldn't talk about it at all, and Lilly said she hoped it was all done with now. They had seen the dresser drawer with its message carved for Kenny and Luka, and in some way, it seemed like they thought this must make anything about Kenny and Luka none of their business. Anthony was the least useful of all. Despite his terrifying encounter with the madman who had shot me, he barely seemed to believe in all of it. Peg was all he was interested in, not that she treated him with all that much tenderness.

Still, I spent a lot of my nights in the carriage house staring at that mirror, wondering if someone was coming through again to kill me.

On days when Wald was hunting alone, I took out the July box Luka had given me and wrote a long account of my time in 1947. Though I hadn't yet admitted to my hosts in this time why Prince Harming had shot me, I mused about it in my letter to Luka. I also told her about Peggy and Lilly, the one so snappish and mean, the other so kind.

"Am I that bad?" said Peggy one afternoon, surprising me as I wrote. I had just described a conversation I had seen with Anthony the night before. It was sad sometimes to watch them talk. Anthony was fattening up again after his ordeal in the cave, but if he had ever been brash and confident the way Jimmy described, that part of him was not rebounding. His eyes still darted furtively about any room, and he constantly pulled at his fingers while he spoke. Half of what Peggy said to him was composed of commands to "ease up" and "cool down."

I folded my paper over quickly, but was at a loss for what to say. How much had she read?

"Don't fret yourself, kid," she said. "I guess I'm a little hard on him. Here, I brought you lunch."

I took the sandwich plate and glass of milk she offered, and studied her as she slumped on the couch near the mirror and took out a cigarette. She was a good-looking girl, though

I guess I didn't notice it that much. Her sharp words and thin-lipped disapproval of almost everything distracted me from her deep, heavy-lidded eyes. From the carriage house, on the few days when her mother was around, I could hear little but yelling between her parents; then, when her mother left, the place was like a graveyard.

You never think about how your own parents are until you start paying attention to other families. Mine didn't see eye-to-eye on everything, particularly the constant house-hopping, and I went through long periods in my life wondering if they wished they hadn't bothered having a kid, but I'd take a year of the worst days in my house over a week in the Garroway place.

"You're going to disappear," I said. Just like that, it came out of me.

She flashed a thin smile and drew lightly on her cigarette. "Been carrying that one around for a while?"

"It's true," I said. "In September. It's—everyone in the neighborhood knows by my time. It was in the newspapers and everything. September first. They never found you."

"Never did, eh?"

A long moment passed. She smoked. I looked at my sandwich.

I tried another way. "Jimmy Hayes said Anthony said he talked to you about it already, and you didn't want to talk about it."

She waved a hand. "It's 1947, kid. Anthony's just ten years up. That was the first thing he talked to me about. His folks bought the place from my dad."

"So … what's going to happen?"

She shrugged. "Whatever it is, it's going to happen." She turned and looked right at me. "Kid, some things aren't for you to worry about. If I'm going missing, that's my beeswax. I know you and the Nancy Drews up in the future think we're some kind of charity case in the past, some sort of adventure mystery for you to come and solve, but we're not, okay? We have our own lives, our own ideas, and our own plans." She reached forward and stubbed her cigarette out on my sandwich plate. "I'm not your summer project, Kenny. Think about your own problems."

With that, she got up and walked down the stairs and out of the carriage house.

Even with my new determination not to end up like Wald, my burning need to just *get out of that time*, I don't know how I would have got moving if Peggy hadn't chosen the next day to break up with Anthony. Lilly said later that the signs were all there if you knew how to look. I hadn't even, I figured, been within hand-holding distance of my first girl-friend yet, so I didn't know what the signs were, much less how to look for them. I wasn't on the same road as those signs.

Lilly used a doorstop to come forward that night, then took it out in time for Anthony to come backward from his time. Peggy's mother had come back home that day, and her parents were loudly drunk, so it was no problem for her to sneak a feast out to us in the carriage house.

After dinner, Wald took Lilly and me out to instruct us on the making of owl calls, though I guess his real purpose was to give Peg some time with Anthony. None of it came as a surprise to Wald. I guess he must have seen his share of through-the-mirror first loves over his uptime centuries.

Our first clue that something was wrong came in the form of sobs as we approached the carriage house. In the noisy summer dark, Anthony's crying rang out above the crickets and the nightjars, inconsolable and, well, embarrassing.

I tensed at first, fearing a return of the crazy gunman, but Wald put a reassuring hand on my shoulder and told me it was only the "cracking a' that confracted heart."

We waited a few minutes in the dark, but when we saw a light in the main house, we hurried in and Lilly broke the news that Anthony would have to be quieter or else duck through to another time. We turned Peggy's kerosene lamp low and stood in an uncomfortable silence.

"Fine then," Anthony said, his voice dripping with bitterness. "I'll just go back into that mirror and never come out again. I'll stay in my year. I won't ever come back. That's what you're saying, isn't it? That's what you want."

Peggy murmured that she wanted no such thing. She just thought they ought to "cool it a little."

"Look," she said, in as gentle a tone as I had heard her use. "In your time I'm in my twenties. Probably married. I'll be thirty when you're done school. Ask John if he ever sees anything like this work out. I ... I just don't want you to get hurt. Is that so bad?"

Anthony looked up at the rest of us. "What about you? Were you just laughing at me, is that it?"

"Nobody's laughing at you, Anthony," said Lilly.

Wald ran a hand through his hair. "Mayhaps, 'twere best to bide this pair alone. I wouldnay—"

He was interrupted by a call from the main house. By now we all knew Peggy's father's voice.

"Hush now, all of you," she said, and doused the lamp the rest of the way. "I'll duck around and come up from the creek, but there's going to be words for me in there." In the thin moonlight, I could see her turn to Anthony. "Buck up, AC. This was going to happen sooner or later."

We stood and waited, silent and uncomfortable, until Peggy made her way around to the far side of the house and apologized to her furious father. When the door slammed, Wald spoke up. "I'll hie out," he said. "'Tis a fine night for walking. Goodnight to all."

Lilly relit the lamp, but kept it shrouded.

"Did you know about this?" said Anthony, more to her, I guess, than me.

Lilly sat down. I couldn't see her face from this angle, but I could imagine her sympathetic expression. She was always the one who wanted to make things okay. "Peg never told me anything," she said. "But that's not what you mean, is it? Oh, Anthony, didn't you know there was something coming? She was getting cool, wasn't she? I haven't seen her let you hold her hand in weeks."

"I thought ... I thought it was just her dad and mom and all that," he said.

"Maybe she'll change her mind," I put in. "Maybe if you ... give her time." The words sounded stupid the moment they came out of my mouth. I don't know what I had been thinking. I didn't know about how girls made up their minds in the first place, much less about how they changed them.

He stood up. "Forget it," he said. "I'm finished. Why should I keep sneaking out for you people? You know how much trouble I got in when I came back muddy and half starved from a week in that madman's stupid cave? But did any of you ask? Time? I'm taking some time, all right," he said. "I'm taking it all. I'm going home and getting rid of that stupid mirror." He turned to me. "Better figure out something to do, pal, because you've been hanging around long enough."

"That's hardly fair," said Lilly. "Kenny is trapped with us. You can't—"

"You're right, he's trapped." He turned to me. "You're trapped, Kenny. Might as well face it. They're not saying it, but they're tired of nursemaiding you here and there. If I were you, I'd just pick a decade. You're an orphan boy now, kid, a hobo. Better get used to it."

He stomped upstairs and thrust himself into the mirror.

"Oh, Kenny," said Lilly after a few breaths of stunned silence. "It's not true, what he said. We feel for you very much, Peg and I. And Anthony. He just isn't himself right now."

"He's kind of right, though," I said. "I can't go on this way. I have to get home or—something."

She didn't have much to say to that, and just stood for a moment pursing her lips. "I suppose I'd better be going. It's late. You should sleep, Kenny. Everything will seem different in the morning."

Despite her advice, I didn't get much sleep, but she was right. In the morning, everything was different.

TWO

That night, I stayed up late and killed two sets of flashlight batteries finishing my letter to Luka.

At five in the morning in the predawn light, I wrote my last line and began to pack up. I don't know where I thought I was going. Wald's lean-to? Ten years on? Ten years back? As I folded up the few extra clothes I had come with, and which I had been rotating through as Peggy sneaked them into her laundry, I tried to run through my choices. Lilly's family sounded the nicest. In the middle of the Great Depression, they didn't have much, but of all the mirror kids, she seemed the happiest. She was an only child whose parents had always wanted another. Maybe they'd adopt me.

Stupid. Never work. And I didn't think I could keep going without television.

Staying with Peggy was out. Even without Anthony's blow-up I had sensed my welcome wearing thin. Her mother and father had been in a constant battle ever since the war, each skirmish usually resulting in her mother taking off for her sister's place for a week, leaving her father to drink, shout, and punch the wall.

Hanging out in Anthony's time was the least appealing idea of all, but at least I'd be closest to home. I could keep checking out the mirror and hope that it would end up on dry land before my year was over.

My watch showed almost six by the time I had erased all signs of my presence. I had twenty minutes before Lilly poked her head through the mirror to see me on her way to her morning chores. I headed out across Manse Creek with a shovel borrowed from the carriage house and found the place where I was supposed to bury the box. Maybe when Luka found it in 1987, she could look up my parents and tell them. Not that they'd believe her. Hi, remember your son that disappeared ten years ago? He and I used to time travel through a mirror in your old house. He's not dead, but he's in his forties or fifties by now.

I lay the box in its hole next to a midsized tree that would be a gnarled giant in thirty years, and looked at it for a long time before covering it up.

It was only when I had patted down the loose dirt on top that I realized I wasn't finished digging yet. It's funny when I look back at this now, just a year later, and think about all the things I didn't realize then, the questions I didn't ask. Why didn't I find out more about Lilly? Why didn't I try to figure out how Peggy was going to disappear, or how a newspaper from 1947 was going to end up wrapping a dead baby that might be from many years before? Why didn't I wonder how

Luka's initials were already carved into a piece of wood that I found not long after arriving in this time?

That last one I did finally start wondering about. Took me long enough.

The initials. She had carved them. We saw them when we dug the tabletop up in 1977. I saw them again in this year. So she had been back further.

Trembling with anticipation, I walked to where I remembered her July box was supposed to be, next to a large, half-buried rock, and without another moment's thought, began to dig with mad energy. It was impossible that the box would be there. Wasn't it? But I knew it was there in 1977, which meant she had buried it further in the past than my home time. Surely that meant that sooner or later, sometime before the year was over, she was going to travel again. And if she was traveling back, why stop at 1967? Why not go back far enough that I could actually use whatever it was she had to tell me?

"Hi."

Startled, I almost dropped the shovel.

A tall, slim man in neat clothing had climbed up from the creek bed. I didn't recognize him, but that wasn't saying much. The area was a lot less populated than it would be in my time, and I had tried to avoid the few farmhands and landowners I saw. Kingston Road wasn't far, and there were a lot more houses and people there, but in the forties Manse Valley had more cornfields than commuters.

"I, ah ... " The man gestured behind him. "I thought I'd take a walk. It's nice around here. Not a lot of people." He looked down at the hole I had been digging. "Treasure hunt?" His clothes didn't look like what you'd wear if you were going to take a walk along a creek. White shirt, pressed grey suit, jacket slung across his arm, yellow tie, and a fedora.

"Kind of a time capsule," I said, hoping they had such things back in the forties.

He grinned. "Oh, like at the World's Fair? That's keen. When did you bury it?"

"A couple of years ago." I dug my shovel into the dirt again. Its weight felt reassuring.

"Oh, yeah? Isn't it a little early to dig it up? Don't you want to wait a few years?" He held up his jacket and took out a cigarette case and a lighter.

I continued digging, but kept my eyes on him. What was he doing here? "We're moving soon," I said. "My dad bought a house in the city. I don't want to leave it here."

The thin man nodded. Did I know him? He was clean shaven. Younger than my parents. "Sure. So you live around here?"

"Just past those trees," I said. "You?"

"Used to. Moved away for a while. War, you know?"

My shovel struck the top of Luka's box. The man must have heard the sound or read my expression. "Well, there's your time capsule. What's inside? Photographs? School essays?"

"A letter," I said.

He lit his cigarette and smiled. "Well, don't let me stop you. Go ahead."

Watchfully, I edged around the shape of the box, then

reached in and struggled it out. The thin man smoked his cigarette and leaned against a tree, looking off at the creek. "Place hasn't changed," he said. "Same old neighbors. Mostly. Not sure if I remember your family, though. What did you say your name was?"

"I didn't," I said. He seemed taken aback. It was useful to be a couple of generations ahead of everyone on smart-ass movie lines. I relented as I stood up with the dirt-covered box. "Bond. James Bond." Something clattered to one end of the box.

The man smiled. "Beckett," he said, and stepped forward, holding out his hand. He must have seen my eyes go wide, because he stopped, hand outstretched. "Sounds like more than a letter. Your name's not familiar. What about mine?" He seemed more sure of himself now than when he had first climbed up from the creek bed.

I gulped, trying to think fast. "Sure. Beckett. My grandpa knew a Clive, but he died in the war."

The thin man nodded, let his hand drop. "Aren't you going to look? At the box."

I had put it protectively under my arm. "I guess. I better head back home. I told my dad I was just coming for a few minutes. He'll come out to find me if I don't."

"Aw, come on. Satisfy an old soldier's curiosity. Maybe that box ain't even yours."

He was between me and the creek. Down one side, across, then up the other? A mad dash through the woods? Could I even get past him, much less to the carriage house?

But why was I worried about him?

"Okay," I said. One-handed, I thrust the shovel into the ground in front of me, and set about opening the box. The hinges, which I had seen brand new only a few weeks ago, were stiff with rust and dirt, and the wood was warped, but I managed to wrench it open without spilling the contents: a large heavy coin, a folded piece of paper, and an envelope addressed to me.

"Hey, a coin," said the man, who had taken the opportunity to step closer. I took a half step back, keeping the shovel between us. "Whoa, take it easy," he said. "I'm just— hey, you know what that is?" His eyes narrowed. "That's a Dead Man's Penny. What's a kid doing with one of those?"

He didn't pass the temporary barrier of the shovel. I tried to keep my hand from trembling as I unfolded the paper. Despite the tension of the moment, I felt a twinge of annoyance at Luka when I realized how little she had written. All night I had stayed up finishing mine. But the mood went away as soon as I saw it actually was hers. Her handwriting. Her voice, after all this time. Talking to me. I tried to keep my wits about me, and held the paper high enough to watch the thin man as I read.

Dear Kenny,

Everybody's okay. I don't think I can say much more than that or you won't be able to read it. I opened your July box early and the paper was rotted so I couldn't make much out. I think you're okay. There was something about a John Wald. Broke my own rules and look what it got me? There is one thing I can do, though. I can give you the letter. It's from your grandmother. She said I should put it in the box for you. She said you have to open it right away.

Good luck. I miss you. I'm coming to get you.

Your friend for all time,
Luka

PS: Okay I can't resist two things. One, your parents know everything and they're waiting for you to come home.

PPS: Look at the name on the big coin. Keisha said the man who attacked her dropped it.

"Do you even know what that is?" said the man. "A Dead Man's Penny? It's funny, I have one. Always carry it." His gaze never left mine as he reached into his pocket and brought out a newer coin. I could see why he called it a penny. It was copper, but larger than any coin. I looked down at the one in the box. A woman stood, a helmet on her head, holding out a wreath. A lion at her feet faced off to the right as did she. Below her hand, a name had been engraved.

Clive Beckett.

"That's funny," said the thin man. He rubbed his fingers on the coin. "Tingly. Like electricity shooting through it."

I didn't touch the coin. Fingers still trembling, I put Luka's letter back in the box, and withdrew the envelope. Sure enough, that was my grandmother's handwriting, same as on every birthday card and Christmas card. I shut the box and tucked it under one arm.

"What's that?" said the thin man. His voice was showing some strain now. "The thing is, do I know you from somewhere? You ever… I don't know… you ever wonder about your memories from a long time ago? Hey, what am I saying. You're a kid. You don't even have a long time ago, right?"

The seal on the envelope was old. It opened easily. Inside was a short letter.

Dearest Kenny,

I have a message I have waited twenty years to tell you. You are the little hobo boy. Come see us.

Oh, and I'm afraid you're going to have to run. I think a bad man is coming to get you. He has a yellow tie.

With love always,
Your grandmother,
Harriet Maxwell

"Maybe I do know you from somewhere," said the man. "I think I can help with something. I think you're Kenny Maxwell." He stepped forward again, frowned, and looked at the coin in his hand. "Hey, there's that tingling again. What does that mean? I think I used to know."

That was enough. I took the box from under my arm, the large coin still rattling inside it, and stepped forward, thrusting it toward him.

He screamed. Blue sparks flashed in his hand, and he almost dropped his coin. The box insulated me from the shock of same-meeting-same, but I could feel the coin struggling inside it. Using the distraction of the blue sparks, I slammed into the man's side and rushed past.

It felt a little like the last part of that "Going on a Lion Hunt" song the kids who go to camp always come back knowing. Down the creek bank, through the mud, across the creek, up the bank. At some point, the man calling himself Beckett took up the chase, while all along the large coin that bore his name clattered around in my wooden box. As I ran, my brain raced faster than my feet. Wasn't Clive Beckett dead? Why did this man call himself Beckett and carry a coin with the name on it? He seemed more charming than the madman in the raincoat who had shot me. Was he Prince Harming? Were we wrong about that other man?

I risked a glance behind me as I reached the overhang above the hiding hole, as John Wald called it. Beckett wasn't running. "It's okay," he shouted to me. "I just want to sort it out, who the man was. I can't remember all of it. I just want to talk."

I didn't slow down.

When I reached the hedgerow that hid the carriage house, I ran into Lilly and Peggy coming out.

"Oh, there you are," said Peggy. "What on earth is wrong with you?"

I almost collapsed onto them, heaving shuddering breaths.

"Kenny, is something wrong?" said Lilly.

"Man," I gasped. "Chasing. Mirror."

"Come on," said Peggy.

As they pulled me through the hedges, I looked back, but I had lost him in the woods.

Only when we got inside the carriage house did I notice that the two of them were carrying large suitcases.

"What is this?" I said.

"Never mind," said Peggy. "What are you running from? What man?"

"Prince Harming maybe. I think it's a man who's supposed to be dead. I don't know." What to do now? We couldn't all just jump into the mirror, could we? Physically, of course, we could. If Lilly went in, she could pull us all back to 1937. If I went, I could take us in the opposite direction to Anthony's time. But that would leave the mirror unprotected. What if Beckett took it and sunk it in the lake just as the other man had?

We had to do something.

It was Peggy who took charge. "Come on, then, help us up the stairs with these. We'll talk once we're through in Lilly's time. I suppose we can find something to do with you."

When she said "these," I saw that she had a lot more than just the two suitcases I had seen them heaving through the door. Smaller overnight bags, a makeup case, and three pillowcases that looked stuffed with clothing and all sorts of knickknacks covered the floor.

"No," I said. "We have to go."

"Hold your horses, charley horse," said Peggy. "Who're

you rushing? I have a lot of important things in these, and I'm not leaving them behind."

Leaving them behind? I shook off the strangeness of the remark. "Look, whoever's coming, it's probably bad," I said. I looked to Lilly for help.

"I think we should listen to him, Peg," Lilly said after meeting my gaze for a moment. "Just—let's get in what we can. Come on."

I grabbed one bag to show my willingness to help, and herded them up the stairs, each of them carrying a suitcase.

The mirror and the sofa I had been sleeping on for the last three weeks were at the top of the stairs. Just being on the same floor as the thing calmed me a little. Whoever this man was, he didn't seem to have it all together. We had the mirror and we knew the mirror. While Lilly and Peggy each lugged a suitcase into the mirror, I ran to the hayloft window. The hedges were shorter now, and over the top of them I could see the thin man. He was standing in the yard of the main house, looking around. I ducked back down and returned to the mirror in time to see Lilly and Peg come back out.

"What is this?" I said again, looking from one to the other. Lilly pursed her lips worriedly and looked to Peggy.

"What do you think it is?" said Peggy, fixing me with a stare. "Aren't you the one who told me I'm disappearing?"

"But it's not … it's not until … "

"Not until September, right? The hell it isn't. You think I'm going to wait around for that? I'm not disappearing, I'm escaping."

"But where will you … ?"

Lilly cleared her throat and gave me a shy smile. "She's coming to stay with me, Kenny. We've talked about it and made a decision. Her parents are horrible, you know? They can't make peace and they won't stay apart. They insist on using Peg as a sort of cattle prod to stick each other with. If she's going to disappear anyway, I'd rather take her with me."

"But it's not September," I said.

"I have an idea about that," said Peggy. "Mother went off again last night. Might not come back for a month. All it takes is for Father to not report me gone for a few weeks. Maybe he'll think I've gone with her." Her mouth twisted bitterly. "Maybe he won't even notice."

"Kenny!" came a shout from outside. "I just want to talk."

Peggy narrowed her eyes at me. "Do you know who this man is?"

I shook my head. "He's using the name of someone who died thirty years ago."

"Come with us," Lilly said. "I don't know what we'll do, Kenny, but it turns out Peg's thought this through. She's found a few investments my parents can make that will bring them some money. We both want to be nurses, and what with the war coming as Peg knows it is, she says there'll be work for us. I don't know how we'll fit you in, but we must."

"No."

It's funny about yes and no. I think I figured out that day that you make yourself who you are by what you choose to say those two words to, and maybe no is the one that really makes you. I had been saying yes just about all year long. Yes to going into the mirror. Yes to other kids' plans.

Peggy had already begun her migration. She got Lilly to shove her hand in, opening the mirror up, and began moving the large suitcases inside. "Come on, kid, there's no time for this. I guess Lilly's right."

"No," I said. "What if he sinks this mirror in the lake? Then I won't just be cut off from 1967, I won't even be able to get back to now. I'm not going any further back. I'll go see Anthony and at least be closer to home. Just go. There's no time."

Lilly opened her mouth to say something, but Peggy cut her off. "He's right, Lil. Say goodbye."

Lilly closed her eyes and nodded. "Goodbye, Kenny. We'll watch for you. We'll miss you."

"Me, too," I said. "But you have to go."

I was practically pushing them through. At our best forward thrust, it took a good six seconds to make it through the slowly expanding Silverlands and out the other side, and that was without heavy suitcases. Just as Lilly's trailing foot went through, the door to the carriage house opened.

The thin man stepped forward, staring right up the stairs as though he had known I would be there. "Please stop running," he said. His neat clothing was mud-splattered from his trip through the creek. He held up his hands as though to show he was harmless. "I'm not chasing you. I just want to make sense of it. You're the boy from the future, aren't you?"

I didn't say anything. It was all I could do not to run into the mirror after the girls.

"I have so many questions," said the man. He sounded so reasonable, I started to have doubts. Was I wrong about him? He stepped farther into the dusty light, but tentatively.

"Don't come any closer," I said. "What's your real name? What are you doing here?"

He raised a hand and ran it through his hair. "It's all real, isn't it?" he said. "I know it is, but it's hard to keep that in my head sometimes. I can't remember it all. Ten years this way and that, right? Kenny, it's me. It's so strange to see you after all this time. It's bringing back memories. Was—there a baby?" He reached a trembling hand up and wiped his brow. "I have so many questions. So much happened. What don't I remember, Kenny? You know it's me, right? Look at me. Kenny, don't go away this time. Everything worked out okay. You always seemed so sad, but it worked out okay."

I grabbed my backpack and tensed myself to climb up onto the dresser and push into the mirror. Would I get through in time? Six seconds. Was he a mirror kid? Could he follow me?

Clive Beckett. CB. Rose Hollerith's boyfriend? Clive Beckett was Prince Harming? How old must he be? When was he born?

He took a step forward. That was all the encouragement I needed. I almost threw myself at the mirror. "No, Kenny!" he shouted. "Wait. I want to tell you how it all turns—"

His words were muffled by the Silverlands. I pushed in harder than ever, ignoring the pain. It wasn't like I'd be stopping to check if anyone was in Anthony's basement before I stumbled in. I strained against the hot molasses of uptime travel, expecting any second to feel a hand on my collar or the punch of a bullet against my back.

My plan was to jump out in 1957 and head for the stairs. Halfway up, I could assess whether or not I needed to make an escape.

What I didn't think about was falling.

THREE

I didn't fall far, but it hurt like hell and taught me a lesson I had somehow gone seven months without learning: just because the mirror has up and down the right way when you go in, that doesn't mean it's going to be the same on the other side.

I cried out with the shock, but my yell was quickly cut short as I thumped sideways into rocky mud and then rolled down to splash face-first into water. I got up, choking and soaked.

I was in a rainstorm. In a river. No, it was too shallow for that.

I looked around and saw the mirror, perched halfway down a familiar turn in Manse Creek a quarter of a mile from the Hollerith place. Fat raindrops drummed the water around me. I felt like I had swallowed half the creek.

I grabbed my sodden backpack before it floated down the creek, stood in a half crouch and watched the mirror, wedged into the mud of the bank above me.

No one came out.

Was he standing there in the Silverlands, waiting until I came closer? I edged to the side, sloshing my way through the creek and up onto the muddy bank and continued to watch the mirror.

Anthony had really done it. He hadn't taken the mirror out of its frame, but had instead ripped the frame itself off the dresser. I wondered if he had actually tried breaking it, and just thinking that made me angry. I would never do that to him.

The rain showed no signs of abating, and no one seemed to be coming out, so I trudged forward, picked up the mirror, and headed upstream. It was harder to carry than the cold night Luka and I had taken it to the junk house, but I found as long as I kept my hands on the edges and the nontraveling back, I could struggle it along.

By the time I got to the old hand-excavated cave, I was scratched all over and soaked to the bone. The frame around the mirror hadn't fared well on the trip, but the glass itself was as flawless as ever.

The collapse of the hand-dug cave had begun, but there was enough left to provide me shelter from the rain. I guess it's okay for me to admit that right after I got in there, propped the mirror over the entrance, facing outward, and moved my backpack to the driest extreme I could find, I leaned against the feathery roots that made up the side of the cave and began to cry.

I was twenty years from home. No Anthony and no doorstop, so I wasn't going back, and without someone fishing the mirror out of the lake in 1967, I wasn't going forward either. I had no friend in this time. How would I get by? Thirty dollars remained in the bottom of my backpack, some in coins not yet minted. My other possessions included two changes of clothing, five wooden boxes, a map of the city, a penknife, a so-called Dead Man's Penny, and a Coke in a green glass bottle.

That last item was about the most useful at that point, and so I spent a good half hour crying into my Coke the way some people cry into their beer. I cried about my mother and father, teenagers right now, not even aware they would get together someday and have a kid who would disappear. I cried about a lost life I never appreciated. I cried about the way the whole world of time travel had receded from me. I wasn't a mirror kid anymore. I was a stranger, unknown to anyone, more odd and out of place than anyone on the planet.

Crying that way in front of anyone is embarrassing, but if you do it all alone, no chance of being seen, it does some good. Once the last sobs and tears had worked their way out, I was exhausted, but at least it was done.

For a while afterward, I didn't move, just let my cheek rest against the dirt and roots, and my mind wander the labyrinth of my problems.

Rules of time travel. Ways of getting around them. Clive Beckett. Prince Harming. Dead wife. Me a murderer. Luka's box, buried in the past, further back even than 1947. Mirror kids getting concussions. The mirror itself, an unanswerable mystery that just stared stupidly back at you.

Eventually the rain slowed enough that I could move to the mouth of the hole and read Luka's letter again.

I liked the closing. *Good luck. I miss you. I'm coming to get you.* Because she knew, didn't she? If that thing was buried further in the past, she knew she was coming to get me. Somehow, in the next few weeks, or maybe months, Luka was going to get further back than now and leave that box.

She was coming for me. Shivering, muddy, soaked to the bone, I held on to that thought. What was the first thing I would say when I saw her. Would I kiss her? Could I do that?

Sometime in the late afternoon, the rain stopped. I stood and stretched. A lot of time had passed since I tumbled out of the mirror Anthony threw away. It would be dinner time at the Currah household. That was good for what I wanted. I left my backpack inside the hole in the creek bank, propped the mirror over the entrance, and headed back to the Hollerith place.

The old house was looking better than it would in the future. The lawns were cut, the hedges trimmed, and every bit of exposed wood stained or painted. I gave three hard knocks and waited.

"Hi, Mrs. Currah," I said when Anthony's mother opened the door. "I'm sorry to interrupt, but I really need to see Anthony."

She gave me a *Do I know you?* frown, then said, "I'm sorry, dear, Anthony's—well, he's not ready for visitors right now. Maybe you could call tomorrow."

I found it difficult to be disrespectful to someone's parent, but I had to. "I know he's upset about his girlfriend," I said, loud enough that I hoped Anthony would hear. "But I'm sure he doesn't want to let down his friends."

Surprise, annoyance, and maybe a little suspicion crossed Mrs. Currah's face before it lapsed into an impassive expression. "I think you must be mistaken, dear," she said. "Anthony doesn't have a girlfriend. Maybe—are you thinking Anthony Chuff over on Bennett? I've never seen you before."

"No, I mean Anthony Currah," I said, getting even louder. "He's got a girlfriend, all right. I could tell you all about her if you like. We're good friends."

Before I could say anything else, Anthony shoved his mother aside, burst through the door, and grabbed my arm.

"I'll take care of this, Ma," he said. "Kenny's a kid from school is all."

"Anthony, what's all this about?"

"It's okay, Ma," he said, guiding me away from the house as he spoke. "Kenny and me, we like to joke around, don't we, Ken?"

"I don't know about joking," I said. "Sometimes your friends really count on you, and they end up getting covered in mud, you know? Hey, do you think your mom knows about those magazines under your mattress?"

My voice was still loud, but his was a hiss. "Hey, cool it, man. That's against the code. You don't talk about girls to a guy's mom."

"Oh?" I said. I let him drag me off. "And is trying to drown someone in mud cool with the code? Is leaving John Wald stuck in the past cool with the code?"

"I told you I was done," said Anthony. "I wanted that thing out of my house."

But I wasn't finished. "Is leaving us by ourselves when Prince Harming comes back cool with the code?"

"What?" he said. "Prince Harming came back?" All the anger drained out of him in an instant.

"Not through the mirror. I don't think so, anyway. It was a younger him. He wasn't the same, but he was. Look, I'll tell you everything. Sneak out tonight and meet me by the cave."

"No," he said. "I'm done. I'm not coming back. This is crazy, and if we don't stop, you won't be the only one who can't get back home. We're lucky it hasn't happened lots of times before now."

"You're not done," I said. "You can do whatever you like after tonight, but you're going in one last time, to put a door-stop in for John. I'll even take the mirror away. You'll never see it again."

Anthony bit his lip. "Is Peg okay?"

I almost answered him, but then I set my face in as hard an expression as I could. "Bring some food. I'm starving."

He came. Sometime in the evening my water-logged watch quit working, so I sat in the dark, getting bitten by mosquitoes and convincing myself that it hadn't worked and midnight must have passed, and what was I going to do now? But he came.

I called to him when I heard him blundering through the undergrowth, and he turned on his flashlight. "All right, fine, here I am. I don't know why I bothered."

"Do you have a doorstop?"

He held out a long piece of string with a dessert spoon tied at each end.

I showed him where I had leaned the mirror against the bank of the creek. "Let's set it," I said. "I'm leaving it for John Wald so he has a way to come forward. Then I'll tell you everything."

I went in with him, just in case anybody was waiting on the other side, but the carriage house in 1947 was empty and still. We set each spoon in the lower corner of the mirror, figuring it would have a better chance of being unnoticed that way.

When we came back, we sat down on a fallen log and I explained everything. When I got to the part about Peggy going through to Lilly's time, I took a glance at him, and I was pretty sure there were tears running down his cheeks.

"I really am done with it," he said after a long while. "I'm sorry about where I put the mirror. That was rotten. But I don't want to do it anymore."

"Okay," I said. I got up and slung my backpack onto my shoulder.

"You're going?" said Anthony. "Don't you wanna—I can probably get you into the little house for the night."

I shook my head. "I spent the day doing nothing. It's time I got going."

"But where? What is there around here you can go to?"

I picked up the mirror. It wasn't easy to carry by myself, but at least I didn't have to worry about breaking it. "You said it yourself," I said. "What else can a little hobo boy do? I'm going to find my dad."

Part Four

The Little Hobo Boy,
August 1957

ONE

One Saturday in early August 1957, I got the opportunity to take part in a story I had been hearing all my life. Three older boys in a downtown neighborhood started in on a vagrant kid who had been staying in an abandoned house.

My grandmother still lived there in my time, so I remembered what she had told me about the old Tarkington place, whose shell-shocked war-vet owner had been moved into a home by his kids. A bunch of local kids had been going there to drink or make out for a couple of years. When I arrived on the street in the early hours of a Wednesday in late July after having walked more than ten miles, it was the natural place to hide out.

I spent two weeks there, avoiding other kids, spending my last bit of money. I was glad when I finally got jumped.

The kids who did it had worked up a sense of outrage at this stranger invading their neighborhood. Despite the fact that in the last couple of years they had tossed their share of rocks through the windows of the Tarkington house, they decided that I was going to have to pay for defiling the house of the local war hero. They caught me crawling out of a basement window on a sweltering August afternoon.

I wasn't a pushover, though, the way you'd figure a skinny little fifteen-year-old would be when confronted with three older boys. I fought back like I had nothing to lose, and I guess also like I knew I'd be rescued, knew the whole script of how this fight would go. When Boyd Fenton broke my nose, I stepped back, pulled it as straight as I could, and asked if he was done yet.

"What the hell is going on here?" said Brian Maxwell, striding around the corner into the Tarkington backyard where they had taken the vagrant kid. "Fenton, what are you doing?"

"Hi, Brian," said Fenton, straightening up from his fighting crouch. "You seen this little thief? He's been breaking in and John saw him stealing from Tuck's the other day. Little gypsy or something. We're giving him the run-off."

Brian examined me. "Kind of blue-eyed for a gypsy, Fenton. How're you giving him the run-off if you don't let him, you know...run off?"

"Making sure he doesn't want to come back," said John Timson.

"And teaching him respect," said the third kid. "He's gotta learn he can't just break into Mr. Tarkington's house like that. Guy was a war hero."

Brian shook his head. "Bines, two years ago, you said I could be the leader of your gang if I'd break in here and set up a clubhouse. I don't think you're the guy to teach respect. Find something else to do."

"No," said Fenton. "We found him first, Brian. We'll let him go in a couple of minutes anyhow."

"Good. So it's a couple of minutes."

Fenton squared his shoulders and thrust out his chest. "I didn't say we were done yet."

Brian Maxwell smiled. "Okay, you're not done yet. But I think that's enough of this three-on-one." He strode forward into the triangle made by the three boys. "Hey, kid, what do you say? Timson's the littlest one; kick him in the balls, I'll give you fifty cents. I'll take the other two."

"Fine by me," I said. "Make it a buck if I break his nose?"

"Deal."

And that's how I did it. I followed as close as I could to the letter of the story the way my grandmother told it. I did break John Timson's nose, and my dad, Brian Maxwell, tore Boyd Fenton's shirt so badly pulling it off his back that Mrs. Fenton actually came around a couple of days later asking my grandmother to pay for a new one.

Grandma declined.

Eventually, my dad's best friend "Chuck" Charles came along. He didn't interfere with the fight, saying that would have made it too lopsided, but he commented from the sidelines and gave me some pointers. In the end, I think it was his input that drove our enemies off. Fenton muttered something about us ganging up on them as they left.

It seems strange to keep calling a seventeen-year-old kid my dad, so I'll call him Brian. Before our attackers were around the corner of the little bungalow, he was on the ground laughing.

"Funny to you," said Chuck, coming over and handing him a Coke. "But Emily's sweet on Fenton. What if my sister goes and marries him and he becomes my brother-in-law? You think I wanna be hearing his version of this historic battle over Christmas dinner for the rest of my life?"

"She won't marry Fenton," I said. "She'll marry a guy called Ben Goldstein."

Chuck raised an eyebrow. "Goldstein? You saying my sister's going to marry a Jew?"

"Do you care?"

He grinned. "Nah, but it don't matter how welcome I am in the family, none of them better try cutting part of my pee-pee off."

Brian laughed. "What about me, kid? Who'm I gonna marry?"

I took a long look, pretending to consider. My grandmother hadn't said anything about the little hobo predicting the future, but I already knew nothing I did could alter things. Things turned out they way they would, the way they already had. "Mary Nelson," I said.

His jaw dropped. "How—did someone put you up to that? How'd you know about her?"

This caught Chuck's interest. "Mary Nelson," he said. "How come I don't know about any Mary Nelson, Bri? Holding out on me?"

Brian shook his head. "You just don't remember. My aunt's cottage last year. I went up for a couple of weeks. She was cute, but three years younger. What was I gonna do? I'm a gentleman. How you know about that, half-pint?"

"You'll meet her again," I said. "University. You'll fall in love."

"Hey, how about me?" said Chuck. "I mean, while we're telling the future and all? Who'm I gonna fall in love with?"

I shook my head. "Lots of people."

That got them both laughing. "He's got you all right," said Brian. "Come on, give the kid a Coke, Chuck, and let's figure out what's next."

Just like that, I had become their problem. They agreed I couldn't keep staying in the abandoned house. Either Fenton's guys would tell an adult or they'd come back for me.

"I heard there was some kid hiding out in this house," Brian said as he tried to straighten my nose.

"I heard that, too," said Chuck. "Everybody says he's an orphan whose dad died in the war. That true, kid?"

"A lot of kids' dads died in the war," I said.

Chuck looked quickly over at Brian. "You got that right, kid. So?"

I wanted to phrase what I said carefully. I was off-script now, since my grandmother's stories had never filled me in on exactly what conversation had gone on between the vagrant boy and my dad, just general impressions Brian had picked up and later related to his mother. I didn't want to lie, not exactly. "So some people picked themselves right up," I said, not looking directly at my dad. "Some people's mothers were real strong, and worked two or three jobs to keep it together. They took in washing from the richies up on the Bridle Path, and they got some crappy factory jobs, and they kept right on providing for the families they had." I closed my eyes, not wanting to give anything away. Everything I had just said was true of his mother. Everything that came next was the short life story of the little orphan boy as told to me years from now. "And some people's mothers just quit. Didn't get no job, they didn't take in no work. Just sat in the kitchen and drank until they keeled over one day when their kid was ten, long after the war was done."

I knew I was a lousy actor, so I kept my head down when I said all this so they couldn't see the lies written all over my face.

They didn't say anything for the longest time, and even though I knew they were going to buy it because that was how my grandmother always said it happened, I started having doubts.

When I finally looked up, Brian was already standing. "I've got an idea," he said.

"Uh-oh," said Chuck. "That means trouble."

TWO

Brian's big idea was his coal cellar. He and Chuck drilled me on how to get in and out through the narrow chute that led in from the side of the house. The two of them had done it for years in war games and hide-and-seek, so they knew how to wedge yourself in the chute in order to reach up and close the hatch. It was a tight fit. I found myself thankful that it had been more than a month since I had been fed on anything more than table scraps.

I left the mirror in the Tarkington house, and visited whenever it was safe in order to check the 1967 mirror. As the Silverlands continued to expand, it was becoming impossible to ignore the other clouds of image-fragments to either side of our own. I got into the habit of checking carefully to the right and left as I went in, but though I thought once or twice that I might have heard someone's distant voice, I never saw any other mirror kid. Just as well; I had enough trouble with my own set of mirrors without getting caught up in anyone else's story.

With my doorstop left in, I figured any former mirror kid could come through from 1947, and if anyone did, I wanted to know about it, so I scattered flour, and checked often for footprints. No luck. Had Wald been arrested in connection with Peggy's disappearance? No, she wouldn't be reported missing until September. Had Prince Harming made trouble for him? It was hard to imagine that younger, overly friendly Beckett I had last seen in 1947 being any match for wily old John Wald.

Brian always made sure he was first up in the morning. He'd sneak down to where I'd been sleeping in the throat-clogging cellar, toss me a set of hand-me-downs, and two sandwiches wrapped in brown paper, then head off to wake his mother and sister. I was lucky, I figured, that my grand-mother, like so many of those who had lived through the Great Depression, never threw anything away. A shelving unit in the garage held at least a decade's worth of clothes her chil-dren had outgrown.

After the neighborhood had quieted down, I would sneak out and hop a few fences so as not to be coming out of the same yard every day, and head to the public library to wait until it opened. In a study carrel at the back, I'd take out the letters from Luka and my grandmother, and pore over them for answers.

Over a lunch eaten out on the library steps, I would chat with the librarian, Mr. Weston. He was a veteran of the first World War, a guy who had been a farmer before he went off to fight in a trench in France, and came back wanting to be a librarian. "They shoot bullets at you long enough," he once told me, "you figure out what you want in life." As far as he knew, I was a kid who had messed up in school last year and been assigned a couple of summer research projects. He showed me the newspaper archives in the basement, and left me there for two or three hours reading and looking.

Pretty soon, I trusted him enough to show the strange, large coin from Luka's box. "I'm supposed to find out what happened to this guy," I said, showing him the name "Clive Beckett" stamped into it.

"He's dead is what happened to him," said Mr. Weston.

"How do you know that?"

He took the outsized coin from my hand. "Dead Man's Penny. They used to send these out to the families. More like a plaque really. Grim. People used to put them on the walls. My mother got one of these for my brother, Steven. Sure, I'll help you look into it."

In the mid-afternoon, I would pack everything up, drop my backpack down the coal chute, hop a few more fences to the Tarkington house, and check my scattered flour for footprints.

On a Friday near the end of August, I made a chilling discovery: two sets of footprints. They hadn't even tried to cover their tracks. I could follow them all the way to the front door, and when I peeked out a window, I could even see a few white marks down the front path.

I felt I needed a wall at my back. Better yet, Luka. She wouldn't be scared by this. Neither would I if I could only have her with me. I shivered. It was January all over again. Someone had come through the mirror, two someones, and

I had no idea who. My heart hammering, I told myself to calm down. I went back to the living room where I had left the mirror and took a closer look at the footprints. One was definitely bigger than mine, the other about the same size. No patterns in the treads. There were a lot of scuffed prints, but that didn't tell me anything. I too would have spent a little time shuffling my feet and looking around if I came out into this abandoned house.

Anthony's doorstop, the string joining a spoon on this side to another in 1947, was still there.

Someone had come through the mirror.

The enormity of it stayed with me the rest of that day and all through the weekend.

On Sunday, as soon as everyone left for church, I slipped out, dusted myself off, slung my backpack onto my shoulder, and started hunting for an unobtrusive place to spend the morning. After some deliberation, I settled on the space between two of Brian's across-the-street neighbors, both of whom were on vacation. An azalea bush shielded me from the street, but enough light got in that I was able to sit back and read some genealogy books Mr. Weston had recommended. I wasn't satisfied with the story so far regarding the death of Clive Beckett in his teens during the first World War, and these books contained lists and diagrams with details about marriages, births, and deaths. Could Beckett have had a kid brother? He would have had to be a lot younger, but maybe it was possible.

Around eleven-thirty I started paying attention to who was coming and going on the street so as not to miss when

Brian and his family returned home. I knew he planned on washing his beat-up old Chevy Fleetmaster that afternoon, and I wanted to be on the scene to give him a hand.

I kept a low profile when I saw Boyd Fenton coming down the street. It wasn't that I was afraid of him, but I didn't want him to have anything over me. I tried to go back to the genealogy charts, but a moment later, I looked up and saw him in conversation with a woman in a floral summer dress, maybe in her mid-twenties. She wore a pillbox hat with enough of her hair tucked under it that I couldn't tell the color.

I couldn't make out everything they were saying, and as he answered her questions, Boyd kept pointing to the Tarkington house.

The woman thanked him and moved on. I tried to get a better look at her. There was something familiar, like the feeling I'd had the week before when I went with Brian, Chuck, and a couple of their girls to see *The Curse of Frankenstein*. The guy playing the mad scientist was the same one who would one day play the creepy admiral in *Star Wars*, and I was the only person on the planet who knew.

Fifteen minutes later, when the Maxwell family returned from their weekly religious topping-up, the woman was still on the street. I saw her approach Brian and his mother and sister as they got out of the "sloppy jalopy" as he called his car. He took the photograph that I had seen her showing to several other people, but shook his head and turned away. A little too fast, I thought. Grandma and Aunt Judy also looked at the picture, but their head shakes seemed more genuine.

For half an hour more, the woman stayed, asking questions of all the church-returners, car-washers, and hedge-trimmers on the street. When she finally wandered off, I hadn't turned a single page in my book. I was sure that if I could see the soles of her shoes, I'd find a few grains of flour on them.

When Brian came out to wash his car, I cased the street for a while, then put my baseball cap on, brim low, and casually walked across to him.

He laughed as he saw me. "You'll never make a spy, hobo boy," he said, tossing me a sponge.

"Did she say who she was?"

He shook his head. "Nah. Kind of funny. Where'd you say that orphanage was you lit out of?"

"Downtown."

"What street?"

"I was only there a couple of months."

Brian took a long look, but then he shrugged and gave me small squirt of the hose. "Whatever you say. Hey, she said your name's Kenny."

"Jimmy's what my mom called me. My middle name is James."

"Get washing, James. But maybe wash from here in the shade. We don't want the neighbors getting a good look at you."

Brian put his friends on alert, and a couple said they'd seen the woman as well. This made me more interesting, and by the time we all met that night in the baseball diamond to hang out, all the better hangouts being closed on a Sunday, Chuck had invented several stories to explain my identity.

I was a Russian spy, Marilyn Monroe's secret love child, a criminal mastermind, the runaway kid of a war criminal. He amused us trying to fit together a story that made every single one of those true.

I smiled, but couldn't keep from wondering what he would have said if he'd known the much stranger truth, that I was the son of his best friend, that just three years from now he'd be best man at Brian's wedding, and two years later, he'd become my godfather.

When we got back to Brian's house, he told me to give him a few minutes to get some noise going in the house so there was no chance anyone would hear me sliding down the chute. "But don't hang around long," he said, eyeing the street, "unless you wanna get pinched."

I didn't want to get pinched, but nor did I want to go back to the coal cellar. What was I doing here, waiting until someone gave my dad a concussion the way my grandmother said it happened? The appearance of this woman and whoever she was with made things serious all over again.

Three fence hops brought me to the Tarkington house. I entered as quietly as I could and stood before the mirror. I pushed my hand inside and felt the downtime chill. If I took out that doorstop, I could possibly never go back. But at the same time, didn't I know I was going back? I was going to meet Rose, wasn't I? Luka was going further back.

I knelt and touched the spoon. If Luka and I got further back, that surely meant that Anthony helped us again. Either that or it meant that I wasn't about to take the doorstop out.

Which would mean Luka couldn't get back here.

I groaned aloud in frustration.

"What was that?" came a voice from upstairs.

"I don't know," said a quieter voice, a woman's.

"Hello," said the first voice. "Is there anyone there?"

I didn't move.

"Hello," said the man's voice again. Then a little lower, "I'll go check it out. Probably just some local kids. Don't get your hopes up."

"Kenny?" said the woman's voice. "Is that you?"

THREE

Think fast, I told myself. They had come through the mirror. They could only have come from the past. If I went through…

"Honey," said the woman's voice, "maybe I should go down. We don't want a repeat performance of last time."

"Okay. I'll be right up here if you need me."

"That's fine. Kenny? I'm coming down to talk to you. It's me—"

If I had stayed just a moment longer, I would have heard her name, but by the time her foot creaked on the top step, I was already pushing my way into the mirror. I've always wondered what would have been different if I had just heard her name.

I took the doorstop with me as I went. As desperate as I was to get out of there and close the mirror before anyone followed me, I paused in the Silverlands to make sure I wouldn't be stepping out into a long fall or a watery grave. I couldn't see anything, but when I stuck my hand through, I felt only air, and, crouching, I could touch the familiar wooden floor of the carriage house. I wrapped the string around my hand, wished for luck, and pushed the rest of the way out into a humid 1947 night.

Assuring myself that no one was in the carriage house, I felt my way down the darkened stairs, and made my way to the front door, just in time to see a flashlight emerge from the mirror. Either they were able to get into the mirror without me or they had pushed in before I left. I wanted to run straight to the trees at the edge of the creek, either lose myself in there or run along the path that led to the bluffs. Manse Valley was wide. While they were searching, I could work my way back to the mirror.

But no. It was dark. That would keep me safe enough. In the meantime, I had to know what was going on. I willed myself to hold still outside the carriage house door, pressed against the wall.

"Kenny?" said the woman's voice again. She had come through the mirror. So they both had access? "This is all going to be a little shocking to you, I think. Are you there? We think you know a lot about what happened in the past that we don't. We can help each other."

Then the man's voice. "He's not coming. Probably gone by now."

"The place down by the creek?"

"Who knows? You must know it better than anyone."

The woman shrugged. "Ancient history. To him, it's just a while ago."

Where had I heard that voice before? It was just on the edge of my brain, but catching it was like grabbing a fistful of water.

The man's voice: "Should we stay? Look around?"

"I don't think there's any point. We couldn't find John Wald. There's too many places to hide. I wish he'd just talk to us."

"Too afraid he's going to get knocked over the head."

"Don't joke about that. We have to find out what happened. That poor little girl."

"I'm sorry. I wasn't joking. Let's get back, then. We don't even know for sure he went into the mirror. This could be the wildest of goose chases, taking us away from what's important. I want to know what he was doing up there in 1957."

"What should we do about the mirror?"

"Let's just leave it."

"Okay. We're lucky, aren't we? That it owes me a trip forward and you a trip back?"

"Lucky. Yeah, that's what I'd call us."

And silence. It was tempting. I could call out to them before they left. Run if they tried to come after me. But had I heard they'd been hunting for Wald? That didn't inspire confidence.

I waited for a long time before going back into the carriage house. Eventually, boredom took over, and I wandered outside of the hedges that bounded the little property and took a look at the main house. Peggy had been missing for almost a month. Was her mother back home? Did her father even realize his daughter was gone?

I shivered despite the humidity.

It owes me a trip forward and you a trip back.

So they were from two different times?

It must have been after three in the morning when I went back into the carriage house and approached the mirror. Could they be waiting in the Silverlands? If they were, it was dark enough that they wouldn't see my approach. Having left my backpack in the coal cellar in 1957, I didn't have a flashlight to brandish as a club, so, feeling foolish, I took Anthony's length of string and wrapped it around my hand, working it so the two spoons ended up on the outside, a makeshift and ridiculous set of brass knuckles.

I edged around the side of the mirror. I'd stick my head in first, open my eyes as soon as I could, and try to see if anyone was in the Silverlands. If it was empty, I'd go right in and survey the abandoned house, but then I wasn't sure what I'd do. Tumble out and hope that the element of surprise would get me past? Wait until they left? I was determined about one thing: I wasn't letting myself get stuck one more mirror into the past. If they tried to grab me, I'd kick, bite, and scream, anything to get on my feet and running.

I took a few deep breaths to get myself worked up, running through an internal pep talk all the while, then rounded on the mirror and stuck my face in.

The mirror was cold.

Cold, as in downtime, the past, heading to 1937. Not hot as it should have been if I was going up. That was wrong. I was out of my time. Whenever I went into the mirror, it should be uptime hot. I didn't get to go further back. That was against the rules.

Panicked, I pulled my face out and stumbled back. I tripped on a chair leg and fell onto the sofa where I had spent so many nights as Peggy's secret guest the month before.

I lay there in silence for a moment, thinking about this new development.

The mirror was cold.

This was impossible. Against the rules.

I lay on the sofa and looked at the mirror for the longest time. It was supposed to take me home, or at least in that direction.

I felt stupid wearing my improvised spoon knuckles, so I unwrapped the string and put Anthony's doorstop on the floor beside me. It was all I had. I was reduced from my backpack full of boxes, flashlights, a map, and a dwindling supply of money, to two spoons and piece of string. If I went back to 1937, would I find that Lilly's mirror also opened only backward for me? Would it open only backward for Peggy as well?

I don't know how long I lay there and looked at the stupid mirror, but I found no answers there. What was there to do in the end but go in? John Wald was missing in this time, maybe scared off by the interlopers or perhaps just steering clear while Peggy's parents searched for her. I had no other friends in this time; my dad was seven.

I got up and with a weary sigh pushed my hand into the mirror.

Which was hot.

I jerked back.

What the hell was going on? For the first time all year, I was beginning to get angry at the mirror. How did it go all these months operating on the same rules, and then suddenly go back and forth. What had I done differently?

Other than keep a doorstop in it for a month.

Frowning, I bent down and picked up the string and spoons. For a month, these had kept a mirror open leading back from 1957 to 1947, Anthony's passage. We had never done anything like that before, because it blocked access to the kids one jump further up and down. I held the doorstop up to the dim starlight leaking in the hayloft window, but it hadn't changed in any way. Ordinary white household string, six feet of it, a tarnished spoon tied to each end.

Holding the doorstop, I stretched out my hand to the mirror and pushed in.

Cold.

I put the doorstop down and tried again.

Hot.

Put it in my pocket.

Hot. It had to be touching my skin to change the mirror to downtime. When I tried it again, I noticed something else. When I held it in my hand near the mirror, the whole thing, string and spoons alike, felt like it was vibrating, almost living. The feeling was subtle, not like the buzz of an object meeting itself from another time, more like the trembling of a pet mouse when you hold it in your hand. When I moved it away from the mirror, the feeling diminished. But it didn't go away.

"Oh, man," I said aloud, and my voice startled me in the

empty little house. I held the string and spoons in my hand. "I know what you are. You're better than a doorstop. You're a key."

FOUR

Before I went through the mirror next, I stood and asked myself what Luka would do. I imagined it was her and not me who had run back to 1947 and discovered the rule of keys. I imagined she was the one chased by these mystery people from different times. Would she let herself be scared by them, stick around a couple of days watching the mirror, tell herself she was gathering information?

No way.

I broke off a chair leg, stuck the spoons and string into my pocket, and shoved my way into the mirror. The Silverlands were wider now, maybe as much as seven feet.

On the 1957 end, I could see nothing but darkness. I stuck the tip of my finger out to make sure I wouldn't emerge into water, then pushed the rest of the way through to an immediate shout and a grab from the side, but whoever was grabbing me got a vicious swipe from my chair leg. I tumbled out of the person's grasp, kicked, and felt a satisfying jar as my foot made contact.

There were shouts of "No, wait" and "Kenny, you don't understand," which I couldn't argue with, but I wasn't going to stop for people who chased me through time and grabbed before they talked.

After all those hours, I must have had the element of surprise, because by the time one of them had the light on, I was already out of the living room and slamming the door. I threw a kitchen chair at them to confound pursuit and escaped to the backyard. At this point, I was good enough at fence-hopping and familiar enough with the neighborhood that getting out was as good as getting away. Just in case they followed, I took a long, roundabout way back to Brian's place.

Back in the choking dark of the coal cellar, too tired to crack my brain against new mysteries and new rules, but pleased at my escape, I fell asleep.

I went out late Monday and Tuesday, crouched down in a yard next to the Tarkington house, and held my string-and-spoons key, moving it closer and farther from the last place I had seen the mirror. The gentle half-alive buzz in my hands told me it was still there. As a bonus, I found myself growing more and more attuned to the vibrations of that key. By Wednesday morning, I could sit in the coal cellar, stretch my arm out, and use the thing to find the direction of the mirror.

I felt more in control of events than I had all summer.

Which I suppose should have been a warning.

I hadn't seen the mysterious couple again, though two of Brian's friends reported talking to the woman. I knew that the house was enemy territory, but I needed answers. And just as they seemed to think that there were answers in this time because I was here, I figured my best source of information must be the past. Mr. Weston in the library had continued to be helpful, but he couldn't find much. On the Beckett front, he found one family in the Manse Creek area in the nineteenth century, their only son was the Clive who died in the war. Since then, as the area grew, there were other births, deaths, and marriages of Becketts in the local churches, but not a single Clive.

The other project I told him I was working on was the local legend of Prince Harming, and he managed to dig up a mention of the story in a small-press chapbook from just a couple of years before, but it didn't tell me much I didn't know. A Manse Valley bogeyman, probably made up in reaction to the stories of children disappearing or being knocked over the head. The author had been able to find people who remembered skipping to those rhymes as far back as 1908.

As interesting as all this was, it wasn't satisfying. Finding things out wasn't the same as doing something.

The mirror was in enemy territory. It was time to take it back.

Five o'clock on Thursday morning, having packed for travel, I got up, skulked next door to the abandoned house, and climbed up to the roof of a shed, certain the strangers were upstairs. I wondered what could get adults out of their lives like this. Me, I was trapped. And I was a kid. What better things did I have to do than travel in time? But them? Didn't they have jobs? What were they doing, out of their time, hiding in an abandoned house, hunting for answers from a kid who didn't know any?

That mirror wasn't supposed to be for them. It was for us kids.

I had to wait three hours. It was a miracle I wasn't discovered. The man whose shed I was on came out around seven to pick tomatoes, and I had to freeze in place for long, cramped minutes. An hour after that, my two came slinking out the back door. I saw the man first, peering out, but I was low on the shed roof and he didn't see me. A moment later, he and the woman slipped out and around the side of the house. They shared a few quick words in the space between that house and its neighbor, too quiet for me to hear, then he kissed her quickly and they headed in separate directions.

The man seemed agitated and poorly rested. He was definitely the same man with the yellow tie I had seen a month ago, nervous despite his quick smile.

The woman was different. She was worried too, but it was all focused on him. Before they parted, she fixed his collar and neatened his hair.

I let ten minutes go by before coming down. This was too important to mess up. I hopped the fence and approached the back door. Unlocked. Once inside, I saw that they had been trying to be smarter. Something was in the mirror's place, a sheet covering it, but the real mirror, my spoons-and-string told me, was upstairs. I guessed the decoy was to lure me in, maybe give me a sense of safety.

Thanks to the weak-then-strong buzzing of the doorstop-turned-key in my hand, I found the mirror easily. They had kept the ruined frame on it, and just tilted it against one wall. The first thing I did was test my key. It worked exactly as it had in 1947; when I held it, the mirror was downtime cold, but if I put it in my pocket, the glass turned hot.

From the evidence, this was the room they had been squatting in. Though they had made the bed before leaving, I could see signs of their presence. They had come through with suitcases and changes of clothing.

I wrote them a note:

"Once I'm done with the mirror, it's going back where it belongs. You know where that is. Who are you, and why are you following me? I'd stick around, but I don't trust you. Please stay away. I'm going back to 1917 to save the baby. Then home. Leave me alone and let me do this. Kenny."

I left it on the bed, hefted the mirror, and went downstairs.

There was no way I was going to hop fences in broad daylight carrying a four-foot-tall mirror, so I took my chances out the front way.

What I didn't count on was Boyd Fenton and John Timson stepping out from behind the Tarkington fence just as I reached the sidewalk. "Well, look here, Johnny," said Fenton, "we got some kind of burglary going on."

"Look," I said, "I just want to go my way in peace. I'm not hurting you—or anyone, really. Mind your own business."

Fenton snorted. "Pal, you are my business. I'm getting five bucks a day to watch this place, and a twenty-dollar bonus if I catch you."

"And how are you going to do that?"

Timson's hands had been behind his back. Now he took

out the baseball bat he was hiding. "Threats, probably," he said. "But anything's possible."

"You'd be surprised," I said. I took the spoons and string from my pocket and wrapped them around my hand.

Fenton laughed. "Look, Johnny, the little nosebleed's got silver-spoon knuckles. What are you gonna do, reject, tap us to death?"

When you've dealt with bullies a lot, you fight twenty different battles in your head for every one you concede in the real world. You come up with a million fool-proof strategies you never have the guts to try out in person. And if you have a time-travel mirror whose rules you've figured out, you can add about ten more to that million.

I snaked my hand out as quickly as I could and tugged the end of the bat toward the mirror. It sunk inside.

Fenton took a half step back and made a tiny, quiet choking sound. I think Timson would have fallen back as well, but he was holding onto the bat. My arm went into the mirror up to my elbow, and though he got tense and almost began to tug back, he didn't let go.

I did, and quickly pulled my arm out of the mirror, closing it.

As I had hoped it would, the part of the bat that was outside of the mirror pulled away, its top half lopped off in the Silverlands.

"Now," I said, "want me to try that with your hands, or do you want to get lost?"

Timson's face turned dark and he twisted to look at Fenton. "That was a two-dollar Louisville Slugger."

Fenton, still staring at the mirror, said nothing.

Timson shook his head and turned to me. "I better be getting all the reward money for this," he said, and launched himself at me.

I shoved the mirror toward the onrushing Timson, smashing it into his face, then grabbed it back, tucked it under my arm, turned, and ran to the backyard.

Next to the Tarkingtons was someone with a real love for berry bushes, and I held the mirror high as I thrashed my way through. Their fence was low. I tossed the mirror over and took a flying leap.

Almost made it, too.

Timson caught my ankle as I went over. I kicked him free, then tumbled sideways over the fence.

I went in so fast I was halfway to 1947 before the Silverlands slowed me down. I steadied myself against the cold, then stepped back uptime, to warm it out of me. When I turned to the swimming images in the 1957 exit, I could make out a patch of petunias the mirror had fallen into, and above them, sky. It was strange to be standing in the Silverlands, looking out and up at the same time.

John Timson's face appeared in front of me, above the mirror. Without stopping to think about it, I pushed my hand out of the mirror and punched him in the face.

Then I wondered all over again what Luka would do. I had never seen her shy away from a fight, but I'd never seen her actually beat someone up. She found other ways of doing things. She talked to people. She cajoled. Sometimes she lied.

Maybe there was a way to be like Luka.

I reached for Timson's shirt. He jerked back, but not fast enough. I grabbed a fistful, and dragged it back into the mirror. It was easy, since in the world of 1957, he was leaning over and gravity was on my side. As I pulled him closer, I pushed my face out.

"Come into the mirror, John Timson," I said. "Come in and be with us forever. We've been waiting for you, John Timson. And we're hungry."

Timson cried out, a strangled kind of scream, and pulled away.

From my vantage point in the Silverlands, all I could see were his feet as he jumped the fence. I waited a moment, not wanting to take the chance of Timson or Fenton having a change of heart, then pulled myself out. With the different up-down orientation, I had to put out my two arms, brace myself against the dirt and petunias, and heave with all my might, gritting my teeth against the uptime heat.

Once out, I shook myself off, picked up the mirror, and clambered two fences to Brian's house.

I checked my watch. The Maxwells would have left for work. I took the mirror down to the coal cellar, and planned for what was next. A quick check uptime told me the 1967 mirror was still submerged.

I steeled myself against the pain that came when you mixed mirror-heat and water, and stuck my hand through to feel around. Sand and mud. I felt a slimy bit of weed and yanked it through, but what good was that? In the last couple of months, I had come up with a hundred schemes for getting back out of that mirror, but none was any good. I could have put a scuba suit on and gone through, but what if John Wald was right, and it wasn't a breathing thing, just the shock of the water mixing with the mirror-heat?

So there was still no hope of getting through into the future. Not yet.

I had an appointment in the past.

I went back into the coal cellar and left a note for Brian, asking him to leave the mirror and promising I'd be back. Then, making sure I had everything, I held my key and headed into the mirror.

It was the longest, coldest downtime journey I had taken. Out into the carriage house, turn around, hold out the key, and back in. Out into what must have been Lilly's room in 1937, turn around, hold the key, and back in. Out into the same room in 1927, nobody around in the midmorning, but I could hear sounds from the hallway, so back in again.

Hold on, I said in my head to the baby my father had taken out of the wall, here I come.

I stopped in the Silverlands and watched 1917 before bursting out into it. Just as I had expected from Rose's diary, the mirror was back in the carriage house where her mother had sent her to live. Half-finished lath on the wall. A neatly made single bed. A pile of books.

A crying girl huddled in a corner.

Time to be like Luka again.

Without another thought, I stepped out of the mirror.

Rose's head sprang up and her eyes grew round with surprise. "Who on earth are you?" she said as I stepped down off her dresser.

"I'm Kenny Maxwell," I said, trying to channel my inner Skywalker. "I'm here to rescue you."

FIVE

Rescuing, it turns out, is a lot harder than in the movies.

As soon as Rose got over the shock of seeing me, she went right back to sobbing. I had no idea what to do. I stood on the low dresser the mirror was mounted on, and felt like an idiot way out of his league.

"You might as well come in," she said after a long while in between choked sobs. "What do you mean? I've never met you before in my life, Kenny Maxwell." She pushed herself up, feet braced against the floor, back sliding up the wall, and I saw just how right Luka was about Rose Hollerith's "condition."

She had the condition all right. Big. Seeing the direction of my gaze, she sniffed and looked away. "Am I a sideshow attraction, then? No wonder Mother keeps me shut up here. I remember your name now. Past Margaret Garroway and Anthony Currah, am I right? I've been making a list of you all. What are you here to rescue me from, Kenny Maxwell?"

She looked down at her stomach. "I haven't exactly been captured by the enemy, have I?"

I opened my mouth to speak, but couldn't think of anything. She motioned again and I stepped down from the dresser.

"It's … Prince Harming, I think. There's … something bad is going to happen. Didn't anybody tell you? A baby dies." We were on the second floor of the carriage house, just as I had been in 1947. I looked at the place where one day my father would draw out that tiny blackened parcel. Someone had left it half built in just about the state my dad would leave it half destroyed.

"Oh," said Rose. "Yes, I've heard about that." She gave me a look that was half pitying, half impossible to interpret. "Lilly told Curtis. Curtis told me." She touched her stomach and suddenly looked exhausted. She pushed past me to sit on her unmade bed. "But that's nothing to do with me, Kenny Maxwell from the future. It's not mine." She stared at me when she said this. I could see something desperate in her denial, but hard, too, as though she were daring me to disagree.

How do you know? I wanted to ask. But you can't ask that of a pregnant girl. How do you know your baby will live? All babies have to live, don't they? But then whose baby was it? When did it come from?

I guess she must have read the question in my face. She shook her head. "You're just a little bit of a ninny, aren't you? He can't die because he's alive. I've known it for months. Don't you see? I see my son all the time. Every second day, through the mirror."

"Every—? But that's Curtis. Your brother."

She smiled and spat out a bitter laugh. "And isn't that just like Mother? She knows, you know, but she won't acknowledge it. In a secret part of her mind, I think she's planned this all along. Father joined up for service. Two months ago, just as he was starting to fix this place up. He's German, and it's never been a bit of a problem to our neighbors until the war began. He finally couldn't stand it, the looks, the pointed comments, and he went and signed up. Mother didn't fight him about it, and after that, she's hardly been out. She has one of the local boys run errands. She's going to tell them it's hers. She's going to tell them all, and my Clive must be dead."

At that, she collapsed again into tears.

I sat awkwardly beside her on her bed for a moment. "I don't—I don't know what to do."

"You don't do anything," she sniffled. "When someone cries and there's noth—nothing to be done, you just put an arm around their shoulders and shut up."

So I did that for a while, wondering how long it had been since someone had just sat with her.

How could she be right about Curtis? His age was right. Her diary described him as eight or nine back in January. But if he lived, who died? Who was the baby whose head would be smashed in, and why had Rose written a note asking me to save him?

And who was the Beckett who was chasing me?

Eventually Rose straightened up and brushed the hair out of her eyes. "Well, nothing to do but do, as Mother says. Would you like to help, Kenny?"

The tears I had seen when I first came through the mirror were of frustration more than anything else. Rose had finally set to finishing the walls, but it had turned out to be at least a two-person job. She assigned me to holding the thin strips of lath against the wall as she nailed them up, making the very wall I had torn apart half a year before.

"Curtis tried to help," she said, "but the dear isn't much use, and he found it so dull. I can't blame him. He wanted traveling the years to be an adventure, and here he ended up surrounded by girls."

"So you've known for a while?" I said. "About him?"

She tapped at a nail a few times before answering. "I can't even tell quite when I realized. It's as though the knowledge had been building in me, like a little ghost house, assembling itself in my mind until one day there it was. That pouting, whining little boy I'd been tolerating for months had transformed into this lonely little ... son."

I didn't know what to say, but she was the one, not facing me, getting out another nail and measuring its place with her fingers, who said what was on my mind.

"I know I'm going to die." Tap, tap as she firmed up the nail's position, then a larger whack to drive it into place. She glanced at me briefly and took another one. "Did you think I didn't know? I go and read things in Curtis's time. Old newspapers, mostly. Mother keeps them in the attic. I expect it's Spanish flu, but I haven't the heart to ask. He looks at me sometimes with the most haunted eyes, and I know he wants to tell me, just as I have something I want to tell him, but how can I?" She looked at her stomach. "I, who wasn't there to raise him, who couldn't even pick a father to be there to raise him. How can I tell him that my mother isn't his?"

I thought she was going to start crying again, but she took it out on the nails instead, hammering five or six in quick succession, bending and ruining half of them.

I stayed until evening with Rose. Her mother delivered a delicious roast beef dinner, necessitating my hiding under the bed while Rose answered some curt questions about how she was and was she keeping indoors, because it wouldn't do for her to be out when she was so clearly unwell. I felt guilty sharing her meal, but she said Mother always brought too much, and would be glad to see it eaten. It was the best I'd had in weeks. By lantern light, she showed me her lists. There were two, it turned out, a separate page showing the names of mirror kids reaching seventy years into the past. I was more interested in the almost-new version of the one I had seen six decades up. I helped her add names. She knew everyone up to Luka, so I gave her Melissa and Keisha, but all I knew about the kid from 2017 was that his initials were C. M. I had overheard Melissa and Luka talking about him once, but they clammed up when they saw I was listening. I ran my fingers over the bottom corner of her list, the place where someday soon she would write a message for me.

Later, when there was no chance of her mother coming, Rose threw on heavier clothes to hide her stomach, then asked me to take her uptime so she could introduce me to Curtis. This wasn't easy; the dresser in 1927 had been moved back to Rose's old room in the house, but after Mrs. Hollerith had gone downstairs, we ghosted down the hall and slipped into Curtis's room.

He was playing listlessly with some tin soldiers when we came in. "Look, Curtis," Rose whispered, "it's Kenny Maxwell from the future. The one we've been hearing about from Lilly."

He perked up right away, dropped his tin soldiers, and motioned for us to come in. "I've heard about you," he said. "You have to get that mirror out of the water."

"I just wish I knew how."

He frowned. "If you had a submarine, you could do it."

I nodded. "That would be good. But I don't think I could fit one through the mirror."

"Oh." His shoulders slumped.

It was the question of wars that most interested Curtis, specifically the big one that would come when he was of age. Grandparents on both sides had told me enough about the World War II, and I had seen enough movies, that I kept him entertained for more than three hours with stories. We were interrupted once when Rose and I had to hide from her mother coming in to wish Curtis goodnight.

When her mother was in the room, I watched Rose's face in the gaslight let in through the sides of the ill-fitting closet door. Stoic, I suppose, would be the word. I had seen all kinds of parent-and-kid relationships in my travels through the glass, but this one was maybe the worst, harsher even than the slaps Luka got from her mother, more hurtful than the way Peggy's parents paid more attention to their own battles than their daughter's well-being. Here was the woman who had known that her daughter was pregnant and decided to hide that condition from the world.

Rose didn't stay much longer. Grimacing in discomfort, she told me she ought to get home and rest. "There's room enough in the carriage house," she said, "though you'll have to continue the indignity of hiding like a gothic suitor every time Mother comes calling." Curtis barely acknowledged her going, though he did thank her for bringing me through.

Curtis had been raised on tales of how his father and other courageous men had served their country well, so he responded eagerly to my half-remembered accounts of D-day, the freeing of concentration camps, and the Battle of Britain, as well as the fiction I supplemented them with, mostly composed of various war movies all cobbled together in my mind—*Where Eagles Dare*, *The Guns of Navarone*, and *Sands of Iwo Jima* combining to make some kind of whole narrative.

Eventually, Curtis was too tired to ask questions anymore. "Will you tuck me into bed?" he said, then turned away, embarrassed. "I mean—just—will you say good night? And will you come back?"

I promised I would. "Good night," I said. "Sleep tight."

I closed his door and skulked back around the corner to Rose's old room where the mirror waited.

Back at the mirror, I took a moment before stepping through, and quietly slid out its top drawer. There, underneath, was the message to Luka: *Luka, help Kenny. Trust John Wald. Kenny says he is the* auby *one. Save the baby.* Even here. Even now.

I had a decision to make. I could go back up to 1957

where a coal cellar was waiting for me, along with the possibility of a hot breakfast in the morning and another conversation with my future dad. Or I could take my spoons-and-string key and go back to Rose. Further from home, it was true, but all year something had been pulling me back there. *Save the baby.*

I clutched the spoons and went backward. Rose was fast asleep. Again, I slid out the drawer, and for the first time saw it without the message.

Well, at least I knew I was in the right place.

I spent the next three uncomfortable nights on the main floor of the carriage house with only a couple of blankets to protect me from the bare floorboards. Each morning, after a brief stint under Rose's bed, I gobbled half of a hot breakfast, and spent the morning helping her with the walls of what she called her "Monte Cristo mansion."

In the afternoons, Rose asked me to go through and spend time with Curtis. "He's lonely," she said. "I know you came charging in to rescue me, but he's the one who needs you, I think. Mother keeps him shut up at home for the most part. He is her shame."

What else was there to do? I could go as far downtime as I liked, but my own time was still closed to me. On my first day with Curtis, I went with him down to the creek, where he showed me his cave. "It was Clive's," he said. "He was my sister's sweetheart, but he died in the war. He and my sister used to come here to be alone."

I could see he had done a good job. The desktops and chair legs that seemed haphazardly embedded in the mud in other decades were now set up with a clear plan in mind, like struts in a mine. Holding up the slight vault of the widest part of the cave was the table with the initials carved in it.

Rose, Clive, Curtis.

And Luka.

I blinked a couple of times at it and shook my head with wonder.

"I put mine there, too," said Curtis. "I wanted to be part of it. You should put yours, too. You're one of us as well, the mirror children. We're like a family."

It's always going to come down to just you and me, she had said. But where was she? Why weren't we rescuing the baby together?

I carved my initials next to hers like I was cosigning a promise.

In the evenings I went all the way uptime past the coal cellar, just to check that 1967 was still inaccessible. It always was.

On the third day, Curtis and I passed a lazy afternoon by the creek. I entertained him with stories about submarine warfare, illustrating with my diving and surfacing hands stories that I knew from comic books and movies. We got bogged down slightly when he asked me to explain the mechanics of submarines.

"How do they float up?"

"They have stuff in them that floats. Air and stuff."

"So why didn't they float before? How did they sink in the first place?"

"It's—I don't know. It's like hot-air balloons, but in reverse. They must have to drop stuff so they can rise up."

"Oh. So they must have to carry heavy stuff to sink. It would be better if they could have light stuff that made them float and they could just bring that out from somewhere."

"But if they had it somewhere, it would make them float up, wouldn't it?"

It was cool being the person with answers, even if not all of them were entirely accurate. I got to play the older brother for a while.

"Is war stupid?" he asked at one point. "Rose says it is. She says that's how father died and Clive as well, and it was all for nothing because this other war is coming. They called it the war to end all wars, but they were wrong."

"Somebody telling you to go kill some other guys because the people in charge can't agree?" I said. "Yeah, that's pretty stupid."

"But you said the Germans were killing people in those camps. Jews and everyone."

"That was stupid, too."

"And the men who went and saved the people in the camps. They were good, weren't they?"

"Yeah, that's true."

"That's going to be me, then. I'll do that. You can tell me what army division to get into, and I'll go over there when it's my turn and free people from the camps."

"It's not that simple," I said, trying to sound grown-up. "Sure, some people saved prisoners and stuff, but a lot of people died. There's lots of … other jobs you can do that would help with the war."

He raised his eyebrows at my lame finish. "Other jobs? I'll be twenty-two when that war starts. That's the age when you should be a soldier. It's okay to do other things if you're an old man."

Suddenly being a big brother got a lot more complicated. Rose had asked me to be good to her son. Had I just talked him into going to war?

SIX

On my third morning of plastering, we finished the second short wall, and started preparation for the long back one, the one Mr. Hollerith had abandoned when he enlisted. I had been avoiding that part of the task; a third of the way along that wall was the dark place out of which that baby had been drawn. I knew there was nothing there yet, just a shadowy hole filled with newspaper insulation.

I spent half an hour after breakfast bringing up the lath strips, and then an hour mixing plaster. Rose had done the mixing on previous days, but today she was tired.

She got up when I was done to inspect the result, but gasped and fell back to the bed.

My heart almost battered through my rib cage. "Is it— are you—?"

She held one hand over her stomach, and the other up like a traffic cop. "No—no, Kenny," she said in between another couple of gasps. "I don't think so. He's moving and it's sore, that's all. It hurts. My back hurts, my feet hurt, and I cannot get a breath just right."

I had an urge to march over to the main house and give her mother a good talking to. She needed a hospital, a doctor.

She needed her mother.

I said as much, but she made me promise not to interfere. "Just stay here," she said. "Hold my hand. I don't need my mother. All I need is something for the pain."

"Oh," I said. "Wait." I hurried downstairs to fetch my backpack.

When I brought out the small leather pouch, she gave a weak smile before even seeing its contents. "He kept his promise," she said. "I said I didn't know how he could, but he did."

"Who?" I said.

"John Wald, of course."

I remembered Wald's promise that I would find a use for the partridge berries he had helped me pick. *A way to float above the stony world*. "Wow. He really is our Obi-Wan."

As the tea brewed, she told about her time with John. Traveling uptime, he reached 1907 just before the new year, and had to travel his "long path" to get to 1917. He worked as a hired hand in the area, never straying far from Hollerith land. As an able-bodied man, he felt pressure to sign up for the war, finding that none of the farmers in the area had work for him anymore, even in the harvest of 1915.

"If he hadn't been wounded last summer," said Rose, taking her first sip of the foul-smelling concoction we had managed to make, "he never would have made it back."

Shot in the leg at the Battle of the Somme, then left for

dead in no-man's land while the wound grew septic, he had been rescued and spent four months in a field hospital, then more time convalescing in England before he was able to find transportation home.

"That man has an eye for secrets," Rose said. "He remembered Clive and knew my condition at once. It took my own mother longer."

Despite Wald's impatience to move on, he stayed a few weeks to help. "He must have stripped every bush for miles around for those berries. 'I'll get thee more,' he said to me. 'Trouble not.' And will you look at this? He did. How did he know, Kenny?"

I shook my head and watched her sip the tea. For just a moment, I felt something relax in me, a thing that had been twitching and grinding like a bag filled with rocks and frogs.

I had done some good. Maybe Wald had known things would work out this way, and maybe he hadn't. But everything ended up fitting together. Rose needed someone to tell her the future worked out, or maybe she just needed partridge berry tea for the pain. Curtis needed a friend.

But the feeling didn't last. I hadn't come back to plaster a wall or babysit a lonely kid. Where was Prince Harming? Where was the thing that needed doing? Up in 1977, I was due for school in a week. Curtis had a birthday in three days, and a newspaper with tomorrow's date in 1947 was going to be found in fifty-nine years wrapped around a blackened package I could barely think about.

In the afternoon, Curtis helped me sneak a shovel from the carriage house, and we forded the creek so that I could bury my August box for Luka. In it, I had told her about my time with my dad in the fifties, my encounters with Curtis and Rose, and my discovery of keys.

Curtis was in an odd mood. He didn't ask questions as we buried the box. A light rain started, and we retreated to his hiding place under the creek bank. Again, I ran my fingers over the initials carved in the tabletop.

I tried to interest Curtis in the plot of *Star Wars*, but I guess it was too far crazy for him. He didn't interrupt, but he was barely listening.

"I should go into the past tonight," he said after I had given up and just sat with him for a while watching the rain. "I know it would be strange, but I should."

I frowned. "I thought you didn't like visiting Rose much anymore."

"Not to see Rose. She's not so bad anymore, though. She's been nicer. I meant to see my mother."

"Why?"

"Why? Because this is when I was born."

Part Five

Shatterdate

ONE

Leave tomorrow when you're called.

I stared at Curtis as he continued. "When I started, anyway. My birthday's in three days, but Mother says I was hard coming. That's what she says. 'The boy was so hard coming, the girl almost died.' That's a silly way to say it, though. She wasn't a girl when she had me."

I half stood, bumping my head on the low ceiling. "You're coming this soon? I mean you came... this soon? I thought she wasn't due... I mean, she didn't look... Oh, man, I gotta go."

"Why?" said Curtis. "You don't even know my mother. And it doesn't matter. I was born. Why do anything?"

In a sense, that was true, wasn't it? I was going to get home. Curtis was going to be born. Was there anything I could do to change anything?

The boy was so hard coming, the girl almost died.

What was her mother's stupid plan, anyway, to just let

her daughter have a baby all by herself in that half-converted barn? And me, a kid, what was I going to do? I didn't even want to be near the birth of a baby.

I clutched my hands into fists to stop the shaking. Things weren't supposed to sneak up on me like this. I was from the future. I could travel in time.

I wasn't supposed to deliver a baby. Professionals were supposed to do that.

Doctors.

Nurses.

"Curtis, I need a piece of paper and a pen, and I need you to sneak me back into the house, to the mirror. Can you do it?"

He frowned, but nodded.

Five minutes later, we were in Rose's old room. "I've got this figured out," I said to him. "I'm going into the future for a few minutes. When I come back, I'll bring help."

My first stop was ten years up, 1937. Empty as it had been for days. I looked at my watch and left a note:

Lilly,

If you're really a nurse by 1947, meet me at 2:12 PM at the mirror on August 30. Rose is giving birth, and she needs your help. Please.

Kenny

Crossing my fingers, I went into 1947.

And for the first time that year, things started working the way I thought they should.

She was there. Ten years older and eyes filled with wonder, she was there.

She wore a plain blue dress, and her hair was shorter, a little darker. She carried a tightly packed leather bag.

"You got older," I said.

She smiled, that same warm smile from ... well, last month, but ten years ago as well. "You stayed the same."

"You came."

She shrugged. "How could I not? You know, I never saw you again? After Peg and I—" There was a noise outside. Lilly's head whipped around. "Kenny, that might be Peg's father. He's been prowling all around the whole day. I think he's getting desperate to find her. They'll report her missing in a day or two. We'd best go."

I had a million questions to ask her, but she was right. Thirty years ago, Rose needed help.

"Come on," I said. "Let's get going."

"How can this work?" Lilly said. "It's only supposed to open up for Peggy, isn't it?"

I grinned, happy to be the one who knew. "Don't worry," I said. "I've got a key."

The door to the carriage house banged open. I thrust my hand into my pocket to get the key and grabbed Lilly's elbow.

"Wait," she said.

I looked down the stairs. There, carrying another man over his shoulder, was John Wald. He grinned up at me.

"Well-timed, lad. I have him here, though a more tricksy rabbit has never bethump'd my wits." He half turned and let me see the face of the man he was carrying, all tied up, the man who had shot me two months ago, still in what was left of his raincoat. He was, if anything, wilder now, but I knew at once it was him. Thick ropes bound him and a gag stopped his mouth, but he glared at me with silent, fiery hatred. It was, I was sure now, the same face as the man with the yellow tie. But there was something else. What was it?

"You caught him," I said. "But how are you here? How did you know the right time?"

Wald smiled and touched his nose. "Auld John Wald knows many a hidden thing, Kennit. Where pass we that our tales may be expounded?"

"But wait. How is Prince Harming here? He put that mirror in water. How did he come through it? Never mind. I can't deal with this now. We're going back to 1917 to save Rose and the baby."

Wald looked for the first time at Lilly. He grunted and smiled. "Lillian Huff, thou art a woman now, and fair with time indeed."

She blushed. "Thank you, John. But it's not Huff. I'm married now."

"'Tis well and good. 'Tis how the world enblooms anew." He started up the stairs, and for all his age, you would hardly know he was carrying a man on his back. "I know not how this fool fits in along this path, but hereabouts Peg's father searches wild. I feel clasped to thy purpose, lad. I've bound him tight and must, I think me, bring this doom along."

I didn't particularly like the idea, but I couldn't disagree. The idea of having Wald come along was comforting, and at least this way I would know where the crazy man was. For now I shoved aside the question of how he could be here.

At least he was tied up.

John seemed mildly surprised at my downtime access, but there was no time for questions. I let Lilly in first to see if the coast was clear. John needed my help to wrestle the wild man inside. As soon as he realized where we were going, he began to strain against his bonds. John grabbed him by his torn shirt-front and pulled him close. "Peace. Thou must be bound. We'll help that girl to birth her child and then turn back to riddling thee."

He went in first carrying the man's shoulders while I, with my string and spoons, followed trying to help, but mostly just avoiding kicks in the face.

Lilly was waiting in the Silverlands. "I can hear talking downstairs. We'll have to just go out and in again."

As soon as he emerged into 1937, the wild man began to scream into his gag, the frantic shriek of a desperate animal. We carried him out, Wald almost tripping on Lilly's bed, Lilly herself shutting the door to give us a few seconds extra. "Hurry," she whispered.

I held onto his feet by the rope and went right back into the mirror as soon as I was all the way out. The Silverlands widened by the day, and the pain of that long, cold passage was distracting.

As I stepped down from the low dresser, the man kicked me with all his strength. His feet caught me in the chest and I was flung back, tumbling over Rose's bed and falling between it and the dresser.

The wild man was on his feet first, and before I had a chance to react, he launched himself at me. I had nowhere to go. His full weight fell on me. My left arm was trapped under the bed, and my right pressed against the dresser. He thrashed frantically, trying to hit me in any way he could. His head slammed against mine, and some part of him dug into my stomach. I felt what little air I had been able to get into me rush out. A second, then third blow to my solar plexus, and I was about to throw up. All the while, his muffled screams filled my ears.

"Leave him alone!" shouted a voice, and the man was partially heaved away. I tried to push upward, but now there were two bodies pressing on me, struggling and grunting. I tried to punch, but there was no room.

For his part, the crazy man still struggled and screamed as though he were being burned alive. Curtis had him from behind, and was trying to pull him by his bound arms, but his face was contorted in pain.

Then at last, John Wald arrived. He leaped from the dresser directly to the bed, grabbed the spitting wild man by the back of his collar, and lifted him bodily off me and out from underneath Curtis.

Just as Lilly followed him through the mirror, Mrs. Hollerith burst into the room. "Curtis, what on—"

We all froze. Even Prince Harming stilled in Wald's grasp, his head turned toward the newest arrival. Lilly slowly withdrew her arm from the mirror. Neither Curtis nor I, half hidden by the bed, moved a muscle. We must have looked like a bunch of kids caught fighting by a teacher.

It was me she looked at first. The stern expression on her face melted.

"It can't be," she said. "You're that boy." Then she looked at Lilly. "And you. The one who helped. Ten years gone and you haven't aged a day."

TWO

Truth and wisdom deeply walled.

Lilly was the fastest-thinking of all of us. "What was wrong?" she said to Mrs. Hollerith. "I'm going to her now. Tell me. Ten years ago—what was wrong? Why was the delivery so hard?"

Mrs. Hollerith's hand went to her mouth. "It can't— you can't blame—I didn't know."

Lilly stepped down from the dresser and toward the woman. "Tell me," she said. "What was wrong? I can go and help her, but only if you tell me."

"B-breech," the woman stammered. "Early. That and— and—"

And with that, she fainted dead away. Lilly caught her, easing her fall.

"Kenny, what's going on?" said Curtis. He was looking at the man in Wald's grip, and for once, the crazy man's eyes were off me as he returned the stare. "Is this the bad man?" said Curtis.

"Curtis, maybe you should—"

"Rose told me," said Curtis. He was almost hypnotized, unable to take his eyes of the filthy, unshaven face. The wild man had stopped struggling against Wald. He let out a whimper under his gag. "Prince Harming. She said all the mirror children had to watch for him. Like a curse. Is that it? Is that why it hurt to touch him?" He looked at Wald. "Does it hurt you to touch him?"

"Nay, lad," said Wald. Despite holding up his prey steadily in one hand, he spoke as calmly as if we were all sitting under a tree on a shady hill. "These deepnesses are past our wits. Leave off for now." He pointed with his chin to where Lilly was placing a pillow under Mrs. Hollerith's head. "Look to who needs thee, and we must through the glass."

Lilly spoke up in support. "Come help her, Curtis. Here, she's just fainted. You're going to sit with her and stroke her arm. When she wakes up, you'll tell her we're gone and you don't know what happened. It's okay."

"It's you, isn't it?" said Curtis. "Lillian."

"Yes. A long time since I saw you, Curtis." There were tears in her eyes. "You look good. Can you be strong for—for your mother now?"

His lips set in a determined line. "I'll take care of her. I will, Lillian."

"I believe you," said Lillian with a smile. Then she turned to Wald. "Maybe you should leave that man up in 1947," she said. "We're going to help a girl give birth. If he gets free..."

Wald shook his head. "He is too deep a danger to let

loose. I'll curb him better this time. My culpis, Kenny. I didna mean for that."

"It's okay," I said.

"Then let's go," said Lilly. "Breech means the baby is coming out backward. It's dangerous for Mother and child. This isn't going to be easy."

Wald went first this time after I opened the mirror. He dragged the crazy man after him. Lilly and I gave him a moment to get down off the dresser in 1917 and followed.

The first thing we heard was a cry of pain from Rose.

Wald had thrown his captive to the floor and, with a warning foot on the man's stomach, was lifting Rose in a blood-stained gown onto her bed.

Seeing the blood, Lilly immediately took charge. "I'm sure you've seen some births," Lilly said to Wald, "so you're going to have to help me."

Within a few minutes, Wald had tied Prince Harming, now docile, but still shooting fiery glares at me, to a chair downstairs, and set me to watching him from a distance.

"That's good," said Lilly to me. "You might have orchestrated this, but the birth of a baby is no place for a boy. Call John if that man so much as blinks the wrong way."

She didn't talk to me much after that, just busied herself with trying to save Rose's life.

I spent the next few hours listening to Rose's groans and sobs, and to Lilly's directions to both Wald and Rose. All the while, I never took my eyes off the prisoner. He eventually dozed, though he'd wake up now and then to glare at me.

"I didn't kill anyone," I said at one point. "And I'm not going to."

I don't know why I felt it necessary to justify myself. He looked even crazier than he had two months ago when he shot me. His hair was matted and dirty, his sunken cheeks covered in a scrubby beard, and his skin burned by sun and wind.

"You've got it wrong," I said. "I never killed anyone. You're the one all the kids tell stories about. You smashed kids' heads in. There was some kid you brain-damaged. You sent them into comas. Not me. You."

He looked away, as though my words held no interest. Or maybe he just didn't understand. When his eyes locked on mine, it was like there was fogged glass between us, like his madness kept him isolated from the world.

"Is your name Beckett?" I said, wanting something to take me away from the groans upstairs and my own cluttered thoughts.

His eyes narrowed, then he shook his head. Saying no? In disgust? I couldn't tell. He grunted, champed his jaws on the wide gag John Wald had put in his mouth, then looked at me questioningly. I had been thinking of removing it anyway. It seemed cruel to keep it in, and what harm was there to let him speak?

"Okay," I said, "I'll take it off. But no tricks. You don't know what I can do with that mirror. I know all the rules now. If I want to, I can toss you into a million years ago, and forget you existed."

His reaction to my ridiculous lie was strange. His eyes

widened and his brows contracted as though in surprise and a kind of deep sadness all at once, then he lapsed back into dull hatred.

Swallowing my fear, I stepped forward. His hands and feet were still bound together, and the rope that tied him to the chair hadn't moved. The gag was disgusting. I couldn't even tell what sort of garment the stained, spit-soaked rag had once been part of.

He snapped at my fingers when I removed it, but I think it was more instinct than intention. I dropped the gag and retreated to my chair.

I was halfway through asking him his name, when he interrupted me, almost spitting out his words. "Kill yourself. Now."

The boldness of the command took me aback momentarily. "Why—why should I do that?"

His lip curled in disgust. "Said you were my friend. Wanted all to work out for everyone. This is the way. Kill yourself." He shook his head. "You won't, will you? Even if I could show you it's the only way." I opened my mouth to reply, but he cut me off. "Go on, tell me you can't. Tell me what happened has already happened, even if it's still to come. Go on." He spat beside himself. "I thought you were some kind of hero. Now I'd as soon kill you as look at you."

At that, he lapsed into a silence of hours, most of which he spent staring fire at me.

Eventually, Wald came down and said that he and I should make a meal.

"Kill him," the madman said to Wald, jerking his head to indicate me.

"Speak'st thou now?" said Wald. "Better silence. More to speak is more to lang regret."

With the sparse food available, we muddled through a kitchen that was futuristic to Wald and antique to me, and managed to make oatmeal topped with sugar. Wald insisted on feeding his captive, and I was allowed up to see Rose while she sipped the sugar water that was all Lilly would allow.

She was pale and soaked with sweat, but gave me a weak half smile as I sat beside her. "Are you sure it isn't tonight I die?"

I nodded. "I'm sure. If that's any help."

"It isn't."

"I'm sorry."

She sighed. "It's not you that should be sorry. It's that Clive Beckett." She stopped for a moment, gasped in pain, then waited a moment as some wave in her subsided. "Dying and leaving me to this. Well. It's not so long, and I'll be with him."

"Don't think like that," I said. "You're going to have Curtis, soon. He'll live."

A keening snarl rose up from the wild man below.

Rose ignored it and reached a trembling, sweaty hand to grasp mine. "Funny, isn't it?" she said. Another wave of pain rolled through her, this one longer and more intense. "All this year, I've been hearing about all of you in the future. The stories about Peggy's love affair with Anthony—" Another pause for pain. "Kenny and Luka. About Kenny and his friends and their adventures, Kenny trapped in the past. I knew you before you came. About you and Luka and what happened between you." She gave a short gasp, then clenched her teeth together, breathing in short, sharp hisses. Lilly soon hurried me back downstairs.

Lilly took occasional cigarette breaks over the next few hours, and on one of those I asked her why we didn't find a hospital or a doctor. "We can't move her," she said. "She's had bleeding, and the labor has started. As to bringing someone here, how would we explain ourselves? A madman tied up on one floor, a seventeenth-century blacksmith assisting a nurse from the future on the next." She shook her head sadly. "Terrible as it is, I think we're her best hope. I didn't do training in obstetrics. I was a war nurse. But I've had your note for ten years. I knew I would do this. I've been preparing, and I have thirty more years of medical science than whatever country doctor we could find. Anyway, in 1917, nobody reserves the best treatment for unwed mothers. They'll spare the baby if it comes to it, at the cost of the mother's life."

More waiting, more cries. Some sleep. Then I woke in a convulsion of panic when I heard a scream of terror and a crash of cutlery and broken glass.

Standing not five feet from me in the doorway of the little house was Mrs. Hollerith, ten years younger than I'd seen her last, holding a tipped tray and staring at a bloody-handed John Wald halfway down the stairs.

THREE

Head will hurt. Death's a cert.

"What . . ." said Mrs. Hollerith. "What—what—"

"Oh, what do you think?" said Lilly, descending the stairs. "Your daughter's giving birth, you fool. Your daughter, whom you knew fine well was pregnant, is having her baby a month too soon."

Francine Hollerith's mouth opened and closed.

"What was your plan?" said Lilly. She reached Mrs. Hollerith and dropped her voice to a furious whisper. "Did you want her to die in childbirth so your problem would go away? If that's the case, you were doing a fine job. With luck, I'll save her. Is that a problem?"

Mrs. Hollerith's face settled into an expression I don't have a name for. Something like a cold acceptance of the new way things were. "Fine," she said. "And who are all of—"

She was interrupted with a scream. Prince Harming must have fallen asleep some time after I did, but he was awake again. "Kill him!" he screamed to Francine Hollerith. "Kill him! Help me and kill him. He's going to kill my wife. Everything from him's a lie. Let me loose and I'll do it."

Mrs. Hollerith stepped back and held her tray like a shield.

I spread my hands. "I'm not going to kill anyone. I just came here to help."

Wald leaped down the last few stairs, picked up Prince Harming's discarded gag, and struggled it back into his mouth over the madman's screamed protests.

Mrs. Hollerith looked from one of us to another. "Well, let me see my daughter," she said at last, and strode to the stairs, pushing past Lilly as she went up. Then she turned for a last word. "And get this madman out of here."

Behind his gag, Prince Harming gave a heartbroken wail.

"Why is he getting worse now?" I said. "I thought he had started to calm down."

"Sees it coming," said Wald. "Whate'er this thing, he feels its shadow." He took Prince Harming by the shoulders and looked into his eyes. "List me now, witling. Thou wishest to stave some doom, is't so?"

The madman cocked his head to one side, then nodded.

"Well and good," said Wald. He turned to me. "I said we'd riddle this one in time. Mayhaps 'tis now." He met Prince Harming's wild gaze again, hands still grasping the straining shoulders. "Now list again. I will not let ye kill young Kennit, hear? If there is some doom to stave, we might yet aid thee." He spoke slowly, as though to a child. "We must have words, na? Peace and words. I'll loose the clout that stops thy voice. Speak thy bit."

With that, he took the gag away again, and Prince Harming took a deep breath before speaking. "Not kill then," he said. "Tie him up. Tie and hold him here."

Wald shook his head. "No talk of that. Kennit's a friend. Talk of what thou wouldst prevent."

Prince Harming gave a small snarl and spoke through clenched teeth. "Listen. Murderer. No friend. Said he was. Pushed her and she's dead and wouldn't let me follow. Pretends to be friend. Tie him or stop him or you kill her like it was your own hands. Said he was a friend!"

His words grew faster, more furious, and with a reluctant shrug, Wald replaced his gag.

"He names thee killer," he said, turning to me. "I know it is not so. Why thinks he that?"

"That's not the question," said Mrs. Hollerith coming down the stairs. "The question is why have you brought a lunatic into a birthing house?"

Wald and I looked at each other. "We were...rushed," I said. "He's dangerous. We couldn't let him run loose."

She shook her head. "Well, it won't do. D'you hear me? I won't have my daughter upset by that. Get him out." Wald, looking as sheepish as I probably did, opened his mouth to speak, but she didn't let him. "I'm serious. She's sleeping now, poor thing, though it's a miracle she can in this madhouse. Go upstairs, and fetch that dresser down. I don't know where you come from inside that thing, but I want you to take this screaming idiot back into it." She smiled thinly at the shock on our faces. "Oh, you thought I didn't know, did you? Well, a mother's not so stupid as you might think."

Prince Harming's cries had acquired a mournful sound, like a locked-up puppy, but she never looked at him as she spoke.

"But I want to help," I said. "I came all this way to help."

"And you have," said Lilly from the top of the stairs. "You brought me." She walked down wearily and addressed herself to Mrs. Hollerith. "She wouldn't have survived. You'd have found her dead." Rose's mother absorbed this in silence. Even Prince Harming quieted at Lilly's appearance. "I think she's right, though, John. I think you and Kenny have to get him out of here."

But the baby, I wanted to say. The baby in the wall.

Was I wrong about everything? Rose said the baby was Curtis. Curtis was alive.

I looked at Wald. "Where do we take him?"

He rubbed his bearded face. "It clackers my wits." He counted on his fingers. "Curtis, nay. Lilly, nay. Peggy, nay—a watch will be set now her vanishment is noted. Anthony?"

I shook my head. "No. It's not even in his house anymore, and I'm not dumping this man on—it just wouldn't work."

"Past that, the water," he said. "If indeed the glass is still a'drowned."

"I think it is," I said. "But maybe I've figured out how to get it out. Something Curtis said about submarines got me thinking. Maybe we can get him up to Rick and Jimmy's time." I turned to Mrs. Hollerith. "Can you get—I don't know—a small chest? And—a broom handle?" I tapped my forehead with my hand as I thought it out. "And a couple of two-by-fours and some nails? And something airtight that'll float."

She looked at me like I was as mad as our prisoner. "A wineskin?"

"That should do. If you can get that and give us some time, I think I can get us out of here."

She sighed, shook her head, and left.

It didn't take long to explain my idea to Wald and Lilly. As soon as Wald understood, he clapped me on the back. "'Twill out and up, then Kennit. 'Twill out and up."

Lilly shook her head. "He's right. That should work. Why didn't we think of that ten years ago?"

I grinned. "I just did."

She opened her mouth, then closed it again and smiled warmly. "I suppose you did."

It took Mrs. Hollerith some time to gather what we wanted, but when she had it, we set to work. Wald double-checked our prisoner's bonds and then dragged him out to the front yard of the carriage house. For a guy born hundreds of years ago, John Wald had no problem using modern tools—if what they had in 1917 could be called modern. He sawed two lengths of wood, broke the head off the broom, and started nailing everything together according to my instructions. By noon, we had something even better than I had conceived. Light enough for me to carry, and when it was folded up, small enough to fit through the mirror. I shouldn't make it sound more impressive than it was, a chest with a broom handle sticking straight up from its lid. At the top of the broom handle were a pair of two-by-twos that could either scissor together, or open out into a large X hovering over the chest. It was like a helicopter made by a five-year-old. When we scissored the arms together, I could use them to pick it up and carry it awkwardly under my arm. The chest held three air-filled wineskins.

We completed it just after noon. Wald looked at the thing speculatively, tugged, banged, and rocked it to make sure it was sound. "It isn't much nor muckle, lad. A storm will shake it asplinter."

I shrugged and grinned. "Let's hope for good weather in 1967 then."

He nodded and glanced toward the carriage house where we could still hear Rose's cries. Twice in the last couple of hours we had seen her hard-hearted mother come out to lean against the wall and cry.

Now I had to think about Rick. I needed his help. How could I get a message to someone who wouldn't be born for more than twenty years?

"What did you mean by the 'stony world'?" I said to Wald. "You told me there's a way to float above the stony world. What did you mean?"

Wald frowned and spread his hands. "'Tis like they beasties we oft see on the creek, water-skimmers you call 'em. For them, so light, even the water is part of the stony world, what they without the mirrors are sunk into. The mirror makes us skimmers, above happenstance and accident. We can't change the course of the river, but we can see where it's going and pick with careful legs where now to step. We can use what we know."

What did I know that would help? I knew Rick's name. I knew he was going to find out about the mirror in the madman's diary, and that he'd actually believe what he read.

I knew his address.

When Mrs. Hollerith came out next, I asked her if she could give me an envelope, and I wrote a quick note:

Dear Rick,

The mirror is in the lake. He must have taken the shortest route from the junk house to get there, right over the Bluffs. On September 2 at 6:00 PM, the mirror will float up to the surface. You'll probably have to swim to get it.

Sincerely,
Kenny

While I was puzzling out how to arrange delivery, Lilly took a break from her patient and came out to join us in the sunlit yard.

I studied her face, so different and yet so much the same. "Did I really never see you again?"

She shook her head. "Things started moving fast, Kenny. That Peg did her homework. Came through with sure-fire investments to make money right away. My parents thought us batty, but she brought newspapers from a week in the future and we waited while they came true. Within two months, father had sold the farm and invested everything. They moved into the city, sent us off to nursing school."

"Where's Peggy now?"

Her smile grew sad. "I don't know. Funny, isn't it? The friends you make in youth—we think we'll know them forever. I was stationed in England, Peggy in France. She found a fellow from back home, as I understand. We lost touch." Mrs. Hollerith poked her head out of the hayloft window to request some help. Lilly stood up and stubbed out her cigarette. She nodded to the contraption Wald and I had built. "Look, Kenny, I know you don't want to leave, but that man's an unexploded bomb. The battle-axe is right about that. You've brought me here. Maybe your part is done."

"'Tis truth, lad," said Wald. "'Twere my culpis first in bringing him. Let's foot it up the years."

There's not a single day that's gone by since then that I didn't wish I could have argued with them, but it was two adults against a kid. They weren't asking. They were waiting for me to do what they said.

"Okay," I said emptily. "Let's get going."

I was able to say a brief, guilty goodbye to Rose. I wasn't even certain if she knew I was going.

We brought the mirror down to the first floor, just as Mrs. Hollerith wanted.

Wald loosened Prince Harming's bonds and gave first his hands and then his feet a few minutes of freedom to restore his circulation, then tied him up again, this time with some rope between his feet so he could hobble.

I pushed through first and left the contraption in the

Silverlands while I checked 1927. No one was visible, so I motioned for Wald. The next two decades were similarly empty, though there were reminders in 1947 that time was pressing on. The carriage house was a wreck, furniture scattered all around. Even the dresser containing the mirror had been moved, and I had to shift some stacked chairs before I could get out. Then there was the newspaper. Someone had left a bunch of them on a table that they had set in the middle of the floor with several chairs placed around it as though for a meeting.

On the front page was a picture of Peggy Garroway, and the headline "Local Girl Missing: Manse Valley Haunted House Claims Latest Victim?"

Wald came struggling through the mirror with his prisoner. I folded the newspaper up and stuck it in my bag.

The coal cellar in 1957 was empty except for a note on the bottom step: "Hobo boy, are you okay? Just wondering."

Wald stood a moment, frowning as I read the note. "Time to test thy craft, Ken."

I stuck my hand into the mirror to open it for Wald, and then said, "Can you go in ahead? I have to say goodbye here. I won't take long."

He smiled warmly. "Aye, lad. I've had a heaping share a' those farewells. Foot it fleet."

I said I'd be as fast as I could, and looked at my watch. They should all be home. As soon as Wald was in the mirror with Prince Harming, I wormed up the coal chute. I figured I'd just say a quick thanks. I wasn't sure what to do about the mirror. On one hand, I knew it had to end up back in the carriage house by the nineteen sixties so Rick could discover it. But maybe I was supposed to make that happen. I could give Brian the address and ask him to deliver it, but surely that hadn't happened. After all, when my dad bought the house in 1976, it wasn't like he had been there before.

If it hadn't been for the raised voices at the Maxwells' front door, I would have had no warning that anything was wrong.

"Look, we know you're hiding him," said a man's voice. "If not, why don't you let us in?"

"Why would I let you in?" said Brian, keeping his voice low. "Who are you anyway?"

"This is the Maxwell residence, isn't it?" said the man. "Come on, kid, let me see if he's there."

"Look," said Brian, "my mother's just up the stairs, and she don't want weirdos hanging about."

"If you're threatening me with your mother," said the man, "then why are you speaking soft so she won't hear? Kid, if I decide I'm coming in there to look for that boy, you're not exactly going to stop me. You think a teenage kid is going to hold back a guy who survived the Dieppe Raid?"

"Now I know you're full of it. You're, what, thirty? Dieppe was fifteen years ago, reject. You weren't there."

A woman's voice spoke up—"Now, dear…"—but she wasn't enough to stop the scuffle I heard next.

I peeked around the corner. The younger Prince Harming had my father in an armlock, his cheek pressed hard against the wall. "Was I there now?" he said. "Fifteen years to you, maybe; for me it was five."

"Let him go, darling," said the woman.

"And then what? Let's just take him inside—stop fighting, kid, unless you want a broken arm—and find Kenny. We can't keep pussyfooting around. I want to know. I think he hid things from you back then. Why is he running from us? I think he even knows who the crazy man is."

I took a deep, deep breath and stepped out from hiding.

"I do know who the crazy man is," I said. "It's you. Let him go."

Their heads snapped up. Brian took the opportunity of their distraction to try to break away, but this younger Prince Harming was too quick. He twisted Brian's arm, checking his lunge, and brought a quick fist down onto the side of his head, slamming him back against the corner of a brick. Brian slumped.

There it was. Unconscious. Head injured. The story of the hobo boy heading into its last act. *Head will hurt. Death's a cert.*

The woman immediately knelt down to Brian. "We said no one was to get hurt," she said to the man. "Here, help me lay him out." The man obediently bent to help her, and together they laid Brian out at the bottom of his front step. The man never took his eyes off me. I stood and watched them, ready to run if I had to.

His companion tutted and fussed at Brian's head, took a look into his eyes, then glanced at me. "He'll be okay. It's a bad knock, but if we get him seen to, it'll be fine. I'm a nurse. I know these things."

I was barely listening. There was something about the

man's eyes that I was seeing at last, some echo of the past. Maybe it was something about the way he looked at me. *I thought you were my friend. I thought you were a hero. You said everything would be okay.*

"What's your name?" I said to him.

A smile, bitter and uncertain, twitched on his face. "You know. You know who I am."

I took a step forward, and he actually rocked back.

"You said your name was Beckett. That's not your last name, though, is it?"

He shook his head. "I didn't—things weren't easy for me. I got—messed up for a while. I wanted to start over. I wanted—I wanted my dad's name."

"Curtis?" I said.

"Kenny?" There was a shake in his voice, and suddenly I could see it, the little kid under all the layers of him. The good kid who sat on the creek bank with me and talked about the coming war. The kid who his mother never got to know. "I've been having these dreams, Kenny. I wanted to sort it out, ask what happened. I didn't do anything bad, did I? There's things I don't remember."

"Brian," came a voice from inside the house. "Who's at the door? Why are you taking so long?"

I made the decision so quickly, I barely noticed it going through my mind. "Go in and turn left at the end of the hall. The door in the kitchen leads to the coal cellar. The mirror's down there. Go into the Silverlands and wait."

The woman stood. "Kenny, we can't just—"

"Go," I said. "I'll take care of things here."

"Brian," said the voice again. "Do you need me to come down there?"

"Come on," said the woman, and that was enough. Curtis shook himself, grabbed her elbow, and steered them both inside.

I stepped up to the door and felt my hand going up to smooth my rumpled hair.

Time to meet my grandmother.

FOUR

Let me pass, leave the lass,
don't go down the backward glass.

When she saw her son unconscious on her front step, my grandmother got down on her knees and began to examine him.

"What happened?" she said to me, fire in her eyes.

"It was an accident," I said. "He'll be okay."

"Who are you?"

I had trouble answering at first. In this decade, I had only seen my grandmother from a distance before. It was striking to look at her now in her forties, a little like what would happen if you put cut-up pictures of my dad and Aunt Judy in a jigsaw puzzle. "Look," I said. "There isn't much time. I have to go, but I have to explain something. I have to convince you. I'm from the future. My name is Kenny Maxwell, and I'm Brian's son. He doesn't know that and you can't tell him."

"You're a lunatic," she said, and went back to examining the gash on Brian's head.

"He'll wake up in a minute," I said. "But he'll have a concussion. You'll have to take him to the hospital. Everything will be fine, but he won't remember it all, and he'll never know who I am."

"Stay away from me," she said. "I need to call an ambulance."

"Aunt Judy can—" I stopped myself. "Judy can drive. She's been taking lessons from her boyfriend, Mark. She'll pull up in a minute in his DeSoto."

She frowned at this. "I told Judy she wasn't allowed to drive yet."

"She went ahead and did it," I said. "You don't get mad at her because she gets dad—Brian—to the hospital. You have to believe me. Your name is Harriet Lenore Maxwell. You were married to John Maxwell, but he died in the war. He said you and Brian were the most important things in his world or something like that. In his last letter. You never showed that to anyone because you thought it wasn't fair to Judy. Grandma, you have to believe. I'm Kenny. I'm Brian's son."

She rocked back on her heels as I spoke, and a tear began to make its way down her cheek. "Kenneth was my father's name. That's—impossible. You—look like him in the eyes. Who are you?"

"I know it's impossible," I said. "Brian marries Mary Nelson. They have just one kid. Me. I'm going to find this mirror. It's in your coal cellar. It lets me go back in time. It's crazy, but it's true." I pointed to Brian. "He has a scar on his knee. He tells everyone he got it falling off his bike, but really it was Jennifer Painter, the first girl he kissed. Ten years old, and he chased her into a scrap yard and kissed her and she tripped him. He threw a dog at a boy who was beating up Aunt Judy. Please, Grandma. Believe me. I'm your grandson. Please. You used to tell me stories about NogNog the giant and his little friend Po."

Now I was crying as well.

Harriet Maxwell looked from her son whose head was cradled in her lap back to me. She smiled through her tears. "You know, it's funny. Maybe every mother does this. I've always wondered what it would be like to be a grandma. I don't want it right away, but I think about it. What will I knit for them? What stories will I tell? I thought of NogNog years ago. Are they good stories?"

"The best."

"Is he really going to be okay?" she said, looking down at Brian.

"He'll be awake before you get to the hospital."

Her back straightened. "What do you need, Kenny?"

I closed my eyes and thought about it for a second. "The mirror in your coal cellar. Leave it there for a couple of days." I rooted through my backpack, brought out the newspaper I had picked up in 1947, and tore off the front page. "There's a house mentioned in this article. Can you take the mirror there? They've got a carriage house surrounded by a hedgerow. Sneak it in there if you can."

She frowned, but nodded. "Is there anything else?"

"Yes." I handed her the envelope. "But it's complicated.

I put an address on this. You have to wait until the summer of 1967 and send it to my friend Rick. He has to get it—then he can save my life. Then—this is even crazier—in 1987, you have to get a letter to my friend Luka. I don't even know how, but she'll get it to me. You have to tell me—"

Then I stopped for a moment. Couldn't I just tell her to tell me that the man with the yellow tie was okay? Couldn't I tell her to let me know his real name? Wouldn't that stop all this running around? But in my heart, I knew it couldn't. I had already gotten the letter. The path it led me on was the one where I discovered how keys worked. And that got me back to Rose. Lilly said she would have died.

My shoulders slumped. "You have to tell me that I'm the little hobo boy in the story you've been telling for years. You have to tell me to come here, because there's a man wearing a yellow tie, and the second I get that letter, I have to run from him."

She looked at me for the longest time before answering. "Okay, Kenny. I'll do that."

I remembered one more thing and smiled to myself, knowing that it would cause trouble for Luka. *Your parents know everything.* "Oh, and twenty years from now? I'm going to go missing. You've got to show my mom and dad that mirror in the carriage house. You've got to prove it to them."

She frowned. "And how am I to do that? Do I have to go into it?"

"No. Just help them catch Luka coming out of it. Eleven at night, every even-numbered day after I go missing. She'll come through. She'll be mad at first, but she'll explain every-thing."

I wanted to stay longer, but I couldn't ignore the fact that I had sent the Curtis and his wife into the Silverlands where Wald was waiting. There was too much to sort out.

A green DeSoto pulled up. "I have to go," I said to my grandmother. "Thank you."

I tore into the house and leaped down the stairs. Nobody in the coal cellar. I held my breath and stepped into the mirror, bracing against the uptime heat. As soon as I was in, shouts from both sides assaulted my ears.

"Let him go! I won't ask again."

"Hold thy troubling. Thou know'st not how scrambled are his wits."

Wald was to my right, ten or fifteen feet away and half obscured with two intervening clouds of swimming images. He had Prince Harming with him, squirming and held like a shield in front. Immediately to my left were Curtis and his wife, easier to make out because they were so close.

My presence was doing nothing to calm the situation. Prince Harming, the mad older one, began screaming, then stopped and tried to talk. "He's going to—" Then he inter-rupted himself and screamed again in frustration. "That's what I said last time. No. I have to do it different. But I can't, because—No!"

Curtis grabbed my shoulder and turned me to face him. "Are you in on this? Is that John Wald? What's he doing to that man? I can't—this is making me—"

"Kennit," said Wald, "what means this?"

"Wait," I said. "John, hold on. This is Curtis. And so is that. I just want to sort things out."

Prince Harming screamed again. "No! Don't trust him. He's tricking. He's—killer. No! That's what I said. It's me!" Every half sentence he seemed to need to interrupt himself, as though he couldn't get anything out without realizing the words weren't right.

The younger Curtis strengthened his grip on my shoulder. "What's he talking about? Look, Kenny, I've been trying to remember. What did you do? That day when I was born?"

Wald must have loosened his grip on Prince Harming, who now surged back, smashing the back of his head into Wald's face.

I've gone over those next two minutes a thousand times since then. I've asked myself if there was anything I could have done differently, any movement, any decision, any word. I think about all I did wrong. Out of some crazy sense of shame that I didn't even understand, I never told anyone why it was that Prince Harming shot me. I had this idea that I was the person who could fix everything even though I knew nothing could be fixed, nothing changed. I wanted to be the main guy who the whole adventure was about, the boy at the center of the universe.

Instead of just one more kid who got it all wrong.

Wald fell down and halfway through a mirror. Prince Harming, unbalanced and bound, stumbled, then started frantically hopping away from us, looking from side to side as he retreated into the distances of the Silverlands, trying to find a specific mirror.

"Hold onto him," said Curtis to his wife. "If that's me, I should help." He shoved me into her hands and started off.

"You don't understand," I said. "There's—something wrong with you—with him."

The woman put her hands on my shoulders. "Kenny, let him go. He's been needing to do something. He's been having these horrible dreams, trying to remember what happened. That's why we came. That's why we've been looking for you. We never got a chance to find out what happened."

I only half paid attention, more interested in what was going on ahead. Most of what you see in the Silverlands is blackness, like you're floating in space. So what I saw as I looked at Curtis retreating was not easy to figure out: a collection of Wald-fragments sluggishly pulling back from a mirror; the twisted face of Prince Harming looking over his shoulder as he struggled away; the retreating back of Curtis, looking like he was running into a stiff wind.

When Curtis got to Wald, he leaned down to help the older man up. In the jumble of images, Wald must have mistaken him for Prince Harming and gave him a powerful shot in the face. Instantly, the two of them were rolling on the featureless floor of the Silverlands.

This was it. Bad things were going to happen. I had to change them. I was in the moment. I forgot all about Wald's advice to float above "accidents and happenstance." I wrenched out of the woman's grasp and propelled myself forward through the buzzing pain. The Silverlands muffled our voices. By the time words reached me, they were a jumble.

Leave him a—get thee back—Kenny, don't—don't, Marg—curst and laggard air—kill you.

As I pushed forward past two, three, four sets of mirrors, images resolved themselves in the floating silver. Curtis and Wald were struggling as best anyone could in that place. They were between two mirrors. Curtis had an arm around Wald's throat, and Wald had Curtis by the middle, trying to lift him up. Three mirrors past them, Prince Harming hobbled on. As he reached each mirror, he looked to the right and left into the cloud of swimming shards as though searching for something.

"Stop it!" I shouted to Wald and Curtis, but my voice just added to the cacophony of cries, and neither paid any heed. Even looking at them as I approached, I could barely tell who was saying what.

Curtis got Wald's head bent far enough into an image-cloud that he must actually have been through the mirror, but then pulled him back when Wald almost tumbled both of them through. Fresh snowflakes glistened on Wald's head and beard. Where did these mirrors lead?

Neither one wanted to harm the other. Wald had a knife in his boot that he wasn't reaching for, and Curtis looked to be pulling his punches.

I glanced at Prince Harming. He had found the mirror he was looking for now, five spaces beyond where we stood. Its cluster of fragments glowed a warm red.

He looked down the corridor toward us, saw me, and

twisted his face again in anger. Without another pause, he thrust his bound hands into the mirror and screamed in abject pain. For a long moment, he held his hands there, then pulled them out. I could see smoke rising from his burned flesh. He pulled his wrists apart with another scream, and the ropes that had held him fell away.

I had to do something. It wasn't just a matter of changing things now. This was the man who had shot me, the man who had terrorized me and my friends through decades. This was Prince Harming, who had smashed kids' heads in. Prince Harming of the skipping songs.

He'll take you down the backward glass.

Curtis and Wald struggled at my feet, each one clearly intent on subduing the other before dealing with anything else. Careful not to get pushed to one side or the other, I stepped over them.

Prince Harming, finding that his burned fingers were useless at untying his bonds, sat down and thrust his feet into the glowing mirror. He screamed again, but kept his feet in the mirror for long enough that when he took them out, the ropes were burning.

I was terrified, but determined not to let it control me. I glanced back to see Curtis and Wald still at each other's throats, though Curtis again clearly had the upper hand. His wife was hurtling toward me, getting ready to jump over them to get at me.

I faced Prince Harming again.

I paused between two mirrors. To one side there was a sunlit beach, on the other side, darkness. Prince Harming was fifteen feet ahead of me. I don't know what I thought. That I could stop him? Reason with him?

Scraps of everyone's muffled voices still clattered in my ears.

From this distance, I could see Prince Harming's hands, charred black and bloody red, cooked and raw at the same time, like poorly grilled steaks with crippled fingers sticking out of them. His feet hadn't fared as badly, and he stood to face me. His features twisted into an expression that wasn't rage this time, just pure terror, and I realized he wasn't looking at me but rather past me.

Behind me, the woman had cleared the two fighting men and was almost upon me.

The woman crashed into me and half turned me around. This close, her voice brightened and became clear. "Kenny, why won't you listen, it's—"

And before she completed that sentence, so much happened that I could never undo.

I saw Prince Harming lunge at me on his still-smoking feet.

I grabbed the woman by her shoulders just as she was holding me and turned around, trying to use her momentum against her. If I could just get her on the same side as the crazy version of Curtis, I could retreat, get Wald, get things cleared up.

Maybe that's what I was thinking. I've gone over it so many times, I don't even know anymore.

Was I angry at her as well? Was I frustrated at all that had kept me from home?

Did I do it deliberately?

I honestly don't know.

I pushed. Hard. Just as I heard the last word in that sentence, I held her shoulders and pushed and what had she said? Kenny, why won't you listen, it's—

"Peggy."

I can still see it. I guess I always will. Peggy's face, much older than when I saw her last, so I didn't get it until now. I had recognized Lilly's flash of blond hair right away. Why not Peggy? Something had softened in her when she found her Curtis and married him. Peggy's eyes widening in surprise, Peggy's mouth in a round "O," Peggy's hands flailing at me as she fell backward into the blackness of a mirror. I reached after her, but all I could feel was water and pain.

FIVE

Trick your feet down the street.

I don't know how I made it out of there alive.

I screamed her name, and there must have been enough desperation in that scream, enough raw, crazy regret to stop Curtis and Wald.

I flailed my hands inside the mirror and turned my head to look at the two of them. Curtis was on top, his hands limp now around Wald's neck.

"What … "

I didn't listen, just plunged my hands again into the mirror. It was downtime, and though I had thought of it as dark, I could now see glimmers of light in its swimming fragments. I was looking up through troubled water, but nowhere could I see the older Peggy, and all I could feel was the water.

I felt an impact from the side and was thrown clear. Prince Harming.

"No!" He shoved his hands through the cluster of watery

shards and screamed himself hoarse, more from broken-hearted frustration, I thought, than from pain.

Then the other Curtis was upon us. He stamped on my hand and my chest in his eagerness to get past me, and for a few moments, I was too busy dealing with my pain and trying to get out of their way to know what they were doing.

By the time I had rolled away and risen to my knees, an odd tableau had asserted itself. Wald and Curtis were locked together again, but not fighting this time. "Ye cannot go," shouted Wald as he strained, arms wrapped around the other man's waist, to keep him from going through the mirror. "'Twill be the death a' thee."

"Let me," said Curtis. "Let me go. She must be there. She needs me. Let me go."

As they struggled, Prince Harming stood unsteadily on his burned feet and looked at me. I shrank from him, but he shook his head as if to say there was no need. All the wildfire and anger was gone now, as though his fury and reason for living had turned into water and splashed to the floor. He was closer to me than the other two, and when he spoke I could hear him clearly.

"I saw it this time," he said. He looked at his hands and then at me. "I saw it. I didn't before. You didn't mean to, did you?"

"I didn't," I said. The enormity of what I had done was only now coming through. It was Peggy. The woman I couldn't place. Peggy who had gone back in time to find a better life. Who had gone to nursing school with her best friend

Lilly. Who met and married a soldier named Curtis Beckett. She hadn't been killed by Prince Harming. She had been killed by me.

He nodded. "All these years. I went mad. I thought you had done it—deliberately. Knew it was her. When I was little and I met you—it seemed like you knew everything. Then—what I saw. On that night." He looked back at the struggling figures of Wald and his own younger self, but did nothing to interfere. "And this." He looked at me again, all hate drained away. "It wasn't you. I couldn't make it not happen by killing you. It wasn't you. It was me. She died because she met me." He shook his shaggy head.

I didn't know what to say. I was still too stunned by what I had done. I had killed his wife after all, just as he said I would. He warned me, but I didn't believe. If I had just told someone. Peggy, Anthony, Lilly. If Peggy had known, surely she wouldn't have come.

"I'm sorry," I said.

He shook his head again. "I was telling you to kill yourself. It's me who should kill myself." He turned and looked at his younger self grappling with John Wald, and suddenly his face shifted again into bottomless rage. He reached down past John to grab the younger Curtis, but as he did, a flash of blue light erupted in the air between them. The older Curtis—I had to stop thinking of him as Prince Harming—screamed and withdrew his mutilated hands. The younger one flinched from the pain of the blue sparks, and Wald took the opportunity to flip him over and pin his hands behind his back.

Older Curtis stepped back and held his hands up, then looked at me. "That pain. Like when I was younger. I remember now." He breathed raggedly and squinted his eyes as though not entirely seeing me. "I didn't remember until now."

The younger version of him wasn't listening. Wald had him pinned well enough that he could barely move, but he continued to shout. "Let me go. I can get her."

"You can't," said the older one, but he said it so quietly I think I was the only one who heard. "You won't and you can't." He looked at me. "I have to die. That would do it. She would be better if she never met me, if I never existed."

He turned and began to limp away through the thick air of the Silverlands. I wanted to call after him, but what was there to say? He had been right.

"Kenny," shouted younger Curtis, jolting me from my thoughts. "Tell him to get off. I have to save her."

I looked at the retreating back of the man I had been thinking of as Prince Harming, now burned and broken. I wanted to stop him. What was he going to do next? I didn't want him to kill himself. I wanted to stop it, to make it right.

Behind me, his younger self was rocking back and forth under Wald, who looked at me, strain evident in his eyes. "I cannot lose him, Kennit. He'll quell his own life. Help me, lad."

"No," shouted Curtis. "I won't. John, let me go. I can get her."

I knelt down beside him. All our faces were wet with tears. "You can't," I said. "She's gone into water. If you go in there, you'll drown. You can't save her. If John lets you go, you'll die as well."

"You pushed her," he said. "You knew, didn't you? All this time, you knew this was going to happen. You pushed her. When I was a kid—you knew." He stopped struggling as the realizations hit him all at once. "You knew I'd grow up to meet her. You knew who she was. You knew you were going to kill her. You knew everything, and you could have changed it, but you watched it happen and you killed her." He screamed those last words as he again tried to rock Wald off him.

"Kennit," Wald hissed at me, and beckoned me closer with his head while holding Curtis down. "Go up a ways, there, farther from our own glass. Find one for me. A mirror. It's up ahead. It spies out upon an auld stone castle wall. Find it, Kennit."

Uncomprehending, I stepped past them and farther down the hall of mirrors. I passed the cloud of images glowing orange and red. It was, on both sides, a mirror inside a fire, the one Prince Harming had burned his hands in. After that came one inside a dusty old junk shop on one side and a bedroom on the other. Were there ten years between these mirrors as there were between our own? I almost tripped over a strip of cloth connecting the mirrors. A doorstop? Were the rules always the same? Next I passed more mirrors in bedrooms, one in a museum, and one in the middle of a forest. How many stories were here, how many kids in their backward glasses, how many haunted houses with legends about missing children? Here was a mirror looking out from under a waterfall, and there one that looked like it had been bricked up inside a tiny space with, in both of its decades, two skeletons looking like they had died inside waiting to escape.

"Fleet, lad," shouted Wald, and I pushed on.

I found the mirror he wanted, looking out on a stone castle wall. I called to him, and through the clouds of image-shards, I saw him drag Curtis to his feet, an arm twisted behind his back. The younger man was wild with rage and grief. Somehow, though, Curtis hit Wald with his free hand, stamped on his feet, kicked him, and tried to throw them both to the side, Wald steadfastly ignored every blow and kept marching him toward me.

"What are you doing?" I said.

"Saving the fool's life," Wald replied. One of his eyes was swollen closed already, his lips and nose bloody, but that iron grip of his still held.

"Why?" Curtis screamed at me as Wald bore him forward. "You were our friend. We trusted you. There has to be some way to stop it. Kenny, you have to stop it. You have to." His voice rose to a fever pitch.

"Hold!" shouted Wald even louder, and he tightened his arm around the younger man's neck. "Will ye hear?" Curtis stilled for a moment in his grasp. "You cannot fetch her from the glass."

"No," shouted Curtis. "You're wrong. I can get her. I'll hold my breath and go through. I'll find her. I'm going after her. Let me go."

"And if I do?" said Wald, still straining to hold Curtis. "You'll dive into that watered glass? Though it's death for you to do it?"

"What are you doing?" I said to Wald. "What are you going to do?"

"Yes!" shouted Curtis. "I have to. Let me go."

"Aye, lad," said Wald, a terrible sadness in his voice. "I will." His eyes met mine, and I saw in them the sort of decision I'm sure I could never make.

Almost faster than my eye could follow, Wald took his arm from around the man's throat, shifted his own weight, and flung Curtis through the mirror. Curtis might have managed to grasp the edges and keep from going through, but Wald hooked a foot to trip him, and gave him a second shove.

On the far side of the mirror, I saw Curtis sprawl forward into the stone wall. He immediately sprang back up and turned to the mirror, throwing himself at it.

As he crashed into it, Wald, never taking his eyes from Curtis, spoke to me. "There's another rule, Kennit, for that list you're making. You cannot come back through a glass that's not your own. Ten years back and ten years on, that mirror is, but not for us."

"What did you do? What have you done?"

He lowered his eyes. "Trapped him. I couldn't hold him long. He was too much for me, too young and strong. If I let him go, he would have killed himself. Or you."

We stood and watched him. His voice came thickly through to us, crying for us to reach out and let him in as he beat on the mirror with his fists.

"What's going to happen to him?" I said. Outside of the mirror, two people had come along and were trying to talk to Curtis who was almost frothing at the mouth, his hands bloody from beating against the glass. He rounded on them like a cornered animal, and they backed away.

Wald shook his head sadly. "Now? Go mad, methinks, for ten long years. They're all as one, the mirrors. All on the sevens and all for ten years. I know that glass. Two hundred years it's held its wall in that Welsh castle. I had to do it, Ken. D'ye see? He would ha' drowned himself or dashed your brains." He looked around. "Where went the other?"

I looked back down toward our mirror and my heart clenched. "I don't know." Far down the Silverlands? Waiting in the coal cellar? "He saw what happened," I said hopefully. "I don't think he wants to kill me now."

"Nor should he. I saw it, too. Ye did no thing in malice."

"But it's still my fault," I said. I was on the verge of tears and collapse all at once.

"Whisht, now," said Wald. "Whisht. All's done."

"But what do we do now?" I said. "We were supposed to get him away from Rose and now he's gone. What do we do?"

Wald stood up, straightened his back, and shook himself as though to cast off the hurts he had from Curtis. "Back to Rose, I think, though her mother will not thank us for coming. Still and all, with the madman loosed again, 'tis best we set a watch about the girl."

"Are you okay?" I said.

"'Tis naught." He waved away my concerns. He was limping now, I could see, hurt more by Curtis than he wanted to let on, but he led me back down the Silverlands unerringly to our own mirror. On one side, I could see glimmers of light through whatever water it was under, and on the other the dimness of my grandmother's coal cellar. We stepped carefully through, just in case the now-crippled older Curtis was waiting for us. I didn't think he would be, though. He had seemed a broken man when he hobbled away on his burned feet. Seeing no one there, we brought the contraption we had made back through and set it in a corner.

"Back down then," I said. "Let's make it quick." I stuck my hand into my pocket for the strings-and-spoon key to take us backward.

And found it gone.

SIX

Then the years will vanish fleet.

"He took it!" I said to Wald. "My key—he must have taken it out of my pocket."

In the dim light leaking in from the open door to the main floor, I saw his mouth open, then close again. He had nothing to say.

Idiotically, I turned to the mirror and pushed my hand in. It was hot. Uptime to the sixties.

"No!" I said. I wanted to hit the mirror in frustration, but I knew my hand would just sink in. What had I done? I had given a madman the key to the mirror and locked myself out of it. I had moved myself forty years up from where a baby was going to die.

"Can you not make some other key?" said Wald.

"No," I said hopelessly. "It takes time. Weeks, maybe. I left that doorstop in for a month before it turned into a key. If I do that now, it'll be long over before we could—" I stopped.

The hairs on the back of my neck rose up as I thought it through before speaking. "Before we could make it." I looked at Wald in the darkness. "So we need time. That's it. We need time. Come on, John. I've got it now. Bring the floater. We have to get Rick. I hope he got my note."

The contraption worked even better than I had hoped, though we still nearly died getting ashore.

Together, Wald and I folded out the two-by-twos that functioned as its arms, an "X" set like helicopter blades above the chest filled with wineskins. We reassured ourselves that, yes, the mirror was still underwater, though even in this evening light we could see some glimmers of waves. Then, together, we shoved the chest through.

It worked instantly. The opened two-by-twos wedged part of the thing inside the Silverlands while outside, in the lake, an air-filled chest had suddenly come through the mirror. Buoyed up, the mirror began to rise, shaking off its weeks of lake mud. It was a dizzying sight from where we stood, looking at the wave-troubled surface of the lake as it shot toward us. We stepped back as the mirror broke into daylight. Before, we had heard nothing through this mirror, but now we could discern muffled splashes.

The mirror was still a few inches below the surface, so Wald didn't want me to try going through, but he agreed to hold me while I stuck my hand up and waved it in 1967 for the first time in months.

"Hey!" I heard a muffled scream from beyond the mirror. "Kenny! Is that you?"

"It's Rick!" I said to Wald. "It's him."

The shouting continued for a few more minutes. Through the glass I couldn't make out everything, but I understood that he was asking me to hold on, and saying he'd be there soon.

At long last, a hand grasped mine and began to pull. "He's got me," I said to Wald.

Sure enough, we could see the bottom of the canoe through the watery light, and Rick Beech's face, leaning over, a strained expression on it as he tried to pull me up. Rick was good in a canoe, and I guess it helped that 1967 gravity only asserted itself on the parts of me that were through the mirror while the rest of me stood in the Silverlands leaning over.

Wald was right about the danger being more than just the ordinary risk of drowning. When Rick pulled me up through the mirror and the shallow covering of water, my body began to convulse. A wave washed over me and I took a sharp, involuntary gulp. My thrashing almost overturned Rick's canoe, but Wald pushed from the Silverlands and Rick leaned back to drag me in. As soon as he had me, he threw me on my back and pressed on my stomach while I heaved and coughed out water.

"Wald," I finally said weakly.

"What?"

"In the—mirror. We have to get him out."

"Stay there," he said. "Let's get it to shore first. If this Walt guy's any bigger than you, I don't think I can do it. I'll get a rope around this chest and we'll tow it in."

With strong, clean strokes Rick took us to shore. We weren't more than twenty feet out, but I would never have made it. When Rick pulled us onto a tiny scrap of sand and rocks under the bluffs, he and I got our hands around the mirror and propped it up against the cliff wall. Pushing our contraption ahead of himself, Wald walked through.

Rick stepped back on seeing him.

"It's okay," I said. "He's our friend. He's John Wald. He's from the seventeenth century."

Rick's mouth hung open for a moment, then he grinned and shook his head. "Jeeze, you sure know how to make an entrance, H. G. Wells. Come on, I got a fire going. You must be freezing."

He was right. Both Wald and I were shivering. Rick got us blankets and towels, and served us coffee from a thermos. He wanted to hear everything, but first he was dying to tell us about his own part in all this. "Can you imagine me, getting that letter last week? All summer long, Jimmy and me, we've been all over the place looking for that guy, looking for the mirror. Then, bang, a letter from you."

"You did good," I said.

He ruffled my hair. "Thanks, kid. Come closer to the fire. You too, Mr. Wald; it ain't getting any warmer. I wanna know everything. What happened? You went back to the seventeenth century?"

"Not exactly," I said. "Felt like it sometimes. But I can't tell you that now. We have to get back."

"What? You just got here. What do you mean, get back? Buddy, you have to go home."

I shook my head. "No. I still have to do something." As quickly as I could, I outlined for him the events of the past two months. He had a million questions, but I waved them aside. All I wanted was for him to understand a few things: how keys worked, how they were made, and why I needed one. Even with my hurrying, the story must have taken an hour to tell. All the while, I kept looking at the mirror, waiting for my plan to work. Where was Luka? As evening began to spread out over the lake, I kept telling myself it would be okay. Curtis wasn't born until tomorrow. There was still time.

Rick was able to clear up one mystery for me, though, when I told him of Prince Harming's reappearance in 1957. As he had prepared to row out onto the lake to look for me, he had come across an abandoned wetsuit, washed up on the shore. "It was water-logged, like someone had just taken it off in the middle of a swim. There's been a bunch of break-ins at the marina this summer. He must have used it to go through, then tossed it back out."

After that, I didn't let him have many more interruptions, just rocketed through until the present moment.

"But what can I do?" Rick said when I had finished my story. "I can get Jimmy to start cooking one of these key things up, but that won't do you any good right now."

"Not Jimmy," I said. "Luka."

"What?"

"There's a little stand of trees across from that place where the tabletop is buried. You remember it? There's a crooked maple on the outside."

"With the big knot way up high like a face? Yeah, I know it."

"I need you to go dig up a box that's buried there. It's right under that knot, about three feet from the tree. It's got a plaque on it that says July. Inside there's a note I wrote to Luka. Put another note in there. Tell her how to make a key. Tell her I need her to come back with one today, right now."

Rick ran a hand through his hair. "I don't know, future boy. Can that even work?"

"Why don't you ask me that question?" came a voice from behind us.

"Luka!"

I almost bowled her over in the eagerness of my embrace. "Whoa, ease up there, tiger," she said, grabbing my shoulders and holding me at arm's length. "Hey, you're not so pasty once you've had a bit of summer on you."

I don't have the words to properly describe what I was feeling right at that moment. Had her eyes been that bright when I saw them before? I grabbed her and crushed her to me again. "Oh, Christ, I missed you."

Rick put his long arms around us both. "Amen to that," he said. "I love a good summer project."

Luka pulled back again. I think she might have been blinking away a few tears. "Okay, you big crybabies." She looked right at me. "I got the note. I'm here. It was a close thing, though."

"Why? The note was in the July box, right? Didn't you get that a month ago?"

She held up her hand so we could see the string wrapped around it, a small washer tied on either end. "I kept messing up. I was too impatient. The first one I tried, I took it out after a week to see if it would work, but no luck. Then I had to start all over again. The second one I kept in for ten days and still nothing. By that time, I was down to the wire. That was exactly two weeks ago, so I just took it out. Anyway, here I am, just when you said, so what's the mission, Captain Solo?"

I sniffed and wiped my own eyes. Luka. Luka who I'd been denied all this time. I sniffed again. "Same old mission," I said. "Rose Hollerith. 1917. You up for it?"

"Try to keep me away," she said. "So we have to go right now?"

I looked at the warm fire Rick built, buffeted now by a breeze from the lake. How good it would be to just lie down by that fire as John Wald had, rest for a while, and then go home. I shook my head at the thought. "Yeah," I said. "Right away, before I change my mind."

"Wait," said Rick. "How is this working? I haven't even buried the note yet."

"Time travel," we said in unison, then grinned at how quickly we were in synch again.

"So bury it," I said. "We have to get going."

"What about him?" said Rick, pointing to the other side of the fire. John Wald was asleep, curled up with his back to the flames.

"That's John Wald?" said Luka.

"Yeah. We should let him sleep. He's been through a lot. I think his leg might be broken." There was something else, too. His solution, his saving of Curtis's life. I couldn't see any other way we could have done it. He was right. But I didn't want those kinds of decisions on this last leg of the journey. I didn't want anything so harsh. I wanted to follow Wald's own advice, to float above the stony world.

Rick's eyes narrowed. "So you just want to go right back into it? Even though—you know—nothing changes? Even though whatever you do, that baby still ends up dead?"

"Not want to," I said. "I have to. Even if I can't change a thing. Even if nothing—" I stopped, caught in the half-formed thought. "Even if nothing we do makes a difference, at least we can want to make a difference. That's what I get now. It matters what you want to do."

Rick smiled warmly. "You got heart, future boy. I'll say that for you. You know what you're making me think about? Last year this English teacher gave us a poem. I don't remember it much, but it ends up with 'I am the master of my fate, I am the captain of my soul.' I get you, Kenny. It's like you're saying if we know the future or whatever, if we know what's going to happen, we can't be the masters of our fate."

I finished for him. "But we can still be the captains of our souls."

Part Six
———

*The Baby in the Wall,
September and
Everything After*

ONE

Crack your head, knock you dead.

1957 coal cellar, empty. 1947 carriage house, empty. 1937 Lilly's bedroom, empty. 1927 Rose's bedroom, empty and preserved. 1917 carriage house—screams and cries. That was our one-minute journey fifty years into the past.

The sound of Rose's wails made their way into the Silverlands, so by the time we stepped out, we had a good idea of what we were going into.

The mirror and its dresser were still downstairs, but close enough that I emerged within Lilly's field of vision as she stood at Rose's bedside. She saw me, then Luka, and gave a slight frown. Mrs. Hollerith had her back to me, and I retreated to the couch before she saw me.

"Another breath, dear," said Lilly. "Just keep it up."

In whispers, I told Luka everything of the summer. Everything. I confessed to how I hadn't told Lilly and Peggy of Prince Harming's accusation, how I had asked my grandmother to send the note warning me of the man in the yellow tie even though I knew by then he didn't mean me harm.

"You were trying for the best," said Luka.

"But none of it mattered," I said. "He said I was going to kill his wife and I did."

"You didn't mean to."

I gave up thinking and talking for a while and just listened to the noises above. About an hour after we got there, Lilly started sounding increasingly worried. I heard the term "breech" again, along with "prolapsed umbilical" and "oxygen starvation."

There was a brief upset when Mrs. Hollerith found out we were there, but Lilly sent me to fetch clean sheets and Luka to pump water, so she let it go.

After that, it was more of what Lilly called hurry-up-and-hold-your-breath.

I was an anthill of emotions, every feeling inside me running in a different direction. Here was Luka next to me, warm and real and somehow outshining every other thing in the world. And there was Rose upstairs, moaning and crying. And Peggy, bitter, sharp-edged Peggy, who had seemed, in the few moments I had seen her, so tender with Curtis—lost now, forever. Sleep, when it came while I rested on Luka's shoulder, was the shallow kind, where dreams come as fragmented and rearranged memories. Me pushing Peggy. Her grabbing and taking me along to her watery death. Curtis burning his hands in the fiery mirror, then reaching out to me, touching my face with his charred fingers.

Then I was woken by a scream, one more urgent, more filled with heartbreak than I had ever heard. "Get him out. He can't be here. He can't see this. Not like this. Get him out."

I shot awake to a tiny moment of silence followed by, "Rose? What's going on? I took care of Mother like Lilly said. She's been awfully upset. I knew I should stay away— but what's happening?"

I stood up. Luka was still asleep. I realized with a guilty thrill that we had fallen asleep with our arms around each other.

"Curtis," came Lilly's voice, "Rose is ill. I'm helping her. You should just let her be. It's a trying time for her."

"Why is there all that blood?" said Curtis. "Where is Mother? Mother now, I mean. I took care of her in my time. But where is she now?"

"She went to the house to get some things, Curtis. Please, dear, give Rose some privacy. Her mother will be back soon, and you've done such a good job this year of making sure she didn't see you."

I got to the middle of the stairs just in time to see everything dawn on Curtis's face at once. "She's not my mother, though, is she? Is she, Rose? Mother isn't my mother. You're my mother, aren't you?"

"Not like this," Rose sobbed quietly. "I was going to tell you, but not like this. Not now."

I walked slowly and quietly toward him, recognizing that this had to stop but that I was also intruding. "Hey, Curtis," I said. "It's me. Let's go downstairs. We should leave Rose. She's going to be okay."

All the way down the stairs, I kept talking to him as gently as I could. Mrs. Hollerith came in carrying some steaming wet cloths. He stared at the sight of her. She frowned and almost stopped to speak to us, but Lilly called her from above. She dismissed us with a snort of derision and went on.

"Who's the new one?" I heard her gruffly ask Lilly a moment later.

In the hesitation that followed, I could imagine a look passing between Lilly and Rose, a lightning flash of communication and caution. "Just another girl come through the mirror," said Lilly. Mrs. Hollerith snorted and said something about taking the mirror to the dump as soon as she could and how Grand Central Station was no place to have a baby.

"Did you know?" Curtis said in a flat voice that betrayed no emotion.

I nodded. "It wasn't my thing to tell you."

"Wait," said Curtis, everything just catching up to him at once. "So who is my father? Clive?" I nodded. Tears welled up in his eyes. "I don't know why I care," he said. "Why do I care? What does it matter? My father—I mean, Rose's father—he's dead, too. Why does it matter which dead father is mine? But I just—I grew up thinking it was this way and it's not, it's that way."

Luka was awake now. She sat very still and watched me with Curtis, scooching well to the side as I sat him down.

What do you do when someone's crying? You shut up and hold them. I took him by the shoulders and pulled him into an awkward hug. In my arms he babbled away for a bit through his tears. Why had nobody told him?

Didn't they think he could understand? How many other people knew? Did the neighbors know?

At the end of all that, his crying stopped, and the next thing he said came out in the thinnest, tiniest whisper. "Rose is dead, though, Kenny. She's dead. I was keeping a secret, too. It was the Spanish flu. She died eight years ago. I didn't know how to tell her. How can I tell her she's dead?"

Instinctively I put my hand up to his head and caressed his hair. "She knows, pal. She's not stupid, your mother. She's smart, just like you. She knows, and she wanted to talk to you about it. She was going to tell you everything before the mirror closes at the end of the year. You know it does that, right? It only opens on the years that end in seven. All she wanted was to get some time with you. And she didn't want to spoil it."

"How do you know all this?" said Curtis pulling away from me, sniffling and rubbing his eyes.

"I just talked to her, that's all," I said. "I've been hearing about you two for months. I wanted to come back and help. I knew things got bad around now."

"Did you help other people as well?"

The emerging look of admiration in his face made me uncomfortable. "I tried. But you have to be careful when you try to help. Things can go bad even if you don't mean them to." Then it just all came out in a rush, pushed out of me by my guilt and frustration. "Listen, Curtis, I know things that are going to happen. Some really bad things. I've seen them all and I know it's going to get really bad. Some of it's my fault. But maybe it doesn't have to happen. When you grow up, you're going to join the army, just like you said. You're going to meet a girl and fall in love."

As I continued, his eyes never strayed from my face, and his mouth hung open. I told him everything, or as much as I could put together in that crazy rush. I forgot all about Wald's advice to float above the events of the world. Wald, me, Peggy, the tragedy in the Silverlands. I tried to tell him as many ways as I could think of to avoid Peggy's death. Don't go back to the mirrors as an adult. If you have to go back, don't take her with you. Tell me everything as soon as you see me, especially your names. Any of those things, I told him, could set us on a new path.

Just as I was telling him to write all of this down, we heard renewed sobs of pain from Rose upstairs. Curtis looked up. "I shouldn't be here," he said.

"No," replied a voice from behind us, "you shouldn't. I'll take care of that."

I turned to see Curtis, older and in his Prince Harming appearance, one burned hand holding my strings-and-spoon key, the fire of madness in his eyes all over again. He stepped all the way through the mirror, and down off the dresser, just as we heard a voice from upstairs.

"There he is, dear. Oh, there he is. It's a boy. Oh!"

"Just in time," said Prince Harming, and he turned toward the stairs.

TWO

Then Prince Harming's hunger's fed.

"Wait," I said. "What are you here for? What are you going to do?"

He turned back and looked at me, and when he spoke it was in a quiet voice, not the fierce shouts of before. "It was never your fault, Kenny. It was always me. All I need to do is never live. I kill that baby and it's no crime. It's suicide."

He started up the stairs and I ran after him. "No," I said. "You can't change things that way. That's not how it works."

I grabbed his arm, but he smashed my face with his elbow. I fell back and cracked my head on the floor. I opened my eyes again just in time to see Luka run at him and get a solid kick in the stomach. Her feet left the step they were on and she flew down to land next to me. "You can't stop me," he said. "This is the end. I do this and everything changes. That's what I understand. You can only change yourself. Don't make me hurt you. This is mine to do."

He turned and continued up the stairs.

As soon as he got to the top, I could hear the sounds of a struggle. Lilly telling him to stay away, Mrs. Hollerith screaming at him, Rose simply screaming. There were thumps and slaps, the dull sound of punches. "Give that to me!" he screamed.

I willed myself to get up, head still spinning.

"Is that ... is that ... " Curtis, little Curtis as I thought of him in my head, walked to the bottom of the stairs and looked up. "Kenny, who is that? You said I was going to burn my hands in a mirror. Who is that, Kenny?"

What happened on the day I was born? the older Curtis had asked me. "Curtis, it's—it's not safe here. Let me take care of this." Whatever was about to happen, I didn't want him to see it. Be a friend to him, she had asked. His tenth birthday was tomorrow.

I gripped the handrail and started up the stairs.

The converted hayloft was a chaos of voices and bodies. Mrs. Hollerith clutched Rose, who thrashed and screamed at this burned stranger. "It's mine," she screamed. "He's mine, he's my boy. Give him to me. Put him in my arms. He's mine, he's my boy." Lilly stood on unsteady feet, a fresh gash on her forehead covering her face with a sheen of blood. She held her hands out to Prince Harming, imperious and demanding.

He clutched the baby in his raw hands, a bloody and curled thing, skin blending with the hideous fingers that cradled it. Why could he hold the baby? Was he beyond pain? Something was happening here, something I should understand, but it was going too quickly.

"It's me," he shouted. He looked around at us all wildly. "Every one of you has been hurt by this." He shook the baby slightly in his hands as he said that, and my heart clutched like a fist. "All of you. I've done—so much wrong. I can't bear it. It was all me. I tried to control it, to stop it. I tried to hurt other people to make it stop. But it's not outside of me, it's in me." He shook the baby again, but only lightly, and I could tell that somehow he couldn't bear to be rough with it.

"That's not the way," I shouted. I didn't want to shout, but I had to if I wanted to make myself heard over Rose's wails. "You're trying to control again. Give it up. You can't."

Seeing him distracted, Lilly stepped forward and brought her hands up to the baby, but she was too gentle, and that was her undoing. Curtis leaned back, braced himself against a wardrobe, and gave her a push with his foot, sending her flying back into a large chest. He paid no further attention to her, but rather began to advance on me. "Get out of my way," he said. "I'll kill you if I have to, because it won't matter. If I kill myself, none of it will have happened. I can do anything right now because in a few moments this will all be gone."

I fell back before his fury, but I kept talking. "That's not it," I said. "You've got it wrong."

"How else is there a dead baby?" he said, then grinned savagely at my reaction. "Oh, yes. I know about it. I talked to your friends in the future, Keisha and Melissa, before I—I didn't mean to hurt them, though. I just wanted to make them let me back in the mirror. I got lost and I had to get you before—but I didn't. I can't." His expression turned pleading and he looked from me to the baby. "Don't you see? It's better

275

if I just end this thing. I remember everything now. Almost everything."

He had backed me into the room now, and had his own back to the stairs, as if preparing for a quick escape. Behind and below him, I could see the mirror.

Older Curtis shook the baby again for emphasis. "He's the problem," he said. "This one here. All this year, you've been living in two times at once, one with the baby dead, one with him living. Now I get to choose. Dead baby or mad Curtis."

"That's crazy," I said, and immediately regretted my choice of words. "You're not thinking about it. Both things can't be true. You live. You have to live. If you kill that baby— but you can't. You don't want to. If you wanted to, you would have done it. You're not the bad guy." I pointed at the red-and-purple burden in his hands. "How can you go from being that to killing that?"

"But it hurts," he said to me, his eyes full of tears. "I thought I could stop you, and I couldn't. Nothing stops it and it—hurts."

"Hurts?" said the ten-year-old's voice from behind his future self. "Hurts like when I touched you before? Did that hurt too? Let's try it. Get away from my friend."

And with that, he touched Prince Harming's scarred and bloody hands.

I jumped forward. So did Lilly. Blue fire erupted from the place where the Curtises met. Both screamed. Older Curtis began to topple back, and I swear I saw him in my memory cradling that baby, instinctively bringing it close as he fell into his younger self and sent them both down the stairs in a tumble of sparks and limbs.

I didn't see the baby die.

Lilly and I got to the top of the stairs at the same time and scrambled down together, but what we saw on the floor made me stop in horror while she pushed on. Little Curtis and his older self lay spread out on the floor, their hands close enough to exchange bright flashes. Both were convulsing slightly.

But it wasn't the sight of them that stopped me, and it wasn't either of them that Lilly rushed to.

Rose's baby must have been flung clear of those maimed hands at the apex of his tumble. Maybe the blue fire had done it, making his hands and arms convulse even as he tried to protect the baby.

It had fallen in an odd path. Older Curtis must have grasped for it, sending it tumbling to one side, and now it lay on the low dresser, directly against the mirror, unmoving. Horrifically and impossibly dead.

THREE

Holler loud, holler proud,
you shall wear a coffin shroud.

Lilly touched the baby, even snatched a locket from her neck and held it before the tiny face to see if it was breathing, but when she turned to me and shook her head, she was only confirming what I already knew. "Move them apart, Kenny," she said, pointing to the two Curtises exchanging blue sparks on the floor, then picked up that tiny, sad weight and headed toward the stairs.

Luka groaned and sat up as I grabbed younger Curtis by his shirt and dragged him a safe distance from his older self. Just then, as though sounds were coming back into the world one by one, I heard Rose's wail.

"Let me hold him," she cried. "Why did he do that? Why did you let him? Let me hold my baby."

"I have to go there," I said. "Are you okay?" She nodded and waved me upstairs.

When I got there, Rose was holding her baby. Her mother and Lilly knelt on either side.

I didn't understand it. I had been so sure. So had she. Curtis was her baby. Who was he then? Who was the burned man downstairs, and the boy he once was?

"Why didn't you stop him?" she said, looking from Lilly to me. "That's why you came here wasn't it?"

Lilly opened her mouth, then closed it. What could she say? What could I say? Rose was right. We had come all this way, gotten lost, gotten found, met each other at different times, different ages, solved mysteries—but for what?

"Well," said her mother at long last. "Rose, it's terrible, but ... perhaps this is for the best. Everything happens for a reason. With no father ... and you unmarried ... "

Rose's face twisted and she took a breath as though to speak, but whatever she would have said to her mother was cut off by a convulsion and a cry of pain. Her hands clutched and trembled against the baby she was cradling. When she could speak again, she beat a weak fist against the bed in frustration. "Why can't it be done?" she said. With a worried look, Lilly left Rose's side and went back to the bottom of the bed.

I took that moment to approach Rose. "I—I think Curtis is okay," I said. "I mean—downstairs. My friend Luka is with him. I think he's going to be okay."

Another shudder of pain took her. When it was gone, her mouth was twisted in a grimace. "What does that matter to me? I was wrong about him. He's not mine. Why should I care? All this time I thought he was mine. I thought I had been given this gift of the lonely little boy I wouldn't get to see." She sniffled and looked at the dead baby again. "But that wasn't him. My baby is dead."

She drew a ragged breath and closed her eyes. Lilly, looking more worried than ever, ran her hands over Rose's stomach and asked Mrs. Hollerith to come to her.

"I can't hate him, though," said Rose to me. "He was being brave. I should—I should forgive him. He didn't want to do anything wrong. He's a dear little boy. But—oh, Kenny, why couldn't you stop it? Why couldn't you—" Another convulsion took her words away, and the hand that clutched mine almost drew blood. "It's—it's funny," she said around her gasps and sobs. "Remember I said I was going to call him Clive? I suppose I will after all. Clive after his father." She shut her eyes against the pain. "I suppose I'll never even know where Curtis comes from."

"Don't be too sure about that," said Lilly from the foot of the bed. Her eyes were bright again with new tears. "You're not done yet, girl. Oh, Rose, you're not done. It's twins. That's what your mother tried to tell us. Curtis is a twin."

This time they didn't send me away. Even Mrs. Hollerith was too frantic to object to my presence. My only job was to sit and comfort Rose, who had already endured more than anyone should. It was amazing to me that someone deprived of food for so long could push as hard as they were telling her she must or crush someone's hand as hard as she did mine. Her other hand, curled around the dead baby that I was already thinking of as Clive, petted him with feathery caresses.

Less than five minutes after his brother's death, Curtis

Hollerith made his first appearance in the world, yelling and screaming the way his brother never did.

Not long after the second baby was born, Mrs. Hollerith remembered my existence and sent me downstairs. Luka had managed to heft little Curtis onto the couch and was staring glumly into the mirror. The boy's breathing was regular, and his hands showed no damage from the blue fire. Lying there, he could be any ten-year-old kid. I wondered how much of this night he would remember. Enough that it would trouble him later, I was sure. Half-remembered images that would bring him and Peggy back to look for me, that would bring her to her death.

"I thought we could save him," Luka said.

Something strange was happening upstairs. I could hear coos and sighs from Lilly and Mrs. Hollerith, and from Rose sobs that were turning from despair to joy. "We did in a way. If I hadn't gotten Lilly back here, I don't even think baby Curtis would have lived."

Luka groaned. "Time travel gives me a headache." I suddenly realized that older Curtis wasn't there. "Out the door," said Luka, reading my expression. "He got up a couple of minutes ago. I was ready to take him on again, but he backed off. Said nothing matters because as soon as it all gets fixed, he won't exist anymore."

"Did you tell him—" I nodded my head upstairs.

"No. What if he tried again?"

"So where is he now?"

She shrugged. "I watched him run to the woods. I wasn't about to follow."

I looked toward the door. It was a cool night in 1917. I tried to imagine the pain of running in those woods with bare, burned feet.

"Come on," I said.

"Kenny, no," Luka said. "Are you crazy? Look, I came here to bring you home. Your family is waiting for you."

I stood for a long moment in tortured indecision, looking between the girl I had been pining for all this time and the door out into the dark, where this man was, this man who was the boy sleeping there on the couch and who was also the baby upstairs. I thought of the tiny hands I had seen for just a moment at his birth, dark and bloody in the lantern light, each tiny finger a perfect new miracle. Just a few hours ago, I had seen those hands, so much older, shoved into fire and crippled forever.

"Just down to the creek," I said. "He'll be there. He'll be in his cave."

Reluctantly, Luka went with me. I called up to Lilly that we were going out for a breath of fresh air, but I didn't even know if she heard. Luka had come with a backpack stuffed with supplies, and we lit our way with modern flashlights. We followed a few bloody footprints at first, and Luka spotted a handprint on the bark of a silver birch, but soon we lost his trail, and by the time we reached the creek, he could have been anywhere.

Ready to run at a moment's notice, I shone my flashlight beam inside the narrow, hand-dug cave, but the man I had destroyed was nowhere to be seen. He had been there, though; on the ground outside the cave was the strings-and-spoon key he had stolen from me. I picked it up.

Luka and I made a tiny island of light in a deep, star-filled, creek-babbling, chirping, and tweeting night. A mosquito bit me.

Luka put a hand on my shoulder. "You'll never find him. Not if he doesn't want to be found. You have to let this go, Kenny. Your mom and dad are waiting for you. You did it. You came back for Rose. She's got her baby."

I sighed. "Okay. Let's go back."

She held up her hand. "Actually. A couple of things first." She made me hold her flashlight while she took out a pocketknife. "What?" she said at my expression. "You thought I was going to forget to carve my initials? This is fifty-four years before I was born. You better believe I'm giving them something to remember me by."

She disappeared into the cave for a moment, and when she emerged, she took a small and familiar wooden box out of her backpack. "Now for this," she said.

I reached out to touch it lightly. "That's got my grandmother's letter inside?" She nodded. "You ever wonder what would happen if you didn't bury it? What if you just threw it in the creek?"

Luka rolled her eyes. "We know it ends up there. Come on. Your dad gave me these collapsible shovels."

"You've been hanging out with my dad?" I asked as we waded across the creek.

"A lot. And your mom. They're pretty cool. Your grand-mother, too. They miss you. I told them I'd bring you." She sighed. "That'll end it. Won't it?"

"Yeah. They're not letting me into that thing again. Sorry." We reached the far bank and headed up to the thicket of trees.

"What are you sorry for? I'm the one who abandoned you. I let him force me into the mirror, Kenny. I couldn't stop him from throwing it in the lake. I went uptime to save Rick and Jimmy from him, but he had a gun and he forced me back in, up to your time. I stood in the Silverlands and watched as he ran to the lake and threw it in."

Here was a point I had been confused on when Rick first explained it to me. "Why did he do that? Why did he make you go back uptime?"

"Said he didn't want to kill me. He just wanted to trap you. He wanted to make sure you couldn't get into the mirror again. It was—I don't know—confusing. He had just shot you, and that seemed to take some of the crazy away. I don't think he knew what time he was in anymore."

I nodded. "That makes sense. It's kind of the same as now. When he thinks he's changed things, all he has to do is sit around and wait for the world to change around him. It must have been a couple of weeks before he realized he had trapped me in 1957, the exact time he was trying to keep me from. That must have been when he stole the wetsuit and started trying to find the mirror again."

"Who cares about that?" said Luka, her voice a knife-edge of regret. "I let you down. I should have stayed with you. I stood in the Silverlands and saw the mirror fly over the bluffs and crash into the lake."

I tried to imagine the kind of worry and guilt that must have been eating at her all these weeks.

"You did what you had to do. Everything worked out. That's just the way it all happens. What matters is you always wanted to do right." We found the thicket of trees, and as we passed between two dark shapes, we temporarily brushed each other's arms. Emboldened by the darkness, and maybe by the deeper darkness of everything I had just gone through, I did the scariest thing I had done all year: I put my hand on Luka's shoulder. "What matters is you were the captain of your soul. Always."

She stopped. I stopped with her. What was I supposed to do next? Kiss her? Drop my flashlight and grab her with my other hand? What if I lost my flashlight?

The moment passed. Luka let out a long breath. "Come on," she said. "It's over here."

I let my hand drop and followed her to the correct tree. "Anyway," I said, deflated, "I'm sorry you had such a boring time the last couple of months. This was supposed to be our year."

Luka pointed her flashlight at her own face so I could see her raised eyebrow. "Boring? Are you kidding? I got to save a drowning kid in 2017. Twenty years further up, I watched the second mission land on Mars. I found the evidence that got my daughter out of a murder charge. This was the best summer of my life." She grinned at my open-mouthed expression.

"What, did you think I'd just sit on my hands and wait for you?"

I smiled back and shook my head. "I really did miss you."

"Come on, H. G. Wells. Get digging."

A few minutes later, as we walked back into the carriage house, Luka halfway through the story of her adventures in the future, Francine Hollerith came down the stairs, carrying the tiny burden of her dead grandchild. Until that moment, I hadn't thought of it that way. Her grandchild.

"Give me something," she said to me in a quiet voice.

"What?"

"Are you stupid? For the baby. It should be wrapped. I had a swaddling cloth prepared, but that's for the other one."

My backpack was right beside me. The first things I brought out of it were the newspaper from 1947, the one with the story about Peggy going missing, dated September 2, and an old T-shirt I had been wearing on and off for the past two months. I froze in the act of handing it to her.

My Speedy Gonzales T-shirt. That I had been wearing all those months ago when we found the baby and I felt that electric charge that came when an object was in danger of meeting itself.

She wrapped the baby in the T-shirt first, then the newspaper, three, four, five sheets crumpled tightly around it. I opened my mouth to object, but a cold, furious stare from her shut me up.

Luka and I sat transfixed as she walked back upstairs.

"What are you doing, Mother?" came Rose's weak voice a few moments later.

"Just putting clothes away. You're coming back to the house when we can move you."

Liar, I wanted to shout. Liar. She was hiding him. Putting him in the wall. And as sure as I knew that, I was certain that Rose herself would put something in that same small space before her mother got a chance to seal it up. Her list, but now with a message written on it, desperately, wildly, against all sense. A plea for me to come back and make it better. And sometime soon, in another wild fit of desperation, probably forbidden by her mother from ever talking about us, she would take the drawer out of her dresser and scratch a message on it for Luka. *Luka, help Kenny. Trust John Wald. Kenny says he is the* auby *one. Save the baby.*

And we would fail.

"You have a baby to care for now," Mrs. Hollerith was saying. "No more of your secret visitors. We'll pack them off and that will be that." She raised her voice. "Do you hear that, down there? I'll have no more of you. Once you're gone, we're happy to see the end of you."

Lillian, her shoulders sloped and weary, descended the stairs. We sat her down and gave her a quick recap of Prince Harming's disappearance and our foray into the night.

"Francine says there's a discreet doctor she can send for," she told us, barely reacting to what we had said. "She says he'll make the certificate out as she tells him. It'll make life easier for Curtis, not being called Rose's bastard. People can be horribly cruel in this time."

Rose soon fell asleep, and Mrs. Hollerith didn't want us upstairs, so we didn't get any kind of last goodbye, not to her, nor to ten-year-old Curtis, who Lilly pronounced to be suffering from shock. Luka and I picked him up and carried him through the Silverlands to his own time.

Mrs. Hollerith, ten years older and not one day more pleasant, sat waiting for us on her dead daughter's bed. "What have you done to him?" she said, standing up. I wondered how long she had been waiting. Her eyes narrowed as we brought him forward and laid him next to her. "I told you ten years ago it was to be the last I saw of you."

"Shut up," said Lilly. "I've had about enough of you. The boy's in shock. Bundle him up and elevate his legs. Keep an eye on him for a few hours and he'll be fine. I suspect he won't remember much. Maybe that's for the best." She eyed Mrs. Hollerith a moment longer, then turned to Luka and me. "Let's go."

"That's it?" said Mrs. Hollerith. "You breeze into my house once every ten years upsetting everything, carrying madmen and unconscious children, and expect me to accept it? I'm going to throw that mirror into the ravine."

"No you won't," I said.

She fixed me with a glare. "Oh, and you're going to tell me what to do?"

"No." I returned her stare as calmly as I could. "I'm just telling you how it happens. In a couple of years you're going to sell this place—to the Huffs—and you'll leave this dresser here when you do. That's how Lillian here gets to know Curtis in the first place, and that's how we come back to save Rose and Curtis. You'll do it because that's the way it happens."

We left her with her mouth hanging open.

When we stepped out of the Silverlands into 1937, Lilly's bedroom was empty again. She told us that she and her family were probably off looking for somewhere to stay in the city.

Our next stop was the carriage house in 1947. "This is where I get off, I suppose," said Lilly.

"You've got a husband and baby waiting for you, right?" said Luka.

"I do. I suppose Kenny told you. I can't imagine what he thinks of all this, my husband I mean. The little one's only two. Can't expect him to have any opinions, can we, Luka?"

In the early morning light, I saw Luka do something I don't think I'd ever witnessed before. She blushed. "Actually," she said, "my real name's Lucy. I just—made up that other name."

"Oh."

"Don't worry about the opinion thing, though," she said. "He'll have a lot of them pretty soon. John, right?"

"Why, yes. How did you know?"

Luka seemed to come to some kind of decision, and she darted forward to give Lilly a quick peck on the cheek. "We better go now. Into the mirror, Kenny. Thanks for everything, Grandma. It all works out in the end."

And just like that, leaving Lilly wide-eyed and open-mouthed, Luka dragged me back into the uptime heat of the mirror and through to the Maxwells' coal cellar. I guess I must have looked pretty shocked as well. "Have you—?"

"Known all along? Nah. A lot happened this summer, Kenny. I moved back in with my dad. First time I've really been with him much in years. A couple of days ago my

grandma sat me down and told me how she saved a pregnant girl's life once. With the help of a cute boy."

I looked back at the mirror. "Lilly said I was cute?"

Luka rolled her eyes. "Well, she's old, now. You know
how the memory goes. Come on, Romeo, I promised your
parents I'd get you home."

FOUR

Hear the wisdom in the walls.

When we got to 1967, John Wald was already awake and making breakfast for Rick from a huge pike he had caught in the lake with a pointed stick. We ate quickly. Luka said she had to get back before her father woke up since he was a little more on the ball than her mom.

Rick hugged us all goodbye, and for the first time in two months, I headed back home to find my mother sleeping in front of the mirror.

There was a lot of crying and hugging. Mom called for Dad and my grandmother, and they came right away.

When everyone calmed down, we reached into the mirror for John Wald. He apologized to my parents for not bringing me home sooner, and that won my mom over. She said he looked like he hadn't eaten a good meal in more than a hundred years, at which he frowned and said it was probably more like sixty.

Luka had to go but promised she'd come back. Wald said he wanted to go with her, but with him it would be my last goodbye.

He stood at the mirror with Luka and turned to face me. "Fare thee well, Kennit," he said. "A twisty path thou didst thread in the glass, and did what good thou couldst. You learned to float above. Stay thee here, now. Cross not the glass again."

He gave me a final embrace and Luka took him uptime.

My parents tried their best to get me to talk and be normal. My grandmother told what should have been the very amusing story of her back-and-forth questioning of her sanity in the months and years following our encounter. She said she had written down everything I said to her, but never showed it to anyone, and kept telling the hobo boy story so she wouldn't forget. My father then told the story of Grandma coming over just as they were growing frantic about my disappearance and considering calling the police. "I almost sent her to a home that very day," he said, giving her a side-armed hug.

Eventually, sensing my need to be alone, my mother pronounced a quiet time.

My attic bedroom was, predictably, much neater than I had left it, since sometimes cleaning is the only thing that can take my mother's mind away from worries. I lay in my bed and looked at the sea of old furniture, a lot of which I had now seen when it was much newer.

I began to cry.

Sixty years into the past a baby had been torn from his mother's grasp by his own brother, then fallen in an arc like a bloody football and ended his life against a mirror that would not let him inside.

And now I was home. Really home. I had been in this house countless times in the past weeks, but I hadn't been home.

Sleep, when I cried myself into it, lasted until noon the next day, and if there were any dreams, I don't remember them.

My only highlights in the bewildering first days of school, when I suddenly had to be a normal kid again, were visits from Luka. Those required a lot of negotiation. Conceding that the mirror was indestructible, and even that we had done some good inside it, my mother still had my dad put a lock on the closet in their bedroom, and agreed to give Luka a key provided that she respected their rules: she could visit if she asked in advance, and I was never to be allowed in the mirror.

I wanted to object, but my dad sat me down and explained in excruciating detail just how much pain my two-month absence had caused. Since they had discovered the truth of the mirror, either my mom, my dad, or my grandmother had sat watch every minute of every day waiting for my return.

So I contented myself with living vicariously through Luka. Using they key she had made, she started spending a lot of time in the past. The mirror was unguarded all the way to 1947, so as long as Luka's dad wasn't watching her too closely, she could risk trips well into the past. Sometimes she'd even go further and bring back news, some bad, some good.

Young Curtis remembered nothing of the night he was

born. Even his memories of the mirror were muddled. In early October, he made his first friend his own age, a girl from two doors down, and tried to take her into the mirror. When she couldn't pass in, he grew angry and smashed her head repeatedly into its unbreakable surface. She never recovered completely.

Rose did better than anyone might have expected. By the time Luka actually met her, Curtis was six weeks old and Rose was devoted to him. She never talked of the other baby.

Of the older Curtis who had run out into the night, she could find out nothing, though there were stories of a wild man living in the woods, stealing chickens, sleeping in barns. Even fearless Luka didn't stray far on the rare nights when she went as far back as 1917.

For almost four months I kept to my parents' new rules, and I guess it would have stayed that way if it hadn't been for you and the fact that there's always one more rule.

FIVE

Running down the silver street.

My mother had never been crazy about keeping the mirror in the house, but I think she comforted herself with the fact that I was under pretty constant supervision. Grandma moved in with us following the madness of that summer. My dad fixed up the library for her. Between the three adults, I hardly had a moment alone in the house.

So when Mom got an invitation to her office Christmas party on the same weekend Grandma was going to visit a sick friend, she didn't like it one bit, but somehow my dad convinced her they should go. Two days before Christmas, a week and a half before my year was to end, I found myself alone at night for the first time in months.

I tried to be good. I sat in my room and got an early start on my Christmas vacation homework, willing myself to ignore the time-travel mirror downstairs. A couple of times I thought I might have heard Luka passing through one way or the other, but she had been given a stern lecture by my dad about just exactly how forbidden it was for her to stop over here tonight, and I had heard her make a solemn promise, so I knew there was no chance of company.

After failing for a good half hour to figure out any of my math problems, I gave up and headed downstairs for some cookies and milk. I stayed down in the kitchen to eat, enjoying that room's better lighting and the comforting sound of the fridge running. When my mother called to check on me, I just about crushed my milk glass in my hand I was so on edge. I assured her that everything was fine. No, Luka hadn't come through. No, I hadn't gone near their closet. Yes, I knew the number and would call if there were any problems.

I washed my glass and cleaned up my crumbs. Nothing to do but clump back up the stairs.

I guess that's when you heard me.

Just as I walked past my parents' bedroom, I heard a knock and a muffled "Hello?"

I froze. I didn't know that voice. Another knock. Another "Hello?" but this time a little louder. "Listen, I need some help here. I need the diary. The one with stuff from Curtis and Rose."

I put my hand on the handle of my parents' door, then jumped as the guy spoke up again.

"It's not even me that needs it. It's Luka. She needs help with Prince Harming."

That did it. I opened the door and walked to the closet. "Who are you?"

"Oh, man, thank you. Are you Kenny? I'm Connor. From 2017."

"What are you doing here?"

"Look, can you open the door?"

"It's locked."

"I know that, D—Kenny. Luka sent me to get the diary."

I looked at the closet door. Hinges on the outside. "Give me a few minutes," I said, and headed down to the basement for a hammer and an awl.

While I took the door off its hinges, I thought I should find out from "Connor from 2017" exactly what was going on and what kind of help Luka needed, but he kept me so busy with questions of his own that I never got to ask mine. How many channels did we have on TV? Had I ever touched a computer? How many phones did we have in the house? Had I ever heard of solar power?

Peevishly, I fired back, "What about you? Do you have a base on the moon?"

"No point. I went uptime with Luka, though, and we saw the Mars landing. That'll be cool."

So that was who she had been with. I guessed maybe this was Luka's new future boy, probably her boyfriend. My feelings of inferiority were even more magnified when I got the closet door off. He was probably two years older than me, about three inches taller, and possessed a frame that was both gangly and muscular. Behind him was the mirror, removed from its dresser again and leaning against my dad's work uniforms. It was the first time I had seen it in weeks. As wrong as it was, I was itching for the slow molasses of the

Silverlands. Uptime heat or downtime cold, it didn't matter. I wanted to be uncomfortable again.

"Aw, jeez, thanks," the newcomer said. "I was sweating like a sonofa—" He checked himself, looked sheepish, and continued. "I was sweating bad. Look, I'm sorry about this. Luka told me to leave you out of everything because she didn't want you getting in trouble. But—" He stopped himself and looked at a large-faced digital wristwatch with four or five buttons around its edge. "Man, she's been alone out there for more than an hour. Look, will you come back with me?"

"Fine," I said. "But this better not take long."

"You should bundle up," said the new kid. "We're going outside."

When I got my strings-and-spoon key out of my coat pocket, Connor gave a low whistle. "Wow. The classic."

"Pardon?"

"Nah, it's just—I've heard about it, that's all. That was the first key."

I shrugged the comment aside. "Let's get going."

The cold was as bone-chilling as it ever had been, worse because of how wide the Silverlands had become. When I was going in every day, I had hardly noticed the change, but now it must have been fifteen feet from one mirror to the next. We didn't see a single person on our journey back.

In 1917, the dresser was back on the second floor of the carriage house. Even in the dark, I noticed the finished wall right away. I guessed Mrs. Hollerith had put that up as quickly as she could.

Enough of our journey had been either painful or necessarily silent that the new kid and I had barely talked. Now I wanted answers. "So where's Luka?" I said as we stamped our feet and beat our arms for warmth.

Connor turned on a flashlight and aimed it downstairs. "Like I said, we have to go outside. I don't know how much I should tell you. She'll be pretty mad that I brought you, especially if she ends up getting shut out of your mirror for the last week of the year. I hate it when she's mad at me."

I held up the diary but didn't give it to him. "You said she's in trouble. Which way?"

Connor grinned. "The hiding hole."

He led me out of the carriage house and into the snow-covered winter-bare wood at the back of the property, and on the walk he gave me a scattered account of what had led him to this point. His other adventures in the glass had been all over the place, mostly in the future, but this one had drawn him far into the past. "It started a few years ago, I guess, but I didn't realize what it all meant until last week. When I was nine years old, Dana took me to a retirement home."

"Dana?"

He looked at me as though I were slow. "My older sister. I didn't know why she wanted me to go there at first. All my grandparents still lived in their own houses, but she said it wasn't them. It was someone way older, my great-grandmother. I hadn't seen her much at all in my life. She had been in that place since before I was born. At first, she didn't even seem to remember me, but then when my sister introduced me to her, last name and everything, she grins really wide and asks me how old I'll be in 2017. I tell her I'll turn seventeen. Grin gets wider. 'Well, you'll be the one, then,' she says. She looks at Dana and says, 'Don't feel bad it isn't you, dear. It's a lot of trouble in there.'

"I was just going to put it down to, old people are weird. Then she stares right at me. You know, one of those laser-beam stares? And she says, 'Connor, I have a message for you to carry, but I'm old and I can't remember which one of them it's for. I can't remember which one does it. Maybe it's you. Here's the message. Remember it as well as you can. He can still save her. He'll just have to get there before her and wait. Curtis can still save Peggy.'"

I felt like I was wearing my Speedy Gonzales T-shirt. "She said Curtis and Peggy?"

"Yeah. Didn't mean a thing to me. I asked Dana about it, and all she would say is that I'd understand it someday. Then last week, Eric—that's my older brother—he gives me this pile of old journals. I mean, really old, like forty years. They had been caught in a fire we had a while ago, and there was a lot of stuff I couldn't make out, but I could definitely see those two names. That got me remembering that visit to the retirement home. I asked Dana about it, and she says it was just something that—something my dad asked her to do."

"So you asked Luka about it."

"So I asked Luka about it. She got crazy excited."

"And?"

"And . . . " He found the spot he was looking for, slid down the creek bank, and gestured for me to come along. "That led us to this mess."

I slid down and followed his pointing finger with my gaze. We were back at Clive Beckett's tiny hand-dug cave, and outside of it, sitting on an upturned crate, was the most ruined and lost Prince Harming I had seen yet.

Four months had not been kind. His cheeks were sunken and his arms, under layers of rags, were twig-thin. "Don't look," he said to me, and his eyes still burned with a manic fire. "Don't look at me. No one looks at me. If no one looks at you, you don't exist. Brother killer. Shouldn't exist. Wiped away. Shouldn't exist. Nobody look."

He didn't seem like much of a danger anymore. "Curtis, you didn't mean to—"

He stood up and screamed, causing us both to step back. "Don't use the name! Doesn't deserve it. Killed a brother. A baby." After a moment of standing there twitching, he sat back down again. "A little baby. Stood outside the door and heard them talking about it. A little baby. Clive. The better one. Named after the father. So just the bad one lived. Killed a baby."

Behind him, someone unfolded from the tiny entrance to the cave. "No, you didn't," said Luka. "I've been trying to tell you that. Hi, Kenny. Sorry I got you into all this again, but maybe you can help me talk some sense into him. I've been trying, but he won't listen. We need the diary. The shatterdate book. Did you bring it?"

I took it out of my pocket. When he saw it, Curtis cocked his head to one side. "I did that," he said. "Long ago."

"I know," said Luka. "You were trying to make sense

of it, weren't you? When you were ten. Did you steal your mother's diary to do it?"

He nodded, his eyes still fixed on the beaten-up old book. "Wanted to know what—couldn't remember. After hurting the little girl. Whose boy? Kept—waking up from the nightmare where—killed the little boy that was—was me—and then no more me. Used the mirror to visit Rose, she told that it was all a bad dream. She showed me the little boy that was me. She said everything was all right now. But—didn't believe her. Thought she was lying. Bad man was going to come and get me."

Luka stepped out from behind Curtis and took the book from Connor's outstretched hand. "You started trying to find out about the bad man, didn't you? You wrote down the little skipping rhymes."

His eyes stayed on the book as he mumbled out the version of the rhyme I had always found hardest to understand. "Treacle sweet, bloody feet, loudly yelling down the street. Holler loud, holler proud, you shall wear a coffin shroud." He bit his lip for a moment, remembering, then said the next one. "Trick your feet down the street, then the years will vanish fleet. Head will hurt, death's a cert, a dead man's sentence should be curt. Let me pass, leave the lass, don't go down the backward glass."

When he said the bit about leaving the lass, his voice trembled and his eyes filled up with tears.

"That one's about you, isn't it?" said Luka. "'A dead man's sentence should be curt.' You're Curt. And the other one. Holler loud. As in Hollerith."

"But how?" I said. "How is that old skipping rhyme about him? It goes back further than this."

Luka shrugged. "Rose, probably. She only saw the kid from 1907 a few times, but all it would take was once, right? She teaches the kid the rhyme, that kid teaches other people..."

"Oh, wow," I said. "Then someone else teaches it to Rose when she's little."

"The point is," said Luka to Curtis, "you wrote that one. Didn't you? A dead man's sentence should be curt. You're saying you should be dead."

"Killed the brother," he said. "Led the—the girl. Loved her. Married. Then—then gone. Drowned and gone. Let me pass. Leave the lass. Don't go down the backward glass."

Luka handed the book to me. "You remember Kenny, right? Kenny was your friend."

Curtis nodded. "Wanted to kill you, but wasn't your fault. Saw you. You tried to save her."

"So if Kenny was your friend, you should listen to him." She looked at me. "I tried to convince him, but he won't listen. October 27. Tell him what it says. Rose's side."

I flipped through the book to a page near the end that I had puzzled out just a month before.

At first, I thought I could never forgive him. Ten-year-old Curtis, that is. But it wasn't his fault. He was trying to be good. I tried to forget about it. I tried to content myself in the baby I did have, my

Curtis. As exhausted as I am in the nights, I some-times try to stay awake just to watch him sleep. I think it is the only time I ever see him still.

I wonder what the other one would have been like. I am not supposed to. Mother says I must forget the other. Sometimes she tells me there was only one, but I know better.

I think he would have been the opposite to his brother. Probably as sweet and silent as Curtis is loud and boisterous. Mother says you cannot tell a baby from just those few minutes I had with him, but I could tell something. I never even heard him cry, and he did not struggle or kick the way Curtis did.

I knew that entry and had read it many times. It gave me some comfort. I couldn't see Rose again, but at least I got to know how much in love with her baby she was.

It wasn't easy for me to read the last few sentences above Curtis's sobs. "No!" he said. "That one should have lived. The good brother."

"You don't get it, do you?" said Luka, and I could see she was talking both to me and to Curtis. "Think about it. 'I never heard him cry.' She basically said he didn't move."

Curtis nodded. "Didn't move. Little, still, good brother." He looked at me, his eyes pleading for understanding. "Didn't want to kill the brother."

"You didn't," said Luka.

"Wait," I said, "are you saying—"

"Yes. My grandmother told me. Lilly. I went to see her,

Kenny, and we talked about this. She said she never figured it out at the time. Not until years later. She wasn't trained in delivering babies. If she was, she would have known."

"Known what?" The question came from Curtis, who stood now and looked at Luka. "What?" He held his hands out, and for the first time I saw how horribly they had healed. His fingers were thick masses of scar tissue, the palms cracked. "Known what?"

"Oh, sure," said Luka. "You'll talk to him about it. What I've been telling you for the past two hours, that's what."

"That you didn't kill him," I said. "You didn't kill him because your brother was already dead. He wasn't still, Curtis. He was stillborn." And before he could say anything else, I turned to Luka. "But that's not all, is it? You didn't just come to tell him that. You've figured out how to save Peggy, haven't you?"

SIX

Let me pass. Save the lass.

We all stood still for a long moment after I said it, Curtis moving his lips silently over the words.

"Stillborn?" he said at last. "The brother? Didn't get killed?"

"No," I said. "Didn't get killed. Curtis, I think that's right. It didn't move, did it? I mean he. He didn't move. Sometimes a baby is born that way. It's nobody's fault."

"Didn't get killed." Then he shook his head. "But died."

"I know," I said. "And that was sad. Really sad. But not anybody's fault. All you were trying to do was save your Peggy."

He wiped tears away from his cheeks with his ruined hands. "Didn't kill it. And the Rose mother sad, but said no, not your fault. A bad man did it. But who was the bad man?" He looked at the diary still in my hands. "Tried to find out. And down and down the backward glass. Tried to be strong.

A soldier. Met the nurse. And fell in love, Kenny. But the nightmares. A bad man killed a baby. Kenny's our friend. He knows. He'll find the bad man. He'll know. Who's the bad man?"

"Nobody," I said. "Nobody's the bad man, Curtis. Curtis is a good man." I looked at Luka. "How does this fit together? How did this Dana, Connor's sister, how did she know to take him to his great-grandmother?"

Luka shrugged and looked away. There was something she was hiding from me. "Kenny, that was Lilly. She's old when Connor meets her. It took me a bit to work out what she meant. But you've got it, haven't you?"

"Yeah. Get there before her." I stepped forward, and though Curtis shied away, I put my hand on his shoulder. "Lilly sent us with a message for you. You can save Peggy. But you'll have to go the long path."

I don't know how, but with the help of Connor and Luka I managed to convince him. Less than an hour after I left my home time, the four of us stood in the Silverlands between 1957 and 1967 and prepared to say goodbye to Curtis for the last time.

When we took him at first to the mirror, far past our own, where Peggy had been lost, I thought we might need to restrain him again the way John Wald and I had done four months ago, but he slumped at the sight of its swimming image-fragments. "Lost her," he said. "Brought her and lost her." His sunken eyes were wide with the need to confess as he looked at me. "Think how that feels. Brought her here.

Because of the nightmares. About the baby. Then lost her. And blamed you."

"But maybe you didn't lose her," I said. I put a hand on his shoulder and turned him around to face the 1957 end of the same mirror. "This is ten years before." Just as it had been back in September, the mirror was on a beach. I wondered how it got there, what crazy series of events had brought it to this sandy beach lit by a noon-day sun. It must be, I realized, some other place in the world, someplace warm in another time zone.

"To save her?" said Curtis. "And how? Going through here—no way back."

"Look at it," I said. "That mirror is on the beach, out of the water. That's in 1957. But in 1967 it's in the water. So go through to 1957 and—and then you have to wait. Wait until September 1967."

Curtis grinned, almost cackled. "And not let it go in. Not let it go in the water."

"No," said Luka, her patience wearing thin. It was the third time we had explained it. "No. We know it goes in the water. We can see it's still in there. You've got to go with the way things are, but just—make them better than we thought they were."

"Not...to change?"

"Not exactly," I said. "That's not the way to do it with the mirrors. If you try to make sure it doesn't go in the water, we know it will anyway, so maybe that means you'll lose the mirror or not be there or something. There's a way to—float above the events we know are going to happen. Think. You can wait with the mirror for ten years and guard it. Then the day before—before I push her through—then you put it in the water." Curtis recoiled, but I continued quickly before he could object. "A little water. A few feet deep. And you wait for her. You know the date. One day before your birthday. About six o'clock our time. Just wait. Have a life jacket there."

Luka interrupted. "A doctor, even. You could have anything. If you do this, you've got ten years to get a whole team together. Everything you do can be to save her. Look at the 1967 mirror. As long as you try to make it look just like that, dark and in the water—there's no reason this shouldn't work."

"And save her?" said Curtis, his eyes wide and wondering.

"And save her," I said. "And live again. And be Curtis. Because you didn't kill anyone, and if you do it right, you can save her. Nobody has to be sad. Nobody has to lose anyone."

Curtis turned to the cloud of images that showed the sun-lit beach. "I have to go now, don't I?"

And without another word, he did. Just turned and pushed his way out of the mirror, a rag-covered, scarred, and ruined man, stepping onto a beach in an unknown part of the world. When he was out, he turned back as though to say something to us, but his face fell when he saw only himself. Something must have caught his attention, because he turned his head and his face broke into a broad smile. He raised his scar-covered hand to wave and stepped out of the range of the mirror.

We watched for a while, but he didn't come back. All we could see were sun-sparkled waves lapping the shore.

"Hard to go back to winter after that," said Connor.

"We'd better, though," said Luka. "Come on, Kenny. I don't want you in too much trouble."

I grinned and shook my head. "Sure you don't."

We returned to our own mirror and slipped into Granny Miller's junk house, then back home.

"Go upstairs and pretend to be asleep," said Luka. "Then if you've missed a phone call, that's your excuse."

"I don't think so," I said. "I think I better just come clean."

"When there's a perfectly good lie to tell?"

"I lied a lot to them already. There's something—I don't know—something Rick said about the mirror. I might not be the master of my fate—"

"But I can still be the captain of my soul," Connor finished. He shrugged when I looked at him inquiringly. "My dad used to say it all the time."

I turned back to Luka. "Maybe they'll understand. We did good tonight."

"Did we?" said Connor. "Think about how weird it's going to be for them. He's, what, forty now? He'll wait ten years. When she comes out of that mirror and he rescues her, what does she see? Her husband's aged twenty years, gotten all burned up, gone crazy."

I shrugged. "They fell in love once when they were just a couple of years apart. Maybe that still counts. Maybe he'll straighten out in the ten years he's waiting."

Connor and Luka stuck around for a few minutes more and helped me rehang the closet door. It slipped a little at one point and bumped my nose, which hurt like hell. Connor held the door away with one hand and, in an oddly tender gesture, reached out with his other to move away my own hand covering my nose. "It got broken," he said. "Didn't set right. You should get that taken care of." He slipped a bolt into the hinge. "Seriously. It causes this thing called a deviated septum. Makes you snore a lot when you get older."

"When I get older?" I said. "Who are you?"

Suddenly there was a kind of electricity in the air, like when an object met itself. Connor rubbed his messy curls and stepped back toward the closet. "Time travel's funny, isn't it? You got to do a lot of stuff this year. You even found out what your dad once wanted to be. What his dreams were."

I hadn't told anybody about that, not even Luka. "Who are you?"

"He would have been good, too. As an architect. When I was twelve, we built a tree house in the backyard. And not just some crappy platform with a roof. It had two different ladders, three levels, and five rooms. We even tried making an elevator with a bag full of rocks as a counterweight."

We all jumped when we heard the door open downstairs and my mother announce that they were home.

"We should go," hissed Luka.

"Who are you?" I said.

Connor looked toward the bedroom door as though he wanted nothing more than to go down there and meet them. Luka must have read his expression, because she grabbed his shoulders and turned him to face her. "No," she whispered. "It didn't happen, so it won't happen."

His shoulders slumped and he gave a defeated smile. "Okay."

From downstairs, my mother called again. I called back that I'd be right down, but I didn't take my eyes off Connor. Off you. "Are you my...?" I said at last.

"Don't say it," said Luka. "This wasn't supposed to happen."

Your gaze flicked to her. "Hey, I didn't tell him," you said with a grin. "I can't stop him figuring things out. I'm not used to him when he isn't old and slow." You straightened up and held out your hand. "Connor Maxwell," you said. "Born in 2000. Seventeen years old."

"Kenny?" my mom called. "Who's up there?"

"It was great to meet you," you said. "I wish we could have had more time. Get that nose fixed, will you?"

You pulled me into a quick hug, then broke it off, held my shoulders for a second, and backed into the mirror. Luka promised to come back again and followed.

Moments after she disappeared into the mirror, my mother came into the room.

"Oh, Kenny, you didn't," she said.

I tried my best to meet her eyes. "I did."

"What could have made you do that again?"

I scratched my head. "I think it was my son."

SEVEN

You'll go down the backward glass.

My parents were angry, but they still let me have a proper goodbye, and I'll bet you know what happened. New Year's Eve, our last day in the glass forever. My dad moved the mirror to the living room, because it wasn't just my goodbye. Grandma and my parents had come to love Luka during the summer of my disappearance, so they all wanted to say their tearful farewells. Grandma said she hoped she'd get to see Luka again, and Luka said not to be silly, of course she would.

My mom gave her a few last-minute presents—some fresh-baked cookies and a handful of family photographs.

After a long hug, they all found excuses to leave the room, so Luka and I had a few minutes alone, though Mom stayed in the kitchen, clattering dishes to both tell us where she was and cover the sounds of our conversation.

"I can't believe this is over," I said.

"It's never over, though, is it?" said Luka.

"How do you mean?"

She reached behind her and touched the mirror lightly. "It wasn't over for Curtis when his year ended. It wasn't over for Lilly or Peggy. It's not like the story of your life is over."

"But ours is," I said. "Yours and mine together. If I go see you now, you'll be a little kid. We had a good time, though, didn't we?"

"The best."

"I wish you could stay."

"I wish you could come."

"Would you just kiss her already?" shouted Grandma from upstairs.

I wanted to. But Luka was almost two years older than me. And she was beautiful. Was that the first time I was thinking this? Maybe it was. And she was my friend.

"Funny about that Connor guy, though," I said, trying to change the subject.

"What was?"

"Him as my kid. He didn't exactly say that, did he? I mean, I know you always say the mirror kids are all connected, but I don't know."

"Why not?"

I shrugged. "The names. His name was Connor. He said his sister and brother were Dana and Eric. I just don't know if I'd ever pick those names, that's all."

Luka got a huge grin on her face and came to a decision. She stepped forward, grabbed my shoulders, and kissed me square on the mouth.

It was awkward, and it wasn't a long kiss like you see in

the movies, and maybe that's all I'm going to tell you about it, because maybe it's none of your business.

It was good, though.

When she let me go, she stepped back and pushed part-way into the mirror. "Maybe you wouldn't," she said, and then paused for effect the way she loved to do. "But I would. Bye, Kenny. Come and find me. It was the best year of my life."

And she was gone.

You know, after all that happened, I still don't really know much about the future. And I guess that's okay by me.

I'm glad I met you. And your mother.

ACKNOWLEDGMENTS

Though I have already dedicated this book to her, I would be remiss in not beginning by thanking my wife, my first and best reader. Others who have been very influential in the development of *Backward Glass* are my agent, the absolutely incredible Katie Grimm, and my editor at Flux, the absolutely merciless Brian Farrey-Latz. Their insight, wisdom, and good sense have been of immeasurable help. My copy editor, Rhiannon Nelson, was instrumental in both rescuing me from a few embarrassing mistakes and giving some very clever last-minute suggestions. I also want to thank my parents, Ed and Margaret Lomax, whose reading to me in my formative years shaped my whole world; Regan Devine, my tenth-grade creative writing teacher, for instilling in me the sense that writing is rewriting; and Lister Mathieson and the whole crew (students and teachers) of the Clarion 98 workshop, who pushed me ahead on a particularly long path. Finally, my kids were a great inspiration; I wanted to write a fun adventure for them. I even hid their names inside.

ABOUT THE AUTHOR

At age eight, David Lomax was transplanted to Canada from his native Scotland. The same year, his parents read him *Tarzan of the Apes*, and he decided to become a writer. He didn't get all of the cool jobs his other writer friends did to make their biographies sound interesting, such as train driver, elevator repairman, or insurance underwriter. He was, briefly, a waiter. But not a good one. He currently divides his time between four great passions—writing, reading, teaching high-school English, and his wonderful family. He lives in Toronto with his awesome wife and three precocious children.